PRAISE FOR
AMELINDA BÉRUBÉ

"Seamlessly executed... An intricate, subtle, and deeply unsettling read."

—*Kirkus Reviews* on *Here There Are Monsters*

"Fun frights and a well-constructed haunting... It's *Black Swan* meets *Carrie*."

—*Kirkus Reviews* on *The Dark Beneath the Ice*

"The book's haunting, waterlogged atmosphere and Marianne's psychological turmoil will build an effective and growing sense of dread in readers... Hand this novel to those who enjoy spooky, psychological books with strong themes of self-discovery."

—*School Library Journal* on *The Dark Beneath the Ice*

"The vivid descriptions make the tension real. Fans of thrillers will enjoy Marianne's struggles."

—*School Library Connection* on *The Dark Beneath the Ice*

"A sinister exploration of self-doubt, internalized hatred, trust, and a romantic awakening...well-crafted and unsettling."

—*Booklist* on *The Dark Beneath the Ice*

HERE THERE ARE MONSTERS

ALSO BY AMELINDA BÉRUBÉ

The Dark Beneath the Ice

HERE
there are
MONSTERS

AMELINDA BÉRUBÉ

sourcebooks
fire

Published by Sourcebooks Fire, an imprint of Sourcebooks
P.O. Box 4410, Naperville, Illinois 60567-4410
(630) 961-3900
sourcebooks.com

Library of Congress Cataloging-in-Publication Data

Names: Bérubé, Amelinda, author.
Title: Here there are monsters / Amelinda Berube.
Description: Naperville, Illinois : Sourcebooks Fire, [2019] | Summary: Sixteen-year-old Skye must confront her most savage secrets to save her missing thirteen-year-old sister, Deirdre, from stick-and-bone monsters that have come to life in the woods behind their new home.
Identifiers: LCCN 2018052458 | (trade pbk. : alk. paper)
Subjects: | CYAC: Sisters--Fiction. | Missing children--Fiction. | Monsters--Fiction. | Supernatural--Fiction. | Moving, Household--Fiction.
Classification: LCC PZ7.1.B46495 Her 2019 | DDC [Fic]--dc23
LC record available at https://lccn.loc.gov/2018052458

Printed and bound in the United States of America.
VP 10 9 8 7 6 5 4 3 2 1

To Liana and Zélie
Long may we reign

T HE NIGHT MY SISTER DISAPPEARS is wild, with a waxing moon sinking dull and red into the leafless claws of the trees.

Mom bursts into my chilly basement room, startling me awake. I blink in the sudden flood of light framing her silhouette. Even in the split second before she speaks, it's obvious—something's wrong. I'm coiled rigid on my bed, bracing for it.

"Skye, have you seen Deirdre?" She barely waits for me to shake my head before she turns away. Her footsteps hammer up the stairs, her voice echoing through the house. "Deirdre! This isn't funny!"

I'm stuck in slow motion. Maybe I'm still dreaming. If I just wait here long enough, I'll wake up for real. On the night table the clock flicks from 11:37 to 11:38. That can't be right, but my phone, laying on the bed beside me, confirms it. A half-composed message to the group chat is still waiting for me when I swipe at the screen.

How could I have slept so long? I wasn't *that* tired. It was broad daylight.

And Deirdre was outside.

The wind whistles and mutters at the window. Instead of fading, the fear unfurls, blooms into an almost physical thing, a near-definable quality in the air that thickens around me until I can barely breathe. I fumble to my feet. She's thirteen, I tell myself. She wanders around out there on her own all the time. She doesn't need me looking after her. This is some sort of trick. Some sort of game. The sort of thing she'd think was perfect for the night before Halloween.

I'm on my way up the stairs when the front door slams; outside, Dad hurries away from the light, shrugging his coat on. The darkness swallows him, leaving only the muffled echo of Deirdre's name shouted into the night, over and over. Mom yanks closet doors open, hauls the couch away from the wall, slaps at every switch until the house swims with light, every corner exposed.

I watch her in silence, hugging my sweater around myself, winding my icy fingers in the wool. I should help. I should do *something*. But the thought is distant, muted, like it's trapped under a thick pane of glass. Outside, a little cone of white light from Dad's flashlight tracks his path around the yard, the tree trunks flashing thin and gray when he turns it toward the woods.

"Where could she have gone?" Mom cries, throwing the back door open and storming out into the garage. "Deirdre! *Deirdre!*"

The seconds tick by on the grandfather clock as I stand frozen, alone in the living room. Years ago, by accident, Deirdre hit me in the head while she was throwing rocks in the river. That's what this is like: the ringing, muffled space before the pain came crashing in.

They'll find her. Any minute now. They have to.

The door to her room stands slightly ajar, and it swings open soundlessly at my touch. The closet doors are hanging wide from Mom's frantic search, the drawers pulled out from under the bed. The bedside light throws shadows all over the room. Its pale circle falls over Deirdre's dented pillow, the blankets rumpled, tossed aside.

The bed is full of leaves. Pine cones. Gray sticks, forked and bent. They're heaped over the mattress in a little drift; a few of the leaves are curled and scattered on the carpet, ground into brittle fragments. Dad's voice drifts in through the open window with a spill of cold air, a distant shout, thin and ineffectual. *Deirdre! Deirdre!* The leaves twitch and ruffle as if they're stirring at her name.

When tearing the house apart hasn't turned up any sign of her, Mom starts making phone calls. One after another, panic simmering in every word. I head for the closet to get my coat, but Mom looks up sharply from the phone.

"Where are you going?" she demands.

"To help Dad?"

She shakes her head, and I start to protest, but she interrupts me.

"Stay here, Skye!" She takes a deep breath, moderates her

voice. "You're not leaving this house. Understand? Not until we find her."

There's no arguing with that. I sink into a chair at the kitchen table as Mom punches in another number. The wind whines at the windows. Two more numbers, two more weird truncated conversations. Then she hangs up, lets the phone clatter onto the table, and puts the heels of her hands to her eyes for a moment.

"Was she here when you got home from school?"

"I thought so," I stammer. "I mean, I thought she was outside. Her boots were gone."

"And you didn't go looking for her? After *hours*? We went out for *one* evening, Skye! We left you in charge!"

Trapped in my chair, I can't back away from her rising voice. I scrunch down a little lower.

"I fell asleep! It's not like I—"

Mom shakes her head, puts a weary hand out, cutting me off. "I'm calling the police."

I can't bear to sit next to her while she answers questions for 911, explaining how she'd gone into Deirdre's room to turn off her light and found only the leaves in her bed. I get up to look out the patio doors for a moment, at the distant gleam of the neighbor's porch light, then put the kettle on and pull boxes of tea from the cupboard. It doesn't keep me busy for nearly long enough. The glass wall of my calm is spiderwebbed with cracks, bright, sharp threads that fill my head, a labyrinth of what-ifs and maybes.

In my head I trace and retrace every path Deirdre could have taken. I imagine her stalking down the road, the gravel crunching under her ugly black rain boots, turning her head like a deer in the flare of oncoming headlights. There's not many ways to walk away from here. At the top of the hill, between the two old stone farmhouses, you can turn right, where the road eventually ends in a snowmobile trail that winds through the woods, or left toward the highway.

How could I have just fallen asleep? The afternoon was perfectly normal; Deirdre's always outside when I get home. If I'd been awake, at least I would have noticed when she didn't come back. Surely, even if it's been hours, she can't have gone that far. It's cold out. All our coats are on their hangers in the closet.

Unless a car pulled over, unless the passing headlights caught her pale hair in the dark—if she was cold enough, maybe she'd get in. Maybe she told them home was somewhere far from here. She never would have wanted to go back to our old neighborhood—and that's two thousand miles from here, anyway—but maybe anywhere else would do, as long as it was away from us. Away from me. If that's what happened, she'd disappear as surely as if she'd stepped into the river. Swallowed up.

But every time I come to the end of those thin speculations, I find them skittering over the one I can't let go. That she slipped into the forest, a shadow among shadows, to wade through the stagnant pools between the tree roots. Or that she splashed down the narrow path of the creek under the sinking moon. But that's as far as I can follow her. I don't know what's back there—I have only the sketchiest mental map—and she's disappeared into its empty spaces like a fish, or a frog, or a dryad.

Those woods devour everything.

Mom accepts a cup of tea but doesn't drink.

"She'll be okay," I tell Mom as she puts the phone down again, because she's cracking too, trembling on the edge of shattering into a million pieces. Not like it will do much good. I'm putting scotch tape on a broken window. "She's out there all the time."

"Not at night," Mom says, and that shuts me up. She drums her fingers against the handle of her mug for a moment, then gets up to retrieve her laptop from the living room.

"What are you doing?" If she says *work*, I think I'll scream. But not even Mom is that hardcore.

"Sending messages. Just in case."

The computer screen washes ghost-pale light over her face, blue and unforgiving, flickering with all the possibilities.

"How long until the police get here?"

Mom rakes a hand through her hair in a familiar gesture that says *I'm busy, don't talk to me.* "They said they'd send someone right away."

Did a root reach out for her foot? Did a puddle turn into a sinkhole under her step? You can't trust the ground back there. You could break something just trying to navigate it. Especially in the dark. There are *things* back there, Deirdre told me once.

Please let her be crouched somewhere, crying, waiting for Dad's voice, waiting for him to find her. Please let her come home in her own good time, like our cat Mog used to.

But Mog didn't come home, in the end.

The thought twists my stomach. Every time I yelled at Deirdre, ignored her, rolled my eyes—every time I kept my mouth shut instead of asking if she was okay—everything I've done was the wrong thing. The memories go round and round, a nauseating spiral.

Come home. I push the thought out toward the woods as if she'll hear it. *I'll play whatever stupid game you want. I promise. Just come home.*

The police officer has a kind face and a military-wannabe haircut. He listens solemnly to Mom's semicoherent rambling, making notes on a long, white form on a clipboard. The questions are icy in their practicality: What was she wearing? Can she swim? Mom keeps circling back to the leaves in Deirdre's bed.

"That's strange, isn't it?" she pleads. "Isn't that strange? I don't understand what she was doing. Could it have been somebody else who put them there, or…well, I left them where they were. I thought maybe you might need to see them. In case—I don't know, just in case."

"We'll take a look," he says solemnly, again and again. "We'll take a look."

We all turn at the sound of the back door opening, but it's only Dad, empty-handed, looking pale and shell-shocked.

"They sent me inside," he says. "They need something of Deirdre's. For the dogs, so they can track her."

Outside, more flashlights weave back and forth across the yard now, winking in and out of the trees. The night is coming alive with sirens and flashing lights that strobe against the branches.

I stand at the window, watching them. The bare branches quiver against the sky. The moon is almost down now, a scrap of clotted light visible between the trees. I don't turn when the policeman—Officer Leduc—sits in the armchair next to me.

"Do you have any ideas about where she might have gone?" he asks. "Does she have a friend she might have gone to visit, anything like that?"

"Deirdre doesn't have friends," I reply dully. She has make-believe worlds instead. Stick monsters and animal bones.

"She's having some trouble adjusting," Mom adds, her voice high. "We've only been here a few months. Since July. And she's never had great social skills, she's"—the words wobble, and I glance around just in time to see the tears start sliding down her cheeks—"she's just been having trouble."

A flare of anger makes me turn away from her pinched, weepy face. I haven't had trouble "adjusting." I'm not the reason our yard is crawling with police officers at one in the morning. It's Deirdre, as usual, who's in trouble; and it's me, as usual, who was supposed to save her.

And I'm done with that. She *knew* I was done with that.

"She was outside when you got home," Officer Leduc prompts. "Is that right?"

"She likes to explore," Mom says unsteadily, behind me, as I nod. "She was so excited to move here. She loves the woods."

"How about you?" Officer Leduc continues. "Have you done much exploring around here? Is there anywhere we should look?"

"Did you bring hip waders?" I ask. His eyebrows go up. I

sigh. "It's practically a lake back there. I gave up after the first time. Maybe she found a way through that wasn't too deep." Or maybe she just doesn't care if she gets wet. She came home soaked and muddy often enough. "Or you could try the castle, I guess."

"She means that big pile of dirt," Mom clarifies. "On the empty lot next door. Some of the other neighborhood kids like to hang out there."

I rest my forehead against the window. The glass is cold. *Castle* is Deirdre's word for it, not mine. "Yeah. That."

"Okay." He scrawls a few notes, frowning at his clipboard, gives me a sympathetic look. "You tell me if you think of anything else, all right?"

"Sure." They'll find her. Maybe she's just camped out somewhere, curled in a sleeping bag at the foot of the castle. Hill, dirt pile, whatever. They'll drag her home muddy and unrepentant, leaves in her hair, sticking her chin out and daring us to yell at her.

Eventually the door opens, admitting men's low voices, and Mom almost knocks her chair over as she hurries to meet them. Officer Leduc follows her. I stay put by the window, waiting. Waiting.

But Mom's sobs start low and echo up to me, and some police officer is saying something grim and professional, and when I shuffle to the top of the stairs and look down at them, she's cradled against Dad's chest, and he's buried his face in her hair. It's not Deirdre they've brought back.

It's her boots.

PART ONE
DEIRDRE

This land like a mirror turns you inward
And you become a forest in a furtive lake;
The dark pines of your mind reach downward,
You dream in the green of your time,
Your memory is a row of sinking pines.

—GWENDOLYN MACEWEN, "DARK PINES UNDER WATER"

ONE

July

THE NAME DEIRDRE MEANS *STORMY*, according to Mom's old baby name book. It suits her. She's rail-thin and pale as dandelion fluff, and behind her ice-blue eyes there are always tempests brewing. Our parents are perpetually perplexed by her; there are constant strategies, negotiations, teachers' conferences, therapists' appointments. Worried, low-voiced conversations down the hall. She's always been the one in tears at the sad movie, the one who wakes up screaming.

I'm easier. Straightforward, dependable. When they told me we were moving, I said "great!" It was a no-brainer; somewhere nobody knew either of us. Somewhere to start over. Not that things were likely to be any different for Deirdre across the country—or anywhere, really, no matter what our parents told themselves. It doesn't matter how hard you dig your heels in and refuse to grow up; time marches on with or without you. At thirteen, she's almost as tall as Mom, all elbows and knees. She refuses to wear anything but dresses, and she leaves her hair unwashed until it's hanging in lank strings and Mom finally orders her into the shower. She owns a bra, but after the one time last year some loser snapped one of its straps at school, she's insisted on going without.

We've always been at the same school before. Not this year. Here, middle and high school are firmly separated: Deirdre at Hillcrest, me at Lanark Centennial. Mostly, it's been a relief. But though I never let it show, I was afraid for her. She doesn't know how to put on a brave face. Instead of bending in the wind, she snaps like chalk or a flower stem. I'm not exactly a master of camouflage myself, but I can get by. Or at least I can now, since I've kicked loose from having to ride to her rescue all the time. I didn't know how to teach her how to blend in. I never have.

If I wanted to cross to the other side of the street and pretend we weren't related, it's not like it would have been hard. I'm dark and quiet compared to her. Practical, undramatic. I keep my hair cut close to my ears because it's easier, and maybe because she's always refused to cut hers. I've never had much patience for fashion, but at least I wear jeans. On good days it's a family joke, how opposite we are, and we laugh together at the teachers who claim to see a sisterly resemblance.

Our names are about the only things tying us together. My

parents' attempt at instilling some sense of family heritage. When you hear *Skye*, the first thing you think about is the clouds—insubstantial, wispy. Moody and changeable, like my sister. When I was younger, I got so many vapid compliments that I was annoyed at them for picking it. But Dad explained that Skye is a place, an island. If you google it, you see a place full of crags and stony slopes, rocks that stand unmoved as the sea breaks over them. The green slopes are a thin veneer over hard bone.

Riding to her rescue was my job before I ever had to do it in real life. In the kingdoms Deirdre invented, I was the Queen of Swords. All the kingdoms were ruled by queens. Deirdre was the first, of course—originally she was just *the* Queen, which always made me complain because I got stuck being her subservient knight. But then she discovered tarot cards and adopted the figures from the deck: Queen of Swords, Queen of Wands, Queen of Cups, Queen of Coins. But even those weren't enough to contain her stories, and they spilled over into monarchs visiting from faraway lands, outlines blooming on her map. Queen of Feathers. Queen of Leaves. Queen of Fire. Queen of the Sea. There were too many kingdoms to keep track of. Even if we stuck to the ones we knew best, the ones where we'd named the roads, the ones with magic systems and long-standing feuds, there were more than a dozen. The others branched off them—not incomplete so much as undiscovered. Places we hadn't gotten around to exploring yet.

I preferred to play *in big*, acting everything out. That way I got to wield my sword in fight scenes. She loved playing *in small* just as much. Barbies made pretty good queens, with their elaborate dresses, but Deirdre found them limiting. The most magical they got was plastic fairy wings.

She preferred to make the denizens of the kingdoms herself. Clay, Popsicle sticks, feathers, felt, whatever. Construction paper silhouettes would do in a pinch, adorned with crowns of tinfoil or pipe cleaner. If the results were misshapen, so much the better. Monsters were way more interesting to Deirdre than animals, even talking ones.

She built dioramas to house them, decorated with scraps of the river valley—smooth gray stones painted with nail polish, sprigs of pussy willows, peeling sticks glued together to make branching trees or bridges or limbs for magical creatures. Disney princesses and little ceramic figurines vied for space with the monstrosities she made herself. Plastic spiders sat on webs woven from acrylic yarn. Pieces from a broken mirror winked out from unexpected corners. Her walls were covered in long scrolls written in a language she'd invented, papier mâché masks bedecked with feathers and ribbons, painted maps—some of them corresponding to the places in the dioramas, others a world removed.

Deirdre's role wasn't fixed; with just the two of us to direct, she spun all the characters out around me. The Queen of Swords was still more like a knight of the realm, really, protecting her from villainy, following her on her epic quests. But since I got to be a queen and still be a fighter, I accepted that position without dispute. I became sort of a queen-errant, too restless for the throne, lending my peerless martial skills to worthy causes wherever I found them. My kingdom had been attacked and overrun in my absence, I think. It was very tragic. Most of Deirdre's stories turned out that way in the end.

Sometimes she'd accept my contributions—take an idea and run with it, unwinding all the consequences. But the kingdoms were hers, unquestionably and forever. I liked being the Queen of Swords: towering, fierce, unconquerable. But I was always traveling in Deirdre's country. She was all the queens and none of them. She belonged there.

And where I belonged? That was more complicated.

For two months I crossed days off the calendar with big red Xs. Counting down to a fresh start. I wouldn't be Psycho Skye after we moved. Away from Deirdre, at a different school, I wouldn't have to be.

It was a grueling three-day drive, and we pulled into the neighborhood past ten o'clock, all of us tired and frazzled, Mog yowling in her carrier, Mom yelling at the GPS. The new house was only a year old, and it stood alone on its street, an island of welcoming yellow light.

We ricocheted through it, running from room to room to take it all in. It didn't take long. Deirdre and I would be sharing a room, a prospect she claimed to be excited about. I wasn't so sure. I smiled and nodded for Dad's benefit when he showed me the dank little corner room in the basement that he planned to trans-form for me. The floor was bare concrete, a low opening in the far wall revealing a dark, spiderwebby crawl space. A ragged rectangle, traced in marker across the plastic skin of the insulation, would be a window. It looked like something Deirdre might have drawn there, pretending it was a magical secret passage.

"Nothing to it," Dad said, hugging my shoulders and giving me a reassuring little shake. "Right?"

Deirdre kept coming back to the tall windows that filled the back wall of the living and dining rooms. The light from the house vanished across a long, grassy slope, and beyond that the woods were an undifferentiated wall of shadow, darker than the sky. She sat there looking hungrily out at them even after Mom and Dad went to bed.

While Deirdre sat perched by the window, I made midnight fries. Cooking was only going to make the heat more oppressive, but rituals were rituals, and she insisted. The sticky dark pressed up against the glass, and a fan purred in the corner, pushing the air around. I was pulling the tray from the oven when she flapped a hand at me suddenly, her voice an urgent half whisper.

"Turn off the light!"

"Why?"

"You have to see this!"

I shut the oven door, scraped my bangs off my forehead.

"Is it something real?" I demanded. "I'm not budging for one of your—"

"*Yes,*" she hissed impatiently, her nose pressed up against the screen. "Come on!"

I left the fries sizzling on the stove top—too hot to eat yet anyway—and snapped the light off, feeling my way carefully around the haphazard mountains of moving boxes. Deirdre was a spare shadow in the luminous oblong of the window, her hair lifting a little as the fan rotated away from her.

"Look," she whispered. Outside, a point of pale green light winked on and off, on and off, bobbing erratically. And there— another. And another. As my eyes adjusted, the yard became full of them, like a bowl full of stars, stirred and left slowly revolving. Beside me, Deirdre's smile was the faintest gleam.

"Fairies," she said, and I snorted.

"What, fireflies aren't cool enough for you?"

"Come on, they're obviously magic." She didn't see me roll my eyes, too caught up in the dancing lights outside. "They're totally fairies."

Even after she reluctantly agreed we should go to bed, it was hard to sleep. Without streetlights to dilute it, night here was dense and deep, and it was full of sounds I didn't know. I hadn't expected the air to be different—sluggish, clingy. Hot breath on your neck. A room for me was only part of Dad's grand plans for the basement, so at least there would be somewhere cool to retreat to eventually. But the room I shared with Deirdre was stifling, even with the windows flung wide open.

"Skye." Deirdre's whisper slid across the room. "Are you asleep?"

"Not anymore," I growled, although I hadn't been.

"Oh. Sorry." She rolled over, the blankets rustling. Sighed.

"Are you okay?" I relented.

"It's just so dark. You know? It's so different."

"Yeah." Outside the window, beyond the black overhang of the roof, the Milky Way threw a long arm across the sky. "Look. You can see the stars."

She wrestled with the blankets for a long minute, flopped down with her pillow at the foot of the bed, making me snort.

"There," she said. "Now I can. D'you think they should be fairies too? From another kingdom, maybe?"

I ignored her question. "You can't sleep like that."

"Sure I can." She lifted her feet, waved them in the air for emphasis. "Why not?"

I rolled over, feeling for a cooler spot on the pillow, sticking a leg outside my thin quilt.

"Did we move to the Amazon?" I muttered. "It's like breathing soup."

"Maybe it'll get better if it rains. Is that crickets, do you think? That sound?"

"I guess. Or frogs, maybe." I'd never heard them before either. "I guess it was too cold for them back home."

We listened to the singing night in silence for a little while, until I started to think Deirdre had gone to sleep, but then she spoke again.

"The creek can be the gate to the kingdoms." I could hear her smile in the words. "We could even fish for algae. Remember that?"

One time we'd found a stick wedged upright among the river stones, the water chattering around it. Deirdre had declared that it marked the way from the ordinary world to ours. She'd twisted it in place—like you'd turn a key—and pulled it free to use as a scepter, since I already had a sword. After a long morning successfully beating back the invading hordes, she'd insisted we leave it behind, a testament to our reign. And after that, we found a new key at every visit and left it pointing skyward from the river. Layers of ritual accumulated around it: you had to walk around it three times; you had to swear undying loyalty by wood, stone, water, and bone. Anything done more than once becomes a ritual for Deirdre. It's as if she's trying to make reality cooperate through sheer, stubborn force. Wearing it down with repetition.

"I remember the gate," I said eventually, when she made an impatient noise, "but fishing for—what? How do you fish for algae? That doesn't even make sense."

Deirdre sprang upright, the pillow falling to the floor unheeded.

"You don't remember that?" she cried.

"Shhh," I hissed. She ignored me and jumped over to my bed, curled up at its end, shoving my feet out of her way.

"How can you not remember this? I was, like, six years old and I remember this. Look. You know when we went walking in the valley? That little piece of the river that came under the bridge?"

Under the blanket I went tense, something pressing its way up through my memory, rolling over in its sleep. "You mean the lagoon?"

"No, no." Deirdre thumped her head back against the footboard. "It was part of the river. Just slower. And really shallow. There was all that tall grass, remember? And it froze solid in the winter."

"Right." I rolled my shoulders, forced myself to relax. That chattering tributary was the scene of a hundred memories, after all, most of them benign. We'd gotten in the worst trouble one time for walking on the ice there. We hadn't been in any danger—we'd punched through the ice with rocks to see how thick it was, and found just the slick riverbed underneath, the barest trickle of water. Though, of course, it had been no use telling Mom that.

"We used to try to catch water bugs there. But it was too hard, because they were so fast and tiny. And so Dad gave us sticks and told us to fish for algae. Remember? It came up in these long, gross strings, like—" She pulled her hand away from her nose and giggled, snorting. "Remember?"

I smiled back in the dark, unevenly. It sounded like something we would do.

"This is going to be great," Deirdre said with a sigh of satisfaction. Her upturned face was a faint, pale oval in the starlight. "Imagine. It'll be like if we had the valley all to ourselves, just for us."

The valley. Long after Deirdre crawled back into her own bed and finally grew still, her breathing evening into sleep, I lay there listening to the alien chorus in the woods, the memories pulling me along. Down the plunge of the ravine, along the bike path that wound down to the river at the bottom. Beneath the houses perched at the crests of the hills on either side, silhouetted against the thin clouds. I knew when I'd walked there for the last time, past the furry petals of crocuses in the brown grass. But I'd been back in my dreams. Again and again.

It was as if I left part of myself behind. As if it were still there, walking through all the places I used to know. They wound out like tree roots to unknowable depths. Maybe that's what it means to put down roots in a place—laying down paths that you can trace with your eyes closed. All the places that make you who you are. All the things you wish you could forget.

I had no roots here. The forest had its own depth. It was a sinkhole, bottomless. But we floated on its surface like leaves in water, unanchored.

It didn't matter, I told myself over and over. Didn't matter. You could pull up a plant, set it down in new soil. Roots could be severed. I didn't tell Deirdre about the dreams, the footsteps that dogged me, though she'd have understood.

I didn't want Deirdre to be the one who understood.

I'd help Mom plant a new garden. I'd help Dad finish the basement. Left behind in the dark, those roots would disappear eventually. And I'd grow upward, toward the light.

TWO

Officer Leduc takes pity on me, trailing uselessly around the kitchen, and puts me in charge of making a page for the search. I set it up as dawn starts to show around the edges of the sky. Mom manages to track down a picture on her thumb drive where Deirdre's actually smiling. I'm tempted to tell Mom that nobody will recognize her if we post that. She looks so innocent, squinting into the camera in the sun. Her white-blond hair is braided—probably by me—and she's wearing a blue sundress that makes her look about three years younger than she is. But in the end, I can't bring myself to say anything, and I post it dutifully. Retweet the police, share posts from the news stations as they start to pick it up.

The day turns crisp and pumpkin-golden, and the police

go on scouring the neighborhood. Knocking on doors, asking questions. Looking under decks, in sheds. Following dogs back and forth across the face of the forest, in and out of the tangle. I close the window but can't shut out the voices, the barking, the pulse of helicopter blades. Heavy foreign footsteps echo through the house, a counterpoint to Mom's tearful voice.

The doorbell rings more constantly than it ever would for trick-or-treaters, heralding a parade of reporters and neighbors bringing food: lasagna, chili, muffins, bread. I'd kind of forgotten that other people live here, that there are actual human beings behind the blank closed faces of the houses scattered up the hill. We're not even a suburb out here. *Exurb*, Mom called it once. A tiny constellation of human presence, perched on the edge of the swamp.

One of the casserole bearers is a boy with long, wheat-colored hair pulled into a messy ponytail, broad-shouldered in a black-and-yellow Lanark Centennial athletic jacket. William Wright. He stands waiting on our doorstep, his hands buried in flowered oven mitts to carry a big white ceramic dish. I should be glad to see him. I could have summoned him by text anytime today, if I wanted a shoulder to cry on. That's probably what he's hoping for—a chance to be the hero. The thought makes me want to disappear back down the hall above the foyer, so he'll have to leave his offering there and go away.

Before I can act on the impulse, he glances up and meets my eyes through the glass, offers an awkward smile, lifts the casserole apologetically.

"Hey," he says when I open the door. "I brought dinner."

I don't tell him that he's only the latest in our stream of visitors. He's the first one my age, anyway.

"Thanks," I say instead.

"Do you mind if I come in? This is just, um, kind of hot. Where can I—"

"Just put it on the stairs, I guess." I stand back to let him in, and he deposits it on the carpeted step, pulls off the silly oven mitts.

"I'm really sorry," he says. "About your sister. I mean, I hope she's okay."

I'm probably giving him the look that makes Deirdre roll her eyes. When I slip into it in front of other people, they get shifty and uncomfortable. But William knows it by now—he's teased me about my resting bitch face often enough. Anyway, better stone-faced than crying. There's no way I'm crying in front of William.

"I thought…did you want to talk about it? We don't have to, but—"

I shake my head, fold my arms. He returns my stare for a moment, at a loss, then glances back out the window at the giant police trailer filling half the driveway—their mobile headquarters, Officer Leduc explained. Beyond it, the road is lined with vans from the news stations. An ambulance waits off to one side, just in case. Police officers hurry back and forth, and cameramen and neighbors stand around in little knots. Ants milling around a nest.

"Has this all been here since last night?"

"Basically." There, I sound sort of human again. "It's kind of a circus."

"Do they need volunteers or anything? To help look?"

"I don't think so. I don't know. They've got the helicopter, right? And the dogs."

He nods, sympathetic. There's a long silence. Flash forward to what I can expect at school as *that girl with the missing sister.* No one will know what to say, including me. Count on Deirdre to ruin everything, leave me cut off, spreading awkward silence like a plague. I can practically hear her sniff of satisfaction. But William's trying, at least. He's here. He's making a gesture. I kind of wish he hadn't.

"If there's anything I can do, let me know," he says finally. "I'm around, you know, if you want some company or anything. I'm…guessing you're not going to be at Kevin's tonight."

I shake my head again. I would rather be just about anywhere other than here. But my presence at the party would be either a total downer or inexcusably weird. I don't need everyone watching me, waiting for me to fall apart. I definitely don't need to fake my way through dealing with Kevin. "It's not like he's going to miss me."

My tone makes William's eyebrows go up in surprise, though he covers it with an answering shrug. I'm off-balance, forgetting the rules. I shouldn't have let that slip, and I fumble for a way to take it back. I can't mess things up with William's friends. My friends, I correct myself. But the idea feels angular and foreign in a way it didn't yesterday. Like a stone in my mouth.

"He's your friend more than mine, is all," I come up with after a too-long pause.

"Well. You kind of intimidate him."

"That's what Sophie said." I sigh. "I don't know. *You* manage to hang out with me without being a douchebag."

"Somehow." His smile is brief, self-deprecating.

"Look, forget I said anything, okay? I don't mean to be bitchy."

"I think you're allowed. And anyway, it's Kevin. He kind of brings it on himself."

"Yeah. Well. Anyway, I'm sorry. I'm just…"

"Don't worry about it. Seriously." There's another silence. He passes the oven mitts from hand to hand for a moment before meeting my eyes again. "Well. I'll get out of your hair. Text me, okay?"

"Sure." I try not to sound too relieved. "Thanks. I will."

"I hope they find her," he says, retreating through the door.

"Yeah. Me too."

They haul me upstairs out of hiding so the social worker can talk to all three of us together. *To get a picture of the family situation,* she says. *To get an idea of why this happened.* Janelle, as she introduces herself, is an ample, motherly-looking person, with a waterfall of black curls, bright red lipstick, and a soft, high voice. My mom looks cold and hard sitting beside her, eyes red-rimmed and haggard but her back poker-straight.

"You said she was having some trouble, Sarah," Janelle prompts. "Is that right?"

Mom gives a tight little nod.

"Could you tell me about that?"

"She's always had trouble making friends," Mom says. "She and Skye were really close, and that was just...all she needed, I guess."

I study the carpet and refuse to respond.

"She didn't quite know how to connect with other kids. She was just so...lost in her own little world, really. And lately, well, Skye's been making her own friends, and Deirdre...kind of felt like she'd been left behind."

I kick at the legs of my chair. I'm not listening. This is not my fault. My armor is forged from steel plates. Mom's barbs bounce right off me.

"Is that how you'd put it, Skye?"

I mumble an indifferent response. Mom gives an aggrieved little huff, looks away out the window.

"The learning resource staff at Hillcrest said you'd been in touch about seeking counseling for Deirdre."

"She's always been kind of explosive," Dad puts in, "and we keep trying to get a handle on it, but—"

"We?" Mom doesn't raise her voice. Her mouth is a thin line.

"Oh, Sarah, come on, don't start."

"Who's the one who always takes time for appointments? Who's the one making the phone calls?"

"We talked about this. Didn't we talk about this? You're the one with an office job, you're the one with the flexibility—"

"All right, let me jump in here," Janelle interrupts. "Brent, what is it you do?"

"Drywall." He sighs. "With a buddy of mine."

"And Sarah?"

"I'm a project manager," she says stiffly. "For Cambria. It's a tech start-up."

"So you've both been working some pretty intense hours, I guess."

"Hey," Dad protests, "I'm home at four to be with the kids. Usually."

"Sometimes five," Mom mutters, "sometimes six…"

"Jesus, Sarah, they're teenagers now. They can look after themselves. They don't need me around to…"

Dad's words falter and sink under Mom's arctic silence. He scrubs a hand over his face.

"And how do you feel about that, Skye?"

They all turn to look at me. I fold my arms.

"Perfectly fine. *I* can look after myself."

Dad's shoulders take on a defeated slouch, and Mom bristles all over again, glaring at me. I'm done with this. I shove my chair back and stalk from the kitchen. Behind me, Janelle goes on trying to play referee while they snipe at each other.

My room is as much of a refuge as I've got: quiet and sunny, my plants filling one wall on the stand Dad built for me. But even here, there's no escape. When I fling myself onto the bed and pull out my phone, there's a million notifications, all about Deirdre. Sympathy. People asking if there's anything they can do. Sophie has texted—*OMG!!! Are you okay???*—and I don't know how to answer that, so I don't. I scroll through the group chat about

Kevin's party instead. Who's going as what. I hadn't decided on a costume yet. I bet they're too hip to do Halloween for real; it's probably all ironic accessories. I was waiting to see what Sophie and Bethany were planning.

Not that it matters now.

I don't bother to answer the knock at my door, so after a pause, the knock comes again.

"Skye?" It's not Mom. Janelle. "Would this be a good time to talk?"

"Whatever." It's not like I have much choice. I don't look up from my phone as she opens the door.

"Wow," she says. "You must have quite the green thumb."

"I guess." I grew some beans from seed in third grade for science class, and ever since, I've been going nonstop, taking cuttings from every houseplant I could lay hands on. My collection is getting pretty impressive—a balancing act of height and texture, long trailing vines arranged just so, framing the others.

"Orchids, even!" Janelle turns her smile on me like a searchlight, and I wince. "A client gave me one of these once, and I killed it stone dead. Is there a secret to it?"

"Not really." Does she think she's being subtle? Get the sulky teenager talking. Get her to open up. Well, I can play along with that. "All you have to do is soak them in a sinkful of water for half an hour every week. And then leave them alone."

"I thought you were supposed to keep them in a tray of water. So they had the humidity."

"No, they hate that. Like, they're from the rain forest, but they grow in these little hollows in the trees, right? Places that fill up with water every now and again and then drain right out."

Outside my window, the door to the garage creaks open, slams shut. Mom stalks out to the sad, straggly patch of the garden under the apple tree with a shovel, stabs it into the ground.

"Well, you obviously really know your plants. Do you garden with your mom?"

"Sometimes. It's pretty much the only thing we have in common." I was her right-hand man in taming the masterful waterfalls of color she'd orchestrated at our old house. I know more botanical names than she does. She looks at garden magazines for the pictures. I like the Latin words. I found a website that shows you how to pronounce them, even. You can click a button and listen to measured female voices saying: *abelia, stephanandra, galanthus, ludisia, araucaria, chamaedorea*. They're like an incantation.

The garden was where I was most at home with Mom. When she comes up for air between all-nighters at work, she throws herself into other projects. Dad is the muscle in our house, the one who builds and fixes things. Eventually. But it's Mom who makes things happen. Most of the time, trying to help her with something, to be companionable, only slows her down. Her barely concealed impatience is sharp as any rebuke. Back at our old house, at least in the garden, there was space for me too.

But it's different here. Like everything else.

"What about Deirdre?" Janelle says delicately. "What did you two have in common?"

I scowl. "Nothing. Nothing at all."

She fingers the shiny leaves of the philodendron draped over the shelf. "You know, I'm the oldest of four sisters. I know exactly how big of a pain they can be. Even when you love them."

I look away. This is the part where I'm supposed to open up, I suppose. Spill my guts. Confess my sins. She's trying to earn my trust, hoping I'll reward her with information.

"Did you ever wish you were an only child?" I ask, still looking at the wall.

"I think everyone with siblings wishes that sometimes."

"But not everyone gets their wish."

She sits beside me on the bed.

"You feel responsible for what happened."

"I should have been awake," is all I say.

"Are you often the one looking out for Deirdre?"

"I'm the only one." If that comes out a little more forcefully than I meant it to, well, that's fine. It's true. "I don't understand why she's *like* this. It's like she can't even see herself in the mirror. And people…used to talk about her all the time. At school." They did more than talk. But I'm not going there.

"It's an awkward age," Janelle offers. "Growing up is hard sometimes. I'm sure you had your own bumps in the road."

That's one way of putting it. I hunch my shoulders against the thought.

"Awkward. Whatever. She *makes* it awkward. She makes herself a target. She just…refuses to grow up. It makes no fucking sense; it's like she's doing it on purpose. How many times do you have to rescue somebody before they figure out how to save themselves?"

I bite the sentence short. She's getting to me.

"Some things just take time," Janelle says. "Right? Everything grows."

I don't answer, and she sighs and stands.

"Here's my card," she says. "You call me anytime you want to talk, okay? Anytime, and I really mean that."

I wait until she's closed the door behind her, and then I shred the card into little pieces and throw it in the trash. That went pretty well, all things considered. I got through it. I didn't let anything slip. I told her what she wanted to hear.

So why do I feel like crying?

Outside, Mom is still attacking the sad remains of the garden. I watch as she levers up sticky clumps of wet earth, turns them over. It refuses to even crumble, and she has to hack every shovelful apart. You could probably make pottery with it. She hasn't bothered with it since a month after we arrived, when the rosebushes she planted withered in the clay and the deer cropped everything else—from the bee balm to the irises to the nasturtiums—right down to the ground, leaving only ragged bits of stem behind.

Everything grows.

Right. Not here it doesn't.

THREE

Four Years Ago

THE FIRST TIME THE QUEEN of Swords was truly tested
was Halloween too—the first time we were allowed
to go trick-or-treating on our own. I was twelve, Deirdre nine.
And there was a blizzard, an actual, old-fashioned blizzard that
started the night before. We saw it coming as wings of orange-
white cloud stretching over the rooftops, blotting out the stars.
The whole house shuddered as the wall of snow slammed past, a
curtain lashing and howling across the street.

Mom and Dad had promised us we could go trick-or-treating
alone that year, though, and there was no way we were missing
out. Deirdre and I were a united front, my stubborn folded arms

folded arms the bedrock for her impassioned pleading. Our only concession was to wearing bulky snowsuits under our dresses. We made ungainly, marshmallowy queens that way, our bodices straining at the seams, but we still had our dramatic capes and our crowns: mine spiky aluminum foil sprayed with black, imitating iron; Deirdre's painstakingly twisted out of Dad's electrical wire.

And my mittened hand could still hold a sword.

The sidewalks were knee-deep in snow. Hardly anyone else had braved it. The only sounds were our voices, the rasp of our snow pants, the whisper of the snow falling, falling, falling. But the jack-o-lanterns were golden islands on the doorsteps, beckoning us up the walks, and people emptied their bowls into our pillowcases, laughing at our determination, admiring our costumes, telling us not to get too cold.

We made it all the way up the hill before people stopped answering their doors, before the porches and the windows went dark and cold. It was time to return; Halloween was well and truly over, our pillowcases so full we had to sling them over our shoulders as we headed home. We trudged through a playground, where a couple of teenaged shadows laughed and shouted on the monkey bars, back out onto the road. Deirdre kept glancing behind us into the dark.

"I think they're following us," she muttered.

"We should double back," I whispered, thinking it was part of the game we'd been playing. We were seeking provisions for battle against the Snow Queen, and the citizens of the city, long besieged by winter, were overjoyed at our arrival, filling our coffers. "Come out behind them, set an ambush—"

"No, for real," she said. "Behind us."

"What, them?" The teenagers from the park were shambling through the snow at the top of the hill, silhouettes in the orange light. "Give me a break, Deir, they're going home. Just like we are."

"They're following us," Deirdre insisted. "I heard them."

"They are not." I quickened my pace, pulled ahead of her. "Come on, don't be ridiculous. It's not like they're sneaking up on us or anything."

"I want to call Dad." Her whine set my teeth on edge.

"No." If our parents caught wind of that kind of worry, they'd never let us do this again. The Queen of Swords would not be ruled by fear. "Come on, just walk."

She did. But she kept looking back, and irritation flared high in my throat. I didn't bother to let her catch up. Why was she always like this? Why couldn't she be bold and fearless just this once? Worse, the voices behind us intruded on my attention now, growing closer. I wouldn't listen. I wouldn't let Deirdre's fear infect me.

"Skye—!"

"Relax, would you?" I threw the words over my shoulder. "It's not—"

But then she cried out, and when I wheeled around, someone—some girl, no taller than me, anonymous in a jaunty ponytail and parka—had hold of the pillowcase, leaving Deirdre clinging desperately to the other end.

"Give it here," the girl said, the words casual, disdainful.

"Let go," Deirdre whimpered. "Skye, help me!"

It wasn't that I froze, that I couldn't move, that my limbs wouldn't obey me. I just didn't react. I stood there, a few yards down the sidewalk, and calm wrapped me like a blanket. Deirdre was freaking out over nothing, as usual. It was fine. Everything was fine. My sword stayed point down in the snow, my pillowcase clutched in one hand between my knees. I watched. I just watched.

"We're bigger than you," the other girl said, grabbing a handful of the pillowcase. "Come on."

"No," Deirdre wailed, "that's not fair! You can't just take it. It's mine!"

"What are you going to do about it?" the first one demanded. "Are you going to cry? Are you going to call your daddy, princess?"

"I'm a *queen*!" Deirdre's voice rose a notch, and they laughed. "And my sister will *hurt* you! Skye, do something!"

"Yeah, Skye, do something," they echoed, mocking. Daring me to wade in and take them on.

But I didn't. I didn't move.

Together, they yanked the pillowcase back and forth like they were taking a toy from a dog, and Deirdre lost her grip and fell headlong into the snowbank. They retreated back up the hill as she floundered free, spitting snow, her crown askew. They didn't even bother to run. Their laughter clattered back down to us. The snow was falling thicker now, shrouding them from sight, letting them disappear.

That's when it occurred to me that I should speak. That's

when it broke over me: fear. The knowledge that something bad had happened, shouldn't have happened—that she'd been right.

"Why didn't you *do* something?" Deirdre cried, staggering upright. Snow clung to her hair in clumps. "How could you just stand there?"

I had no explanation. There wasn't one. "I thought—I don't know, I just thought—"

"Some champion you are," she sniffed, and soldiered past me.

"Deirdre, I'm sorry," I panted, finally coming unstuck to catch up to her. "I don't know what happened. I just—"

"Whatever," she said bitterly. Not looking at me. We slogged the rest of the way home in silence.

"Wow, that's quite a haul," Dad said when we pushed through the door. "But, Deir, where's yours?"

"Hers ripped," I said, before she could speak. "So I put it in here. This is both of ours."

Halloween tradition demanded that we sit at the kitchen table afterward and eat as much candy as we could stomach. Deirdre took a listless bite of a Reese's Peanut Butter Cup as I fielded questions from our parents, hoping my cheerfulness sounded natural, that they wouldn't notice her silence.

"Mom," I said abruptly, "I want to take karate or something. Some sort of martial arts. Can I do that?"

She blinked, looked up from the computer.

"Uh, sure, I guess, if you want. What brought that on?"

"So I can be the Queen of Swords," I said. "The Queen of Swords knows how to fight."

"We don't have to worry about you getting into fights or anything, do we?" Dad said it like it was a joke, but it was a real question underneath.

"No." I looked at Deirdre. She met my eyes steadily, grave and regal. "I'll only fight monsters."

Mom and Dad exchanged a glance, and Mom shrugged and pulled up a browser window. "I'll see what I can find."

"Here," Deirdre said, pushing a Mars Bar across the table to me. They were my favorite. "Spoils of war."

Some champion you are. After that Halloween, I was the perfect champion, thank you very much. Mom's digging unearthed a little club that trained at the university, run by a grave-faced biochemistry professor, semiretired—Sensei Matt, to me—and his lieutenants, Sensei Ayesha and Sensei Alex. I loved it from the second Sensei Ayesha greeted me at the door to show me how to bow my respect every time I came in. Warm-ups, katas, sparring—all of it was magical.

That was *my* kingdom.

And the next time—when Deirdre stood red-faced, her hands balled in useless fists, outside a laughing circle with some girl in the middle, holding her sparkly pink notebook aloft to read it aloud—I didn't hesitate. I plunged through the line, seized the ringleader's hand in both of mine, twisted down and away until she squawked and dropped Deirdre's notebook in the snow.

It happened so fast. It was so easy. I held her there, staring into her wide frightened eyes, and stood transfigured, draped in righteous calm. It was a whole different world.

"You'd better leave her alone," I said.

I let her scuttle off to join her friends, who had scattered away from me to regroup across the yard, and turned my back on them.

"That was amazing," Deirdre breathed, the notebook clutched to her chest.

"I'm the Queen of Swords," I told her, and let my grin escape. "Just don't tell Mom and Dad."

It worked so well for a while. It was like keeping lily beetles in check, picking them off before they multiplied. But last year Deirdre hit seventh grade—like it was a brick wall—and suddenly she was too tempting a target to ignore. They'd found their champion too; with Tyler egging them on, laughing, fearless, the goblin hordes weren't scared of me anymore. And there was only one of me.

But I don't think about Tyler. I won't follow the path down into the valley, not even in my mind.

I'm thousands of miles away, and I will never walk there again.

FOUR

As twilight comes creeping into the afternoon, leaving the golden light thin and wintery, Mom stands staring into the fridge at all the foil-wrapped offerings with the door hanging open, the cold pouring out onto the floor.

"We'll never eat all this," she says.

I fish out the lasagna William brought earlier—its casserole dish is the one sticking out the farthest—and push the door closed, interrupting Mom's trance.

"We can freeze some of it." I stick the tray in the oven. "Right?"

Mom shrugs listlessly. "I guess." Her lips twist down at the corners. "I'm not really hungry."

Me neither, but I poke at the oven to start it heating anyway. Mom sinks into a chair.

"Shit," she says to the tabletop, "it's Halloween. I was going to get candy today."

"Nobody's coming down here, anyway," I point out, which is the wrong thing to say, because she goes bright-eyed and quiet, looking out at the porch light gleaming through the gathering dark. It's true, though. Even if there's anyone around who's still young enough for trick-or-treating, nobody's coming down the street with one lonely house and a pile of cop cars.

"Anything on the computer?"

Social media has remained mostly my job, though she insisted on dictating some of the posts. "All the news places are sharing it," I report. "And the radio stations."

Dad finally shuffles into the kitchen a tense and silent half hour later as I'm pulling the lasagna from the oven. I've barely seen him all afternoon, not since he retreated to the bedroom, where the sound of newscaster voices has been a faint, constant soundtrack. I cut us all gooey squares, set them on plates on the table. Look at me, holding us together.

"Nothing new," Dad sighs, before Mom can speak. He lowers his head into his hands, his elbows propped on the table. I set a plate in front of him, and he blinks up at me, bleary-eyed.

"Oh," he says. "Thanks, honey. I'm just…I'm not really…"

Mom clears her throat, picks up her fork.

"You need to eat," she says sternly. "We all do. You can't just go for twenty-four hours straight without…without eating."

She seems to hear herself, stumbles over the words, and looks at her plate, poking at the lasagna half-heartedly with the fork. Without the constant throb of helicopter blades, the quiet crouches over us, a living thing perched in Deirdre's empty chair. The clock is as loud as rocks falling. Mom's fork scrapes against her plate. Dad takes a bite, chews dutifully.

"She can't have gone far, Sarah," he continues. "Half of it's underwater. She'd have had to come out at—"

Mom lets her fork fall with a clatter, rests her head on her hand.

"Can we not?" she says, her voice high. Dad stares at her.

"Well—okay, I was only trying to—"

"Let's just eat." The words tremble. "Okay? Please?"

A heavy thump echoes down from over our heads, making us all jump. It's followed by a scrape, a rattle. It falls silent for a moment as we stare at each other, then resumes. An uneven scuffing sound—as if someone's staggering drunkenly across the roof—punctuated by occasional scrabbling noises.

"Is that..." Mom begins. Dad frowns. Their eyes meet across the table, and suddenly they're both lurching to their feet, shoving the chairs out of the way, dropping cutlery on the floor. Dad throws the patio door open and backs up against the railing, craning his neck to scan the roof.

"Brent?" Mom's voice is high.

There's a long, faint scratching sound, like the point of a stick dragging over the shingles.

"We need flashlights," Dad says, and he practically runs back through the kitchen, down the stairs.

"I've got my phone," I offer, but with shaking hands, it takes me longer than it should to fumble for the button that turns on the flashlight. Over our heads, whatever it is taps and shuffles. Mom takes the phone from me and hurries after Dad, out the front door.

"Go around the back," Dad calls. He's in the middle of the lawn, casting his flashlight back and forth across the face of the house. Mom's footsteps crunch on the gravel of the driveway, then in the frost-rimed grass as she disappears around the garage.

The beam of the flashlight spills over pinkish brick, the sea of gray shingles glittering and empty, stretching upward into shadow. Nothing moves. Dad stalks a few feet farther into the yard to splash the light across the roof of the garage. The backwash of it makes his face pale and tight, shadows stretching up from his cheeks. Mom's voice echoes from the far side of the house, shrill with desperate hope, calling Deirdre's name.

"I can't see anything," Dad shouts to her. The wind stirs, a breath against my face. In the bush, something creaks and snaps, falls silent.

"It can't be her," I manage. "Dad, it can't be. They've had a helicopter out here all day." They would have seen her on the roof. There's nowhere to hide. How would she even get up there?

He doesn't answer, just puts an arm around my shoulders, hugs me close. He doesn't look away from the roof.

"Maybe it was squirrels," Dad ventures, breaking a long silence, as Mom reappears around the corner of the garage, shoulders slumped in defeat. "Or raccoons. I hope they're not in the attic or something. They could cause an awful lot of damage up there."

Mom doesn't answer. Dad doesn't voice the possibility that

maybe it's Deirdre hiding up there, but he declares that he's going to go check, hurries into the house.

"Go on in, Skye," Mom whispers as the door falls closed behind him. "I'll just go around the house one more time. Okay? Go in and tell me when you hear it."

The scratching, tapping noises are still there. I yell down to Mom in the backyard from the window, and she flicks the flashlight beam from my phone back and forth while Dad hauls a ladder upstairs, pushes the attic hatch aside. By the time he climbs back down, the sounds are growing fainter, like someone drumming on the roof with their fingers. That's almost worse. It makes me think of spiders. By then, even Mom has to admit that if there is something on the roof, it can't be Deirdre.

"I thought I heard—" Mom shakes her head as she kicks her shoes off. "It doesn't seem possible, but I could have sworn I heard a bell."

"Do you think it was Mog?" I ask.

"On the roof? After all this time?" She makes a doubtful face, but sighs. "Maybe we should put some kibble out. Just in case."

We go back to the table, to our cold abandoned plates, and silence falls again. Mom scans the ceiling anxiously. Dad takes two reluctant bites and then sits back with a sigh. His head droops, and for a second, I'm sure he's going to cry, and I don't know how any of us are going to keep it together if he cries. But he sits up with a jerk; he was falling asleep. Mom's eyes are the ones filled with tears.

"Dad," I say. He blinks at me. "Dad, you should go to bed."

"Yeah," he mumbles, pushing his chair back. "Yeah. Fair enough. Wake me up later, okay, Sarah? I'll take a turn waiting up."

Mom doesn't answer, and eventually he sighs and shuffles from the room. That leaves me and Mom facing each other. She forces herself through half her lasagna before she pushes it aside, her eyes still dangerously bright.

"You can go to bed too, if you want," Mom says. But the words have a brittle edge that tells me there's only one right answer.

"No, it's okay. I'll stay up."

"We have to leave the lights on. All of them. So she'll see them. That's what they told us to do. And leave the windows open. In case we might hear something."

I was there when Officer Leduc explained this before leaving for the night. But I nod anyway. She drums her fingers against the table, then gets up. Sets a dish of cat food outside the patio door, closes the screen.

"I may as well try to get some work done," she says, and for once, it's a relief. Something to take her attention off me.

When she's about to pass my chair, she stops suddenly and leans over to gather me into a hug. I freeze for a startled second before managing to return it—Mom's not usually a huggy person. Her voice breaks as she speaks into my shoulder. "Oh my God, Skye, what are we going to do? I can't stand it."

"It's okay, Mom." It's not. Of course it's not. "They'll find her."

She straightens up, shaking her head, lips pressed tight together, and disappears into the living room. After a moment, the clatter of her keyboard rattles into the silence. Icy air from the patio door spills over my feet. Outside, night is deepening across the yard, imperceptibly as a flower opening, full of whispers and shifting leaves.

I get my own laptop from my room and try to disappear into the internet, but none of my friends are online; they're busy getting drunk up the hill, forgetting about me. Refresh and scroll, refresh and scroll. Eventually the couch creaks as Mom gets up with a long, shaky sigh. I guess her distraction is working about as well as mine. Her footsteps disappear down the hall, leaving me alone with my thoughts. They chase one another in free-falling circles, fizzling into blank, ashy anxiety.

My head hurts. My eyes feel hollow. But sleep is impossible. I'll never sleep again. I should have been awake. I keep remembering Mom's accusing words: *You didn't go looking for her? We left you in charge!* Or Deirdre's sniffle on another Halloween night in the snow: *Some champion you are.* The should-have-dones swoop around me, diving at me, digging in.

It's not my job to protect her. I repeat it like a mantra. It never was, not really. It should never have been my job in the first place.

It was too big a job for me. I went overboard trying to fill those shoes before. And I won't think about that. That wasn't my fault. I had to. I had no choice.

It's not long before I abandon the computer too, desperate to move, to do something. Anything. The training exercises I learned in karate have lost their calming magic since the spring. I should go for a run. Not one of Dad's leisurely jogs, but one of the grueling, never-ending runs that my sensei used to put us through. You can't think about anything else when your legs are made of burning rubber and sweat is running into your eyes.

My pacing carries me down the hall, following the thump and creak of whatever Mom's doing. I haven't been in Deirdre's room since she trashed all her artwork. With the overhead light on, it looks bare and disheveled: the empty shelves, the tape clinging to the walls here and there with a corner of torn paper, the rumpled bed still full of leaves. Mom is picking up clothes from where they got scattered during the search, folding them and putting them back in the closet.

Speaking up is probably dangerous, but guilt prods me into it. "Can I help?"

Mom clears her throat. Doesn't look at me.

"You could clean up her bed, I guess. They took their pictures and everything." She pauses to study the heap of leaves, puts a fretful hand to her temple. "I just can't figure out... You don't know what that's about, do you?"

I hug my elbows. "Why would I?"

She shakes her head, goes back to the clothes on the floor. "Just asking."

I set my jaw and grab the trash can from the corner. Mom is silent as I sweep leaves from the mattress into the garbage. A few spill from my hands, and I pick them up carefully, one by one.

When I go to scoop up a double handful, my fingers connect with something solid at the bottom of the pile, heavier than any of the sticks. Frowning, I close my hand around it—flat, blunt-edged—and pull it free of the leaves, into the light.

It's a sword. My sword. The one Dad made for me, years ago, from a leftover strip of hardwood flooring. I'd badgered him for it nonstop, pleaded, offered to help, offered to do dishes for a million years—whatever it took. He wouldn't let me near most of the power tools, but he did let me run his little sander back and forth over its rough-cut planes until they took on a smooth sheen, showed me how to brush on the finish. By now, the grip is an ugly patchwork of colors, layers of electrical tape worn through and covered up again. It's warm and heavy in my hand, the golden grain of the beveled oak blade a familiar, irregular tracery.

"Isn't that yours?" Mom says.

I nod without looking at her. Deirdre must have found it in the garage where I dumped it. And she left it here, before she went out into the woods yesterday. She never played with it. Did she leave it here for me to find? To…what, to send some sort of message?

It feels like a rebuke. I'm supposed to be doing something. I'm supposed to go find her.

And that's stupid, obviously. I don't have a helicopter or infrared cameras.

Rage sweeps over me, leaving my eyes blurry and my hands cold. I grip the sword so tight my fingers go numb. Did she start this whole thing just as some sort of trick to drag me back into the kingdoms? No. I will not be responsible for this. I refuse. Why is she so impossible?

I will not let her make this my fault.

I clench my teeth and put the sword aside for long enough to finish cleaning the leaves out of the bed. And then I march with the sword across the house, through the balcony doors, out to the railing. Nothing stirs beyond the porch light. There's only the faint murmur of the wind, the tiny noises of little things nosing invisibly through the brush. No human sound at all.

I heft the sword and throw it, as hard as I can, end over end into the darkness. I want to scream. Instead, I let only a little huff of sound escape. The sword cartwheels out into the garden to land with a snap and crash in the tall grass under the apple tree.

I stand there panting, my heart thudding behind my eyes. What was I expecting, that it would bring her running? That I'd hear her shriek of outrage? Maybe I'm trying to throw off the weight in my chest, trying to evict the hollow screaming feeling that I was the one who ran away, who turned her back. That I was the one who left her behind.

I turn blindly back to the house, into the comfortless light, and pull the door closed behind me.

To hell with what Deirdre wants me to do. Or what Mom wants me to do. To hell with all of them.

How's the party? I text William.

Just getting started. You okay?

I pocket the phone again without answering and thump heavily down the stairs, making sure Mom can hear me and assume I'm retreating to my room. Not that she's listening. Not that she'll check.

Instead, I cram my feet into sneakers, open the door as quietly as I can, and slip out into the night. To freedom.

FIVE

August

ONCE WE WERE SORT OF unpacked, our first order of business, Deirdre declared, was to explore. Reluctantly, I agreed. It was irresistible. We'd never had a dominion before. Her kingdoms had always been superimposed over landscapes we visited—campsites, hiking trails, the valley—but they were only ever pitched there temporarily to be gathered up and adapted to the next convenient setting, and always put away in haste when other people approached. The wildernesses we'd wandered through were not places it occurred to us to map or name. We didn't *own* them. We kept to the paths laid out for us. Our old yard, an ordinary city lot, was Mom's territory, and like everything in our house, its rambling exuberance bent to her will. The flowers spilling over rock walls and popping up between pavers were contained. Barely. Cultivated chaos. It was knowable; we had counted every stone, mapped out every good spot for hide-and-seek a thousand times.

These woods were different.

Dad said our lot was two acres, stretching back into conservation wetland in a thin spaghetti strip. Looking at it from the house, there was no end to it, a knotted tapestry of gray and green, caverns receding into fathomless distance. There were no paths back there.

Despite the sticky heat, Mom insisted we wear long pants, long sleeves, rubber boots, and an ocean of bug spray.

"You'll thank me later," she snapped when Deirdre protested its antiseptic smell. "You'll get eaten alive without it back there. Look out for poison ivy. You know what that looks like, right? Leaves of three, let it be? And stay within sight of the house!"

"Yeah, yeah," I grumbled, pulling my shirt away from my back where it was already clingy with sweat.

Mog darted between our feet to slip out the door as we left, almost tripping me, despite the bell on her collar announcing her approach. Mog was a sleek seal of a cat with scornful yellow eyes. She was Deirdre's cat—she slept on her pillow, curled up on her hair, and didn't suffer anyone else to pick her up.

Since we'd arrived, she'd been unstoppable, the terror of the countryside. On our doorstep, gruesome offerings accumulated, lined up neatly in a row. Little furry things with tails. Once, she left us a bird's wing, feathers ripped out in patches, minus the rest of the bird. Now that Mom had her wearing the collar and bell, there weren't as many corpses, but you still had to watch your step going out the front door, just in case.

We'd seen her drop a victim and let it make a run for it before she pounced and tossed it in the air, her bell jingling cheerfully. She'd nudge it with her claws until it tried to flee again, and then pounce. Repeat. And repeat. When I opened the door to intervene, a little nauseated, Mog just snatched up her victim and trotted off around the corner of the house.

"She's a cat," had been Deirdre's unconcerned comment. "That's what they do."

We trooped out across the lawn, grasshoppers springing away from our crashing feet, Mog zigzagging after us. One corner of the yard was occupied by a garden patch so overgrown I didn't recognize it until raspberry canes crunched under my boots. Hard green apples clung to the branches of the stooping tree whose limbs fanned out above us. Beneath it was a gateway; under the eaves of the trees, the ground sloped sharply downwards, like it had been cut with a shovel. Arching fern fronds disguised humped and knotted tree roots.

We had to feel our way down, step by step, shrill mosquitos whining in our ears. After several feet, we came to the forest floor. Tufts of grass and reeds wove around puddles of standing water, reflecting the pale gray sky and endless layers of leaves.

Floor wasn't really the right word, it turned out. It wasn't solid. Even places that looked grassy and safe could suck your foot down unexpectedly. Nothing else walked upright in this place; we had to push through the interlacing branches, and they resented every step, snagging at our long clothes with a thousand clawed hands. Our progress was slow and blundering. Before long, my jeans were soaked and muddy to the knee, water sloshing in my boots. Only Mog threaded the labyrinth with ease, padding up the sloping trunks of fallen trees, hopping delicately from one patch of dry ground to the next, stopping to watch us disdainfully before loping on ahead. Trying to follow her was hopeless—she was much lighter than us, and she could jump farther. After a while she gave up on us and disappeared into the trees. We tried to balance on fallen logs for a while, but those weren't trustworthy either, creaking dangerously under our weight or flaking and crumbling wetly, mushrooms snapping under our boots.

I swore and slapped at mosquitos biting my neck. Deirdre didn't even notice, looking around enraptured, craning her neck and turning around and around to see it all.

"There's a whole kingdom here," she breathed. "Can't you feel it, Skye? It's *magical.*"

"Yeah, sure," I growled. "It's populated by vampire bugs."

"It makes the valley look so tame." She sloshed forward, undeterred. "It's like it's been waiting for us. It feels *alive.* Like a dryad forest. You know?"

I crossed my arms against a prickle of goose bumps, despite the heat, and pushed past her without answering. The maze whispered around us, layered with singing insects, secretive more than peaceful, dense as a closed fist.

After an eternity of crashing through the muggy, airless brush, Deirdre struggling along behind me—"Skye! Wait up!"—I stumbled into the creek that cut between our lot and the next one over. It was sluggish, choked with cattails, its bottom murky and indeterminate, sucking at my boots. But at least it was a space between the trees, a gap in the endless thicket of branches. Even there, they leaned over me, reaching across the sky.

"Skye!" Deirdre called after me, protesting, as I started to slosh through the water. "Not that way! I want to see what's back there!"

"We have to stay within sight of the house!"

"Since when do you care what Mom says? And anyway, we can't get lost if we're following the water, it's—"

"Come *on*," I yelled over my shoulder. After a long moment, she fell into step behind me, muttering under her breath. Eventually, reluctantly, the cedars parted to reveal the house on our right. All that, and we'd only crossed the yard. The empty lot on our left rippled with knee-high grass, interspersed with spires of silver thistles, delicate sprays of Queen Anne's lace, blue fireworks of chicory. It blended gradually into the woods, a swelling tangle of small trees and bushes. On the far side, rising out of it, was a huge mound of dirt, one and a half times taller than either of us, wide as the house. Its peak was tufted with grass and weeds, one side left raw and bare, like a cresting wave.

Deirdre pushed through the reeds that flanked the creek and headed straight for it. I shoved my sweaty, tangled hair out of my face and followed her. Crickets fell silent in our wake.

"This is amazing!" Deirdre's voice drifted back to me as she disappeared behind the dirt pile.

"Deirdre, can we go home already please?"

She levered herself up to the crest of the pile, stood carefully, and walked along its edge, her skinny arms flung wide—not for balance, but in a gesture of ownership.

"We should call it something," she yelled down to me.

"What?"

"This! Doesn't it look like a castle? With ramparts and everything! Come on, Skye, you can climb right up the back!"

I followed her, grabbing handfuls of yellowing grass and digging my toes into the crumbling soil until I could plunk myself down beside her, my feet dangling over the edge into the air. I had to admit, I could sort of see what she meant. The dirt pile backed up against the edge of the forest, and the block spread out before us: the empty lot full of dancing grass, the black twist of the creek, the trees encroaching in a ragged line where the bulldozers must have stopped. The road running away from it, up the hill, disappearing around a corner.

If it was a castle, it was a ruined one. Haunted, maybe. As if at the smallest lapse in vigilance—if you slept, if you blinked—the woods would surround it, flowing around it like a snake. They'd swallow it whole.

Undeterred by my silence, Deirdre scrambled up and down the slope, hunting through the grass, and returned to me, panting, with a fallen branch, snapping off little twigs to make a single, slightly crooked stick with a feathery crown of browned cedar fronds.

"Here." She stabbed the stick into the earth between us so it stood upright. "I declare this our stronghold. By wood, stone, water, and bone." She looked up at me expectantly. I looked away. "Come on, you have to say it too."

"No, thanks."

"But you're the Queen of Swords!"

"I'm not playing that anymore," I snapped. "You know that." She stared at me.

"I thought moving would help," she said, turning petulant. "What's wrong with you? Ever since you captured Tyler—"

The name was like a slap, and I reeled away from it.

"Don't talk to me about that." I focused on my muddy knees. Didn't look at her. "I told you not to *ever* talk to me about that."

"I don't know what your problem is," she huffed. "He deserved it." That sent me to my feet, but she continued anyway, raising her voice into a full-on whine. "And now it's like you're *abdicating*, you won't even—"

"That's right. I won't. I'm going home."

The jump to the ground jarred through my legs, and I almost fell. I didn't look back to see if Deirdre was following.

She chattered on endlessly, those first few weeks, grafting the kingdoms on to the wilderness outside, trying to draw me in. I stonewalled every attempt. There was no more Queen of Swords— just Skye. And I was sick of waging war.

I was measuring dish soap into a teaspoon, following instructions in a garden magazine, when she came galloping into the kitchen.

"Skye! Come be the Queen of Swords! I need you!"

What she needed was a shower. I could smell her from across the room. "I'm in the middle of something," I said, tipping the soap into a spray bottle and swishing it around.

"Come *on*," she said breathlessly, bouncing on the balls of her feet. "It's amazing out there. You're not even going to believe it. Here, I found your sword. Come outside!"

She held the taped-up hilt out to me. Nudged my arm with the pommel.

"Ow!" I yanked it away from her. A crown of wild daisies and chicory and dandelions drooped lopsidedly over her sweaty forehead. Her gold necklace, the one engraved with the tree design, sparkled against the dirt-smeared fabric of her dress. One of these days, she was going to lose it somewhere. God, it was like she was still nine years old. I dumped the sword on the counter with a clatter and aimed a jet of soapy water at the little yellow bugs that had taken up residence in the leaves of my cyclamen.

"You go ahead," I said, as neutrally as possible. She stomped her foot.

"It's not just me! It's our *kingdom*, Skye, it wants to meet you! Pretty please?"

"I'm busy."

"You're just messing around with your stupid plants!"

"At least plants are real." Unlike Deirdre's obsessions. Plants are full of marvelous secrets you can witness and chart. I watched a YouTube video once of time-lapse footage of morning glories growing. As their heart-shaped leaves open and expand, climbing tendrils whirl around in place until they latch on blindly to something. Miraculous and silent and utterly unobserved, unless you're paying attention.

"This *is* real. It's right out there waiting for us. If you would just—"

"I'm not interested!" I flung the words at her. "And you'd better not let Mom see that stuff in your hair. Remember what she said about ticks?"

She hesitated a moment longer; then she tossed back a *fine!* and stormed from the room.

I waited until I heard the front door slam behind her. Then I set the cyclamen aside and picked the sword up from the counter.

The garage was even hotter than the yard, its shadowy depths stifling. Light leaked under the door in a molten line, and a couple of intrepid crickets creaked through the dark. I hurried down the stairs and tossed the sword into the corner beside the pile of firewood the previous owners had left.

I slammed back into the kitchen, turned the tap on, let a sparkling trickle wash the soap off the leaves. I couldn't make her grow up. If she was going to disappear into her imaginary world and make herself a target all over again, it wasn't like I could stop her.

But she wasn't keeping me in there with her. Not anymore.

Dad had been making a determined effort to meet the neighbors, marching up the hill from house to house to offer laid-back charm and a handshake. Look at us, such a nice, normal family. He must have been convincing, because a hubbub of voices spilling down the hall announced the arrival of the Wrights, repaying his visit.

Deirdre scowled and shut herself in the bathroom, the lock clicking behind her. Well, that was just fine with me. This was my first contact with whatever alien life-forms I had to go to school with. It would be easier without her.

Bill Wright was a jovial barrel of a man with a neat gray beard and a crushing handshake. Mrs. Wright—Angie, she insisted I call her—had a polished smile and an even, golden tan at odds with her track pants and the pencil fastening her hair in its loose bun. Trailing behind their parents, quiet and awkward—maybe bored—were a girl I could only describe as *shiny*, with nails and lip gloss gleaming, and a boy whose long hair was pulled into a thick ponytail, little strands escaping around his face and sticking to his temples. Behind a pair of glasses, his eyes, meeting mine, were lively and gray.

"This is William." Bill clamped an arm around his shoulders, jostling him a little.

"Junior?" Mom guessed.

"The fifth, actually. Carrying on a long tradition, eh?"

William Wright V gave a tilted, faintly pained smile, straightened his glasses, and stepped out of his dad's embrace to extend his hand to me. "Just William. Nice to meet you."

His palm against mine was warm, a little damp. "Skye."

"This is my sister, Christina," he said, since the adults were drifting up the stairs without us. The shiny girl gave a little sigh and rippled her fingers at me in a wave before folding her arms again.

"You're at Hillcrest, right?" I asked her, making my voice bright and friendly. "What grade?"

"Eighth."

Same as Deirdre, then. Defensive dismay washed over me in a hot, familiar wave, but I pushed it down, kept my smile on. It was preordained: They were going to hate each other. It wasn't like I could prevent it. It wasn't my problem.

I led them upstairs after our parents, trying to think of something else to say. Bill was regaling Dad with neighborhood history—the Wrights, apparently, were the first family in the area—while Mom exclaimed over the character of their stone house at the top of the hill. Angie laughed and said something rueful about how the place was in constant danger of falling apart.

"Our youngest is feeling a little shy," Mom explained, leading everyone into the kitchen, casting a pointed glance back at me over her shoulder. "Skye, could you go see what Deirdre's up to? Please?" She said it casually, but there was a faint steely edge to the words that suggested Deirdre was getting included whether she liked it or not. "Maybe you guys could start one of those board games she likes, that ought to get her attention."

I left William and Christina to make small talk with the adults and hurried down the hall to our room. Deirdre was kneeling on her bed, leaning on the windowsill. She was fiddling with something, whispering to herself. A little Tupperware container sat at her elbow, full of—what, pebbles? Shells?

"Deir, do you want to play Catan or something?" She didn't answer. "Deirdre. Mom wants you to come out. Come on."

"I'm not going anywhere with *them*," she shot back sullenly.

"Who, the Wrights? You haven't even met them yet."

"I don't have to. I've heard all about them. They're invaders."

"Will you please just drop whatever stupid game you're—"

"It's not a game! I don't want them here!"

The floor creaked behind me, signaling William's arrival. He stood at my elbow, flashed the same self-conscious smile.

"Hi," he said cheerfully to Deirdre. She looked around at us, sidelong through her hair, and didn't answer.

"Come on." I started toward her, trying not to speak through my teeth. "Mom will be after you next, so you might as well—Jesus, Deirdre, are those—"

At my approach, she'd extended her hand, displaying two yellowing little ovals cradled in her palm. Tiny skulls, frail as eggshells.

"I think they were mice," she said matter-of-factly, ignoring my recoil.

"Where did you even—those aren't Mog's, are they?"

"Did you know that when owls eat their prey they throw up the fur and bones afterward?"

"Oh, gross, Deirdre—!"

"They leave these little dried-up pucks around. Like under the trees beside the castle. Or in the long grass. If you take them apart, the bones are inside."

"Cool," said William from the doorway. God, he actually sounded interested. "Can I see?"

Deirdre shied back, cradling the bones to her chest, and scowled at him.

"No," she said, glowering. "They don't like you."

"Deirdre!"

"They don't," she insisted. She got to her feet, not breaking eye contact with William, whose eyebrows had gone way up. "Do you spend much time in the woods around here, *William?*"

"Uh, sometimes, I guess," he began, but she cut him off, her voice a wicked hiss.

"You shouldn't. *They* don't like you either. You're not welcome here."

"Deirdre, are you seriously going to—"

"You go in there, and they'll chew you up and spit you out just like an owl would. Just like *this*."

She brandished one of the skulls at him. I pressed a hand to my face, closed my eyes.

"Um. Oookay." William took a step back from the door. Deirdre turned away from him, stroking the skulls with one finger like they were pets in need of soothing, crooning to them in an undertone. "Sorry. I didn't mean to...well...sorry."

His footsteps faded. I thumped the nearest shelf on the plant stand with my fist, sending a shiver through its greenery.

"What is wrong with you?" I hurled at her, keeping my voice low. "Could you *get* any creepier?"

She shrugged—hiding a smile, I thought—and turned back to the windowsill, where a dozen more little skulls were arranged in a wide arc.

"If Mom catches you with those, she'll make you bathe in bleach. You know that, right?"

She rolled her eyes, but after a moment, she swept her grim collection back into the Tupperware, snapped the lid over it. Feeling like I'd done way more than my duty, I turned on my heel and stalked from the room.

In the dining room, I pulled the lid from the box for Settlers of Catan and set about arranging the hexagons on the carpet to make the board.

"I'm really sorry," I muttered to William. "She is the biggest freak."

The awkwardness in his answering shrug made me wince, and I moved on to explaining how the game worked instead of trying to comment further. I could feel Mom trying to catch my eye, but I kept my attention on the board.

Christina drifted away from the game partway through the rules, but William turned out to be alarmingly good at it, with an eye for strategy that surprised me. I guess it shouldn't have, given his vaguely nerdy vibe.

"Damn," I said as he cornered one of the two-for-one ports. "Are you sure you haven't played this before?"

"Yup." He grinned and passed me a handful of sheep cards. "This is for a city, by the way."

Deirdre chose that moment to sidle into the kitchen, head down, still refusing to meet my eye, glaring at William's back. He saw me looking past him and twisted around. Deirdre's scowl deepened. She was fiddling with something in the pockets of her dress.

"Well, I have the longest road now," I announced loudly, and he turned back to the game. I caught his gaze, rolled my eyes. He smiled crookedly in response. But he was obviously uncomfortable after that, shifting his weight a little bit, his eyes flickering to the side every now and then like he was resisting the urge to look around again. Mom tried to draw Deirdre into conversation with the grown-ups but got only monosyllables. She refused to join them at the kitchen table and shrank into the corner instead. Her presence blighted the room, and eventually the Wrights started to make bright, friendly overtures about heading home.

SIX

I FORGOT ABOUT THE COPS.

I freeze for a second on the doorstep, though there's no way they'd miss me, standing in the bright circle of the porch lights. Past the mobile headquarters still parked in the driveway, two cars are parked on the road, illuminated islands. The occupant of the nearest one is looking out into the dark over the rim of a coffee cup.

Well, for all they know, I have permission. It's not even that late. And they're not here to worry about me, anyway.

So I toss my hair out of my face, fold my arms against the chill, and crunch down the driveway like I have every right to be there. The officer in the closest car catches my eye as I come out onto the road, nods at me. I flash my hand in a wave, but don't slow down, don't look up again until I'm around the bend of the road, out of sight.

It's so quiet. The light of the streetlight at the corner spills down the pavement, but on either side, the woods make a darkness so impenetrable I should be able to touch it, a solid velvety curtain hanging in the air.

Somewhere behind it is Deirdre.

The more I refuse to think about Deirdre, the more I can't help it. And the angrier I get. Idiot. What did she think she was doing? It's as if this whole thing is some sort of joke. She could be right behind me even now, sneaking up on me with bare feet. I can just imagine her leaping forward to grab my hand and laughing, laughing when I scream. I clench my fists in my pockets and walk faster.

Kevin lives at the top of the hill, at the end of the road that disappears eastwards into the woods. Up there, the trees are higher, the spaces between them airier, the ground more solid, more open. Past the cars filling the long driveway, past the dark and silent house, a track of crunching pine needles eventually opens up into a wide, scrubby space, dominated by a broad shelf of flattened rock. They call it the party rock. It's justly famous.

Tonight, though, it's more subdued than I expected, only a dozen people or so, sitting around the dancing light of a fire. I guess having the police cruising past all night would cast a bit of a chill. I hesitate at the edge of the rock, suddenly not sure I should have come, not sure I can pass for one of them tonight. What the hell am I even going to say?

But Sophie, sporting the kind of sparkly butterfly wings that kids wear over her low-cut top, spots me first, and says *hey*, in a perfect blend of surprise and concern. A wave of silence washes over the clearing. I swallow and shuffle farther into the light.

"Hey," I manage.

"We didn't think you were coming," Sophie says after an uncomfortable pause. Sucks to be her, she's the designated spokesperson now. "Is there—? Did they, you know—?"

"Not yet." I can't afford a stone-faced stare. Not here. I need to be brittle, vulnerable. That's what they want to see. I can do that. "I just wanted to get out of the house."

Sophie bites her lip in sympathetic horror. Beside her, William sneaks occasional glances my way, but Sophie holds my gaze. She's good. I guess she has to be, to keep all the pieces of her spiderweb intact. If I play it right, changing the subject won't be weird. I swallow, blink up at the sky for a second, and then offer her a shy, shaky smile.

"Nice wings," I say, and she smiles back. Relieved. She's good, but she's not that good.

"Do you want something to drink?"

"Hell yes," I say fervently, and their awkward laughter washes over me, warms me through.

Sophie scoots over to open a space for me to sit between her and William, who's wearing a cowboy hat. Ironic accessories. I totally called it. And then she startles me by putting an arm around me and resting her head on my shoulder. I stiffen for a split second before I remember to relax into it, rest my cheek against her hair to accept the hug. William, not quite as bold, leans his shoulder into mine companionably. Even Kevin twists his lips into an appropriate grimace.

"I'm sorry," I say into the silence. "This is weird, isn't it? I didn't want to make everything weird."

"Don't be ridiculous," Sophie says firmly. She kind of has to say it, but even so, I'm absurdly reassured. "We're glad you're here."

"We were worried about you," William adds.

Slowly, conversation starts back up around us, though mostly they avoid my eyes. Which is fine by me. I sip at the drink Sophie brings me, one of the vile pink concoctions she likes. I guess it's better than beer. Around me, they relive sports victories, pass somebody's phone around to cackle at an internet video, speculate over the sex lives of teachers. They spend a long time dissecting what's going on between Zeke and Brittany, and whether they're together again or not and how everyone hopes he's not that stupid, especially after she hooked up with that guy behind Jared's back, and what kind of desperate slut is she trying to dress like anyway.

"Don't call her that," Kevin says, suddenly serious, and a brief silence is broken by James and Adam hooting at him. "Hey, shut up, I mean it."

I hide my surprise in a scoff. "Who are you, and what have you done with Kevin?"

He rolls his eyes, takes a moody gulp of his beer, and doesn't answer.

"You were the one who caught them at it," Sophie says. "Come on. If the shoe fits…"

"Exactly." James lifts his bottle in salute. "Thank you."

Adam's not ready to let it drop yet. "Hang on. *You* were the one who saw them? Holy shit, man, I didn't know that! Who was it?"

"I don't know," Kevin grumbles. "Why the hell does anyone still care about this? It was, like, two years ago."

Sophie tosses her hair, a blond waterfall that never seems to turn tangled or stringy, no matter how windy it is, how long she leaves it down.

"So what? Actions have consequences."

"Aw, Kevin's just hoping for his turn." James grins. "Admit it, Kev, you'd totally hit that if you got the chance."

Kevin hits James instead, to general hilarity, though James rubs his arm surreptitiously once the spotlight has moved past him.

"You can't really blame him," Adam muses. "I mean, Brittany's pretty hot."

"From the neck down," Kevin mutters, and that's more like him, so everyone laughs again. I manage to smile enough that I'm participating. But something bristles under my skin, refusing to be soothed. A voice that sounds like Deirdre's.

Seriously? it says. *This is what you chose? Over your sister?*

When I get up to pull another drink from the cooler, a voice at my elbow startles me.

"Hey." It's Kevin, of all people.

"Hi." I eye him warily, wondering what he's about to pull.

"I just wanted to say—you know, I'm sorry. About your sister. That…that really sucks, you know?"

"Yeah." Is this sincerity? From Kevin? How drunk is he? The whole world is upside down tonight. "Thanks."

"Do they know what happened yet?"

"No. It's like she vanished into thin air."

He peers at me. Hiccups. He must be drunk.

"Do you think she ran away? I heard she was kind of, you know, freaky. Like, at school, I mean."

I don't bother to hide my bristling irritation. "You're in on all the eighth grade gossip, huh?"

"Seriously, I heard she was, like, trying to hex people in her class, and got all mad when it didn't work. Like she really expected it to. Maybe she—"

"Look," I snap, "can you just back off already?"

He blinks at me. "You don't need to bite my head off. I'm just trying to, you know, express concern and shit."

"Yeah. Right." I bare my teeth in something like a smile, not caring that it's transparently false. "So, what's the deal with you and Brittany, then?"

"What's that supposed to mean?"

"Why do you care if anyone calls her a slut? Was it you who slept with her?"

Score one for me. He jerks his head back a little, like I slapped him. And then he takes a step closer. Thinking he can intimidate me, maybe? He should know better.

"You don't know a fucking thing about—"

"I'm just trying to, you know, express concern and shit."

"Right. Whatever." He throws up his hands in surrender, retreats. "Jesus."

William claps him on the shoulder as he reaches the fire, and they both glance my way. Kevin says something, intense and scowling, and William protests. Kevin turns a hand out in a gesture that plainly says *fucking whatever*, and after a last reproachful glare at me, he turns his back and sits again.

William, meanwhile, jogs over to me. I focus on twisting the cap off my drink.

"What happened there?" he asks.

"Kevin," I say shortly. "Being Kevin."

William sighs. "Yeah."

"Remind me why the hell you hang out with him again?"

"He's really not as obnoxious as he pretends to be."

You wouldn't know it, considering the assholes he hangs out with. I steal a glance at James and Adam, interchangeable jocks in hoodies and backward baseball caps, laughing again over Adam's phone. Kevin's in his element. I'm tempted to say it aloud, but William might think it includes him. I take a long swallow of my drink instead of speaking.

"Give him a chance," William says. "You guys just…got off on the wrong foot."

"Yeah. And *you* guys keep making excuses for him."

He winces, glances back toward the fire. I draw a deep breath. It's time to go. I have to get out of here before I do any more damage.

"Never mind. I shouldn't have come."

"Skye—"

"No, it's all right." I push my just-opened drink at him.

"I could walk with you, at least." He starts after me, but I throw an arm out to block his way, stop just short of hitting him, and he jerks to a startled halt.

I pull my hand back, a little shaken. Drinking was a bad idea. I've got to get my shit together.

"Just leave me alone." My voice trembles. Great. What the hell is wrong with me?

I glance back just once, as I reach the edge of the trees. He's still staring after me.

I kick myself all the way down the hill. I should have known better than to get in Kevin's face. He was just…being Kevin. I let him get to me. Why is everything getting to me all of a sudden?

But I know the answer to that: It's Deirdre. Like it always is. I couldn't stand the idea of them talking about her. Not just because Kevin's act is too much like certain assholes who came before him. Because I didn't want her invading my life, taking it over. Not again. Not here.

Because for a minute, I fell right back into defending her, into being the Queen of Swords. Without thinking. Like it's a reflex.

Like I never stopped.

I've almost reached the cop cars when a twinkling silver noise makes me jump: a bell. Like Mog used to wear.

I stop dead in the middle of the street, straining my ears, turning around and around. There it is again. I'm not imagining it.

"Mog?"

The street is empty, the darkness of the woods complete. The sound pauses, jingles, weaves closer. I can't tell where it's coming from.

"Mog! Here, kitty!" If it's her, she listens about as well as she ever did. It couldn't be her, not after so many weeks. Deirdre would be beside herself. A picture of her flickers through my imagination: She'd be sobbing, tears dripping into Mog's gray fur as she squirmed to escape Deirdre's embrace. My heart crimps into a small and painful knot.

I turn on the flashlight on my phone, cast its pale circle of light over tall dead grass, brown cattails turning fuzzy, losing their firm shape. The bulk of the dirt castle looms just beyond the light.

The sound of the bell twinkles out through the dark.

I push my way into the empty lot, shivering, calling Mog's name, snapping my fingers, and making encouraging smoochy noises. The bell sounds again whenever I fall silent, pinging on ahead of me.

Something catches my eye, a flicker at the edge of the woods. There, between the trees—a light? Is there more than one? It winks off, then on again. Vanishes, then reappears a little farther on. Pulsing in and out at the edge of my vision.

It's way too late in the year for fireflies.

I lurch after it, about to run, but my next step sends me stumbling over the bank and into the creek, a trickle of water barely visible between the reeds. My running shoes are promptly soaked through, icy water biting into my feet.

"Hello?" Someone calls, an urgent male voice. A car door slams, and a flashlight beam catches me in the face. I put a hand up to shield my eyes. "Hello? Who's there?"

"It's me," I manage. "It's Skye. It's just me."

The officer doesn't move his flashlight. "What are you doing?"

"It's just—our cat went missing last month, and I heard—I thought I heard—" I twist around to look at the woods again, but there's no sign of whatever it was I glimpsed. "And I saw something just now. A light. In the woods. I swear I did."

We stand there a moment, his flashlight scanning the face of the forest, back and forth, searching. Everything is silent. The light splashes over gray tree trunks, tall grass.

Maybe Deirdre heard the same sound. Maybe she followed a dancing light into the woods.

"I heard a bell," I stammer. "Like Mog used to wear. I *heard* it."

"I expect there's other cats around with bells," the officer says kindly. "It does get kind of spooky out here. Let me help you up."

"Deirdre?" The shrill voice comes from the house as he pulls me up the bank. A door slams. Mom. Oh shit. "Deirdre, baby, is that you?"

I'm going to catch hell, but it's not like there's any escape. And I can't stand the hope in her voice.

"No, Mom. It's me. It's Skye."

"What?" Her face, as she runs up into the light of the flashlight, is pinched and white. "Skye?" She leans against her knees, lets out all her breath. "Oh. Oh, dammit, Skye, I thought—" Her voice breaks. She buries her face in her hands.

"I didn't mean to make you—"

She looks up at me, her eyes brimming, accusing, and doesn't let me finish.

"What are you doing out here?"

"I just went for a walk."

Mom leans closer to me, her frown deepening.

"Then why do you smell like a campfire?" she demands. "And—and *beer?*"

The police officer sighs, raises his eyebrows at me.

"I walked to Kevin's," I amend quickly. "I didn't go far! I just wanted—"

"Wasn't he having a party tonight?" Mom folds her arms, her voice going dead level. Bad sign.

"Mom—"

"A party. Deirdre is missing. And you went to a party."

"Mom, listen—"

"We will discuss this later." The most ominous phrase in their parental lexicon. She sags in place, props her forehead against her hand. "Inside. Now."

I scurry into the house, trade my soggy-cuffed jeans for flannel pajama bottoms, crawl into bed. The front door slams again, but Mom's footsteps creak slowly up the stairs instead of down toward me. She doesn't want to have that conversation any more than I do.

The porch light spills through my window, won't let me sleep. It's stupid, but it's Halloween and it's almost midnight, and it feels like something was calling me. Leading me on, leading me into the woods.

Deirdre would have followed it.

SEVEN

September

I T WASN'T THAT I WANTED to be popular or anything. Who would throw themselves into that shark tank on purpose? The top of the food chain was a scary place—all the stormy drama, the breakups everyone talks about, the betrayals that draw lines in the sand and leave feuds simmering for months. But I didn't want Deirdre's place as the class freak, and I didn't want the place I'd left behind either. I didn't want to be the one everyone avoided, whispered about, even if they were too chicken to cross me.

I was an unknown quantity here, and sooner or later they'd test me, to see what I was made of. They weren't any threat to me. That was well established by now. But I couldn't make myself dangerous enough for them to declare me a threat either. I would not be Psycho Skye, not here. I had to be steel, inert. If I earned their respect, just enough respect, I'd drop off the radar, a piece of the landscape, and they'd leave me more or less alone.

We got on a yellow school bus at the mailbox at the top of the hill, in the long chilly shadow of William's stone square of a house. Kevin was the one channelling a sort of jock Kylo Ren vibe, with black curls and a long face that went intense in concentration but broke into a wide, lazy smile. And there was Sophie, glossy and put together, but never so much that she looked like she cared, deflecting the sharpest jokes from the boys with pitch-perfect amusement.

I was wary of William at first. He seemed too nice. A potential liability. I didn't need to end up defending somebody all over again. I'd placed him somewhere on the sidelines—a high achiever, maybe a drama geek. But at school, he ditched the glasses for contacts. He stood straighter, so I suddenly noticed he was a head taller than me. He laughed louder, wrestled in the halls and slapped shoulders and traded crass dudebro jokes without caution. He moved through the day there with genuine ease, bouncing sunnily between cliques with that same self-conscious smile. Everyone seemed to like him.

And he liked me.

It was William who invited me to that first party at Kevin's back in September. Up till that point, Kevin hadn't said much to me beyond *hey*, but still, that invitation was the first solid good sign—it signaled neutrality, at least. I was under consideration. A possibility.

The woods withdrew like a cautious animal from the firelight, the thick blanketing smell of pot and woodsmoke and beer, the music blaring from speakers hooked up to somebody's phone. I sat next to William by the fire, taking occasional swallows—not gulps, not sips—from the bottle in my hand. The beer tasted like old sour socks, but drinking steadily, I'd managed to down one and half of another. Across from us, Kevin was already staggering and gesturing expansively, inspired to deep thoughts by Sophie's halter top.

"Sophie's almost got too much on top, you know? Like, all you need is a handful." He mimed a feel with one hand while his beer tipped dangerously in the other, splashing a little on the ground. "The best is the girls with little tits and, like, these huge-ass cookie nipples. I love that. 'S fuckin' hilarious."

"Jesus, Kev," William said, though he softened it with a laugh, "do you hear yourself?"

"What? I'm just saying."

William glared at him, then gave me a look that might have been apologetic. Kevin grinned. Something about the glance, the edge in William's voice, suggested that Sophie wasn't the only one whose assets they'd discussed. Interesting. I downed another mouthful of beer.

"Aww, don't worry about Skye," Kevin said, stretching. "Skye's cool. She knows I'm harmless. Right?"

"Seriously," William protested. "You can't just say shit like—"

"Relax, William," I interrupted. "It doesn't matter. He's not going to talk about *my* boobs, because I'd kick his ass."

"Ooooooh," Kevin crowed.

"I'm serious." I put on a smile. "I have a blue belt."

"What, like that's impressive? I thought you were going to say you had a *black* belt—"

"I might have had a black belt if I'd gone to some crappy McDojo that just handed out belts to get people to shell out more cash. It wouldn't mean I was any good." I paused. That was more than I'd meant to say. But fuck it. I was feeling expansive myself. A little reckless, even. Warmth tingled in my cheeks despite the chilly night. "I'm not bad. I could take either of you."

"Oh, come on." With the subject safely changed, William was smiling again. "We both outweigh you by, like, fifty pounds. At least."

"So? I've got training. Come on, get up. I'll show you some stuff."

Kevin cackled as William reluctantly obeyed, handing off his own drink.

"Make a fist," I told him, and shook my head when he did. "No, no. You've got to keep your thumb out of the way." His hands were bigger than mine. I pressed his fingers into formation; they were warm against my own. "Make your knuckles flat. Otherwise you just hurt your hand. See? Your feet need to be shoulder-width apart. Move that one up a little. Like that."

We started to draw onlookers, firelit shadows heckling and shouting encouragement, as I showed him how to hunch his shoulders to protect his chin, how to jab without chicken-winging his elbow out to the side, how to step forward to put his weight into it.

"Yeah, yeah," Kevin drawled as William clumsily copied me. "But you wouldn't actually *hit* him."

I turned to look at him, hands on hips, considering.

"I will punch *you*," I said into a sudden hush, "hard enough to make your eyes water. But not hard enough to make your nose bleed."

"You would not," he scoffed. "You can't even do that. No way."

"Sure I can. I will." I beckoned. "Bring it on."

He pushed himself up from the ground, almost fell down again. For a moment, a different face bloomed in my memory. A different smirk, a spiky haircut. The warmth curdled in my stomach, but I stood my ground.

That was before. Kevin was just a garden-variety douchebag. I knew that. And I knew what I was doing. I would not go overboard.

Kevin came shuffling forward, bobbing and weaving exaggeratedly. I watched. I watched. And then when he came close enough, I snapped my hand out.

I didn't even punch him, really. It was more like I shoved his nose with my fist. But he was drunk, and the stone surface was uneven, and he stumbled backward and fell on his ass. He sat there as everyone laughed and cheered, blinking rapidly, and put a hand to his face. He wasn't bleeding.

"I cannot believe you did that," he said slowly.

"I told you." I picked up my bottle and drained it. William helped Kevin to his feet, laughing at his slurred protests. When William met my eyes, his face was full of undisguised admiration. And I grinned back.

Because that was it. I'd done it. I was in.

After the party, everyone knew who I was. I was on edgy high alert at first when people started looking at me and talking as I passed in the halls. But no, history wasn't repeating itself. They were smiling at me, sometimes even stopping me to bestow a high five. Sophie was the one who tracked me down at my locker to show me why—someone had recorded the whole thing on their phone. The comments piled up.

OMG NINJA SKILLZ.
Boom!
#pwned.

"What's your handle?" she demanded. "I have to tag you!"

I didn't have one. I'd carefully erased any trace of myself on social media. But at her urging, I reluctantly created one account, first name only, the profile picture an anonymous quarter of my face.

That's @NightSkye you guys, **Sophie tapped out.** SHE IS THE BESSSSST!!!!

I smiled when she showed me the screen. "Aw." It was the Sophie thing to say, the right thing to say. She swung her hair over her shoulder, looking pleased with herself.

"I don't see what the big deal is," Kevin grumbled at her elbow. He was going along with it—he didn't really have a choice; if people thought he actually cared, the laughter at his expense would turn scornful—but he was still sulking. Sophie gave him a shove.

"Oh, get over yourself. It's funny."

You could learn a lot, watching Sophie. She was one of those people everyone knows, a hub of information carefully stockpiled, casually traded. She said *aw, thank you* with sincere eyes, swapped self-deprecating compliments like it was an Olympic sport or a secret handshake. A few words from her—*guys, this is* hard—were enough to bring all the boys tripping over themselves to contradict and encourage her. William and Kevin included. I watched it happen in biology, torn between being appalled and admiring her technique.

I couldn't decide whether she knew she was doing it or not. That wasn't the sort of thing you asked.

Deirdre was not doing well at school. Surprise. Three weeks in, the fighting at home was going full tilt: Mom attempting to figure out what the problem was, Deirdre resisting with every ounce of breath and volume she could summon.

The only place to escape was outside. With the windows open, Deirdre's shrill voice followed me even there, so I'd walk around the long loop of the block, through the bright golden heat of afternoons whirring with crickets.

One of those afternoons, as I stepped out of the shadow of the house, a sound drew my gaze to the empty lot. *Thok…thok… thok.* William strode through the tall grass, bending to collect

something from the foot of the dirt pile. His hair made him easy
to recognize, even at a distance. As I waded across the yard, he
paused to pull it from its ponytail, shake it out, yank it impatiently
back together into a loose knot.

"Hey," I called, and he looked up with a smile of pleased
surprise and returned the greeting. Maybe that was how he was
on everyone's good side, that unstudied way he had of making you
feel instantly welcome.

"Everything okay?" he asked, as Deirdre's voice drifted into
hearing, hitting an earsplitting pitch. I rolled my eyes.

"Just my sister. You know."

"Ha. Yeah. Been there."

Like shiny Christina had ever in her life pitched a Deirdre-
level fit. I made a face, changed the subject. "What are you doing?"

"Target practice." He lifted a contraption from the grass at
his feet, a webbed double arc of black plastic with wheels at either
end. A bow.

"Oh, *cool*." I forgot to be casual, to check my enthusiasm.

His smile broadened at my instant interest, and he passed
it to me to look at.

"Just don't dry fire it," he said. "You don't ever fire without an
arrow. It damages the bow. If you draw, don't let go of the string."

It was light in my hand, the grip worn shiny-smooth, and it
felt like a weapon. Taut, no-nonsense, elegantly deadly, like a hawk
in the sky.

"Show me." It might have come out as a command, but I
didn't care, and anyway, he took it in stride.

"See over there?" He pointed across the lot to two white oblongs propped up in front of the dirt pile, both sprayed with vivid red circles, then pulled an orange-feathered arrow from where he'd stuck it point first in the dirt. He drew in one smooth motion, pulling the feathers back to rest at the corner of his jaw. He stood for a heartbeat with the sun falling over his shoulders, still and cold-eyed in a way I would never have expected, and then let the arrow fly—*thok*—into the target. He returned my stare with a grin before reaching for the next arrow, sending it after the first.

"I'll go get them," I said when all three were gone.

"Just don't judge," he called after me. "It always psychs me out when people are watching."

But he needn't have worried, because all three arrows were buried in the red. The target, a woven fabric bag that might have once held rice, crinkled under my touch as I yanked them out.

"Holy shit, William, you're Robin Hood," I called back to him, and he laughed.

"Everyone needs a zombie apocalypse skill, right? Like your martial arts."

I jogged back across the lot, arrows in hand.

"Arrows are way better for that than martial arts. You'd get bit for sure if you tried to grapple with a zombie. And anyway, you could hunt food like this."

William's smile tilted.

"You wouldn't want me to be the hunter in a zombie apocalypse. We'd starve for sure."

"Can't hit a moving target?"

"No, I'm pretty good at that, actually." He ran a hand over his hair. "I'm just…not so good with the whole blood-and-guts part of hunting. You know?"

"Really?"

He shrugged. "My dad's always after me to go with him. That was the whole point of teaching me how to use a bow, right? He says it's something you get used to. That it's only 'intense' the first couple of times." He put air quotes around the word, his face clouding over. "Personally, puking over it the once was enough for me. I just like to shoot."

He turned away abruptly, maybe thinking he'd said too much, and fired the three arrows off again in quick succession. I went out again to retrieve them.

"I get that," I said as I made my way back to him, not wanting the confession to be awkward. "It's hard to get used to the idea of yourself as a predator."

"Nah," he said. "I'm kind of a shitty predator is all. I couldn't eat the meat from the deer we killed. Dad just about lost it, he wouldn't let me leave the table—we were sitting there past midnight. And I mean, he's right, it's more humane than factory farming, really. I should probably be a vegetarian. Like, what kind of hypocrite does that make me, if I'll eat meat but can't kill it?" He dropped his gaze to the bow, fidgeting with the string. "But that would really put him over the edge, probably."

"Isn't that kind of the point of civilization?" I handed him the arrows. "Not having to be predators anymore?"

"More like not having to be prey."

"It's kind of the same thing. Some people would never be predators except in self-defense." Careful. I had to be careful, or I'd be the one saying too much. "I bet you could be a predator in the zombie apocalypse. If you had to."

"I doubt it." He drew and fired. *Thok.* "I'd be a zombie, more likely." *Thok.* "You, on the other hand, would be a badass zombie-slaying warrior chick." *Thok.* "Dammit. See?"

"Oh, what, because you were a whole three inches off?"

He handed the bow to me and retrieved the arrows himself this time.

"Here," he said, sticking the arrows in the dirt between us. "You try."

He passed me a little leather tab for my fingers, showed me where to stand, how to hold the bow upright without clutching it so hard I'd throw off my aim, how to sight the target through the circle along the little pins.

"You want to make sure you draw to your armpit—like this—and not across your chest. This is, um, not so much a problem for guys, but, well, the last thing you want to do is hit yourself there with the bowstring."

"One more reason why all you need is a handful, I guess."

William made a derisive noise, but didn't meet my eye, looking away at the targets instead. He might have been blushing.

"Kevin's an idiot," he said, and handed me an arrow. "Anyway. Here. See, there's a notch at the end for the string, and the shaft rests on this little tab here. Draw. Give it a try."

The bow resisted at first, then swung willingly back.

"You want your fingers back here," he said, touching my jaw with one finger. It left a lingering point of warmth. "Yeah. See, then you know you're doing it the same way every time. Like that. And let go."

When I did, I was rewarded with a sudden sting against my forearm, blunt and fiery, a long red welt marking its trail, and the arrow went sailing past the target into the dirt.

"Shit! Ow!"

"Yeah. You have to sort of curve your arm away from the string a bit." He handed me another arrow. "Same thing, fingers to your jaw. Go ahead."

The string smacked into my arm again, but the arrow thumped into the target. Nowhere near the red, but I let out a whoop of triumph. The next one bit the dirt too. Still, I turned to William with a girly squeal that should have embarrassed me.

"This is amazing!"

"There's a proper range in town." He grinned. "You should take lessons."

"Or I could just practice here," I said, "with you."

It came out way too blunt. I scrambled for a way to let him off the hook, in case it was trespassing on his time, his territory, but he beamed approval at me.

"Sure," he said.

"Hey!" A shrill voice cut across the yard. Deirdre came storming through the grass, her hands in fists. "*Hey!*"

"Oh, great," I sighed. William raised a hand to wave, but Deirdre graced him only with a single baleful look before focusing on me.

"What are you doing?" she demanded.

"Target practice," William supplied again.

"Deir, you should totally see this," I told her, William's blunt friendliness shaming me into following suit. "You'll love it."

But Deirdre was having none of it. "You're out here with him? You never want to go exploring with me, but you'll come here with *him?*"

"Will you stop being ridiculous and just listen for a second?" I caught her elbow, tried to pull her over. "This is the coolest thing ever!"

"You're a traitor." She yanked her arm away from me. "Bringing him here to my place! *Him!* How could you? You're supposed to be my champion!"

"Hey," William said, finally getting defensive, "I've been coming down here since before they even built your house—"

"He doesn't belong here!" Deirdre shouted over him. "You're siding with the invaders! *Traitor!*"

"We're invaders too, Deirdre! Nobody even owns this lot!"

Her lip curled. "You like him, don't you?"

Oh my God. I didn't dare look at William. I opened my mouth to say something withering, but she cut me off.

"You do!" Her eyes were bright, threatening tears. "You're choosing him instead of me!"

"Right, because I talked to him for five minutes!"

"Just wait until he figures out what you're *really* like. He won't like you back for very long!" She glowered at William. "You watch it! You just *watch* yourself! I warned you!"

"Whatever, Queen of Melodrama," I snapped, but she was

already pushing her way back toward the house, leaving me to kick my heel down into the grass in thwarted fury.

"Crap," William said, looking stricken. "I probably shouldn't shoot here anymore."

"Are you seriously going to pay attention to her bullshit?"

"It's a safety thing. Nobody used to use this place. But if she was here sometime and I didn't know it…what if she ran out in front of me? What if I missed?"

"Let's go talk to my parents," I blazed. "She can't just throw a tantrum and expect—"

"It's fine. Really. We can use my yard, out back." He hesitated. "Mostly I come down here to get away from my dad, is all."

"I'll talk to them," I insisted. "Look, give me your number. I'll let you know. Okay?"

He brightened at that. Just a tiny bit. He shouldn't have let it show, but still, I saw it. We spent a moment punching digits into our phones, the crickets singing around us. I pocketed mine and waved a hurried goodbye.

"Text me," he called after me.

Beneath my irritation with Deirdre, a weird satisfaction pushed its way up, an optimism. Something sprouting, finding the light.

PART TWO
WILLIAM

Explorer, you tell yourself,
this is not what you came for
Although it is good here, and green;
You had meant to move with a kind of largeness,
You had planned a heavy grace, an anguished dream.

—GWENDOLYN MACEWEN, "DARK PINES UNDER WATER"

EIGHT

I WAKE TO THE PALE beginnings of daylight, to footfalls overhead in the kitchen. It takes me a heartbeat to remember why my pillow smells like smoke, why tension and misery are crouched waiting for me, seeping in with consciousness.

Deirdre. Still not back.

Dad slouches at the kitchen table in front of the laptop, poking disconsolately at it, and looks up as I come into the kitchen.

"I just fell asleep, that's all. The other night." Tears well up at the confession. Some champion. "I didn't mean to fall asleep. I don't know how it even happened."

Dad gets up to pull me into a hug. I fight for composure while he murmurs reassurances.

"Where's Mom?" I croak eventually.

"Still in bed. She was awake most of the night, anyway. Let's keep quiet so she can get some rest, okay?"

I nod, hurriedly wiping my eyes. He gives my shoulders a last squeeze. "I'm going to make some more coffee. You want some?"

While he rinses out the carafe, I lean against the patio door. The green wood of the balcony is marbled with streaks of water. It must have rained last night. That's not good. Officer Leduc said rain would wash away her trail, make it harder for the dogs to pick up her scent. Not that they had any luck yesterday, apparently.

And on the railing…what the hell?

I push the door open, then the screen, ignoring the chilly bite lingering in the air. Lined up on the railing are three, four, five little bone-pale ovals.

Skulls. Like the ones Deirdre collected from the woods.

"Dad?"

I try to keep my voice calm, but I must sound freaked out anyway, because he hurries to join me. "What? What is it?"

I point. "Were those…were those here last night?"

"Not that I saw." He frowns at them, picks one up between two fingers, and then sets it down again, scrubs his hand against his jeans. "Well. That's not creepy at all, is it?"

"Who would do that?" I demand.

Dad shakes his head. "I was wondering more how they'd get up here." Fair point; there's nothing to climb on. "Maybe it was an animal of some kind. You know how Mog used to leave critters lined up on the doorstep?"

I did hear a bell last night. But it was never bones that Mog left behind as presents. The coffee maker gurgles in the kitchen, breaking the silence.

"We'll tell the police about it," Dad says, "just in case. Leave them there and come on inside for now."

I follow him reluctantly, but linger at the door, still watching the bones on the railing. Like they might scuttle out of sight if I turn my back. Dad's hand on my shoulder startles me; he passes me a steaming mug that's almost too hot to hold. I think of the sword spinning out into the dark, the lights beckoning in the woods. An idea kindles coldly into life.

"Dad, do you think the police would let me help look?"

"They didn't let me," he says bleakly, and I wince.

"It's just that—she—I was in her room last night. And I found my sword. On her bed, under the leaves." His brows quirk in weary puzzlement. I stumble on. "I know it sounds dumb, but it was like it was supposed to be some sort of message. I think she wanted me to come looking for her. And last night, I heard this bell, it was just like Mog's, and I thought maybe—"

Dad sighs and rubs his forehead.

"Skye—honey—it doesn't really matter who she wanted to come looking for her or why she went into the woods. We have to let the police do their job. Okay?"

"But what if it's some kind of lead?" I hate the pleading note in my voice. I sound like a little kid.

"Well, I suppose you could tell the police about it. I don't know what kind of lead that could really give them, but no harm in trying." He fixes me with a look. "But you stay out of those woods. Got it?"

I stare into my coffee to avoid his eyes. It's true—there's nothing I could do out there. If she were just waiting somewhere to hear my voice, they'd have found her in about five minutes.

There's a knock at the front door, and Dad hurries to answer it. I trail over to the computer. It's open to the latest post on the search page: Deirdre's smiling face again, a non-update—there's nothing to tell—and a plea for information that's followed by an endless string of useless mealymouthed comments.

I hope she's enjoying this. Having everyone's absolute, undivided attention.

When I stab at the track pad to close the tab, a satellite image of our neighborhood fills the screen. Our street is a gentle curve, the last clean line of civilization before the wilderness takes over. There's the blank, brown expanse of the empty lot, the brush that fades back into the woods, a gray haze at its edges. The zigzag pencil line of the creek slices through the trees, eventually meeting another that snakes off in a different direction, off-screen to the west.

She always wanted to know what was back there. I scroll across to follow it, a thin porcelain crack running through the green expanse of the woods. The creek ends in a huge beige oval— dead grass, maybe?—that eats into the forest like a patch of mold. The water widens into a black swath down its middle.

That beige tumor is the size of the whole subdivision and then some. Miles across. I can't stop staring at it.

Dad returns to the kitchen with Officer Leduc right

behind him. He points out the bones on the railing, prompts me to explain how I found the sword. I leave out the part where I chucked it across the garden. The story doesn't seem to spark any insights, though he listens seriously and jots down notes as we speak.

"You've kept your doors locked? Anyone else have a key?"

"No one," Dad says. "I guess Skye was…out for a bit last night. But other than that…"

"Deirdre had some bones like that," I find myself saying. Officer Leduc and Dad both blink at me in surprise, and my face heats with that same old secondhand embarrassment. "She was collecting them or something; I don't know. She had them in a box a few weeks ago."

"Well." Officer Leduc frowns. "We'll bring the dogs back around, I guess. Just in case. Mr. Mackenzie, maybe you could check her room and see if this collection is still there?"

Dad nods, but it's me he's looking at. *You didn't tell us about this*, the look says, and I dodge it, reach for the computer instead.

"Um…out of curiosity…what *is* that?" I point at the beige oval on the screen. Dad leans over to look, casts an inquiring glance to Officer Leduc.

"The long swamp," Officer Leduc supplies. "At the bottom of the valley, see? That part of the road used to flood every spring."

On the other side of the pale patch, a cross street runs along another expanse of woods, almost as deep. I scroll down past the swamp, down, down. The green sea seems trackless in this direction, bottomless, marked only once by a long, straight scar for power lines. It takes forever before I find another road, all the way out past the next little satellite suburb. When the gray line of pavement finally appears on the screen, Dad sits back, letting out a little puff of breath like someone's hit him.

"It's huge," he says, hugging his coffee cup close. "I didn't realize—my God."

"We're focusing on the immediate area," Officer Leduc puts in firmly. "A two-mile radius. She can't be moving very fast."

Dad stares at the screen, nodding, not looking at him.

"Here, look." Officer Leduc takes over the track pad, drags the screen back to our neighborhood. "This is where we're focusing our search today. Okay?" He points to the few houses scattered up the hill at the end of the street. "We've got our radius divided up into sections, and we're going through them one by one. I'm guessing we'll probably finish up out here"—he circles a patch of the green sea, out past the end of the houses—"for today, if we make good time, but really we just have to wait and see how things unfold. And like I said, this is our top priority. Right?"

Dad nods, keeps nodding, his eyes fixed on the screen. Eventually he sets his mug down, slaps his hands against his thighs, and strides from the room, muttering something about taking a shower. I poke at the track pad, pan back up to the long, pale wound in the green depths. I wonder how deep that water is this time of year. It must be cold.

"Maybe she went that way," I say hesitantly. "Along the creek."

Officer Leduc gives me a somber look, then turns back to the screen with a sigh.

"Anything's possible," he says quietly. "But it'd be mighty cold without boots."

Mom's already on the phone when she comes striding into the kitchen, her hair still sticking up in frosted tufts, her eyes puffy and red. She's giving deceptively brisk instructions to someone at work, something about blockers that need to be dealt with so they don't fuck up the deployment date. Finally she drops the phone onto the counter and scrubs her hands through her hair, drawing a deep, shaky breath. Not looking at me, hunched over my cold mug at the table beside her.

"Have the police already come by?" She's still using her manager voice, sharp and demanding. "Why didn't anyone wake me?"

I pull away from the interrogation. "Dad said you needed—"

"I told him to wake me up!"

"All they said was that—"

"Never mind," she sighs, yanking the ties of her bathrobe closed. "I'll find out for myself."

The front door opens and closes again with a bang that echoes through the whole silent house. The distant drone of the helicopter shivers through the walls. Outside, a bark and jingle and a pair of men's voices announce the return of the K-9 unit. From the window above the sink, I can just see the bushy tail of a big German shepherd weaving back and forth around the feet of the balcony.

After a couple of circuits, it tosses its head, pulls its ears back; its tail curls down between its legs, and despite the encouragement of its handlers, it shrinks backward, into the garden and flattens itself into the dirt, whimpering. Even when they urge it forward, it won't move. As the police officers stand over the dog, making gestures of bafflement, it takes off like a shot, bolting back to the road, leaving the officers to chase after it.

I don't know anything about police dogs, but I don't think that's normal.

Not that you could blame the dog for wanting to get the hell out of here. I know the feeling.

How hungover are you, I text William. The phone chirps with an answer almost right away, surprising me.

Been worse, why

Arrows today?? Rly need to leave the house

I hear you. Can't use the empty lot tho, too many ppl.☹

Right. I sit back, resisting the feeling that the walls are sidling in closer around me. But then another message pops onto the screen.

Fam is out this morning. Come over? Will make pancakes ☺

"Dad?" I yell, stuffing the phone in my pocket. "Dad, I'm going over to William's!"

I'm out the door without waiting to see if he heard me, plunging through the swarm of activity in the driveway, pulling the hood of my sweater up over my ears, blocking out the cameras and the uniforms and the pitying glances from strangers. Mom steps out of the mobile headquarters, letting the door slap closed behind her, just as I'm hurrying past.

"Skye? Skye!"

"I'm going to William's," I toss back at her.

"Are you kidding me?" I recognize the tremor in her voice, and I hunch my shoulders, walk faster. It's the sound of her cool fraying, at its limit. If I stay, I'm about to get thirty hours' worth of fear and wrath and no sleep in a single screaming payload. That's the way she works, hoarding it under a collected and rational shell until it cracks under the strain. "Your sister is *missing*, in case you hadn't noticed!"

"I'll be back later."

"You're just going to leave? Again? This is your *family*, Skye! This is why this happened in the first place, because you couldn't spend so much as an *evening*—"

I raise my hand to ward it off, don't turn around, keep walking. When I finally give in and glance back, she's stalking back inside, her arms folded, her hand at her mouth. Dad's about to get it. Better him than me.

NINE

September

WILLIAM GOT THE EMPTY LOT two afternoons a week, despite Deirdre's furious protests. And sometimes I'd join him. Not often enough to make it weird. But sometimes. We spent the hours shooting mostly in companionable silence. Stealing a sliver of time to escape our families.

But he'd text me other times to hang out with Sophie. Kevin too, sometimes. Kevin was aloof at first, but when Sophie greeted me with a peal of *Skye's here!*, he didn't dare hold out for long. Suddenly, the evenings I used to spend avoiding Deirdre were gloriously full of normal company: playing video games on the Wii in Sophie's basement that made us "dance" to terrible pop anthems till we were breathless and laughing; sneaking bottles from Kevin's dad's beer fridge; roaming the neighborhood like we owned it, though there wasn't much of anywhere to go.

"I hate living out here," Sophie said.

We were leaning on a crumbling fence that roped off a long, green field tumbling down on one side of the road. The sagging gray barn marked halfway to the highway. The field ended, like everything did, at the woods, the murky green border of another country. The sun sank slowly toward the far edge of the valley, gilding the distant pines, turning the humidity into a thin rose-gold haze.

"It's fucking boring," Sophie grumbled. "There's never anything to do."

"Yeah, but we'd survive the zombie apocalypse." Kevin smirked. "Right?"

"Oh my God, don't start with that again." She turned to me. "Have you been sorted, Skye? Survivor or not?"

Beside her, William grinned. "Three guesses, Soph."

Sophie rolled her eyes. "It practically *is* the zombie apocalypse out here. What's that movie where the guy gets out of bed and everyone's been zombified and he doesn't even notice?"

"*Shaun of the Dead*," William supplied.

"Whatever."

"We'd be good for nuclear war too," he went on cheerfully. "There's a reason that bunker's out here."

"What bunker?" I asked.

Sophie groaned. "Don't encourage him."

"It's this place they built underground in the sixties in case they had to evacuate the government. It's a museum now. You should go sometime; it's creepy."

"Only to geeks like you." Kevin slumped over the rail, kicking at one of the posts. "Try boring."

"Well, if anyone ever dropped a nuke on the city—"

"Because they would totally bother," Sophie put in.

"—we'd be pretty safe. Relatively. Because of the ridge over that way, see?"

"The apocalypse is cooler with zombies, anyway," Kevin declared. "The nuclear version's just depressing. We'd be hunting two-headed deer."

"So you're the hunter, huh?" I stole a glance at William, who looked away.

"Sure," Kevin said. "Me and William. You should see him with a bow and arrow. This one time a few years ago, he and his dad brought back this huge buck—"

"I told her about it, Kev," William said shortly.

"Oh," Kevin said. And then, "Seriously?" He leaned back from the rail to shoot me a look of deep skepticism. I smiled thinly back.

"*Anyway*," William said. "It wouldn't be that big a deal. There aren't any two-headed deer around Chernobyl. The animals there are all fine. More of them die of cancer, is all."

Kevin made a face. "Right. Depressing."

"What is it with you guys and the end of the world?" I asked.

"It's just interesting," William said. "Like, everyone has to show their true colors. Everyone knows who they really are at the end of the world. No more bullshit."

"No law and order," Kevin added. "No rules."

Typical Kevin. Did they have a machine somewhere, knocking off copies of the same guy over and over? I'd never had to stay on speaking terms with one of them before. My attempt at it was sort of working. It was enough for William and Sophie, anyway, and that was what mattered; he wouldn't challenge them. He needed their approval as much as I did.

"I bet you'd totally survive the zombie apocalypse," I told him.

"What," Sophie said, "so a firearm is a free pass?"

"You have to admit it's kind of an advantage," William pointed out.

"Not just that. He's adaptable," I said. "Throw him into deep water and he figures out how to float." By pushing other people under, if necessary. "He does what it takes. He's a survivor."

Sophie smacked Kevin's arm.

"Pay attention, dumbass, you're getting a compliment. From *Skye*."

"That's not a compliment," Kevin said.

"Come on," William protested, laughing, "she just said you'd survive the zombie apocalypse."

"It's true, isn't it?" I said, a little bolder. "You know how to look out for number one. That's what counts. Right?"

"Sure I do," he shot back, unsmiling. "And I look out for my people. That's why we'd make it. All of us."

The pause that followed wasn't quite long enough to be awkward.

"I wish you guys would shut up about this," Sophie said.

Always the expert at defusing tension. "I don't have any zombie apocalypse skills."

"That's okay," William said gallantly. "We'd protect you."

That was Sophie's zombie apocalypse skill right there. Sophie would survive anything.

"Besides," Kevin added, his habitual smirk reestablished, "girls automatically have a zombie apocalypse skill. Everyone would have to start having babies, right?"

Sophie rolled her eyes. "Like any girl would pollute the gene pool with *you*."

I matched her tone—snarky, but unmoved. "Why the hell would you want to have babies in the zombie apocalypse, anyway?"

"Repopulation," William said, with a shrug that said it was obvious, at the same time as Kevin said, "Bait." He cackled when William punched him.

"There, see?" I swung away from the fence, back to the road, and they followed behind me. "He's a survivor."

"What's so funny?" Deirdre asked that night, frowning.

I pressed send on my text, didn't look up at her. "Nothing."

The frown became a glower. "You're always on your stupid phone. Who are you even talking to?"

"Why should you care?"

"Girls," Dad said wearily.

"I bet I know," Deirdre muttered.

"I bet you do," I shot back.

"*Girls*. Skye, put the phone away at the table, all right?"

I shrugged and pocketed it, turned my attention to my plate. But a hot little glow in my chest wouldn't let me stay silent.

"Mom," I said sweetly, "I'm going to Bayshore with Sophie after school next Wednesday, okay? Her mom said she'd pick us up."

Deirdre shoved her chair back and stormed from the room, leaving her dinner half-eaten. Mom and Dad exchanged a look, their own private version of chicken: Whose turn was it this time? Dad won. Mom sighed, pushed herself up from the table. Just as well. Mom would have given me a lecture about being kind and considerate when Deirdre was having a tough time. Dad was too wrung out to bother.

The phone in my pocket buzzed again. I stopped myself from reaching for it, but the heat in my chest flared higher. It wasn't my problem if I finally had a life and she didn't. She had the same chance to start over that I did. If she refused to take it, that wasn't my fault.

"Who *are* you talking to all the time, anyway?" Dad asked eventually, wagging his eyebrows in a tired attempt at teasing. "Boys?"

"Just William," I said. "And Sophie and Kevin, sometimes, I guess."

"William," Dad said. "Oh."

"He's nice," I told him, warding off parental concern, and Dad smiled.

"I know," he said.

"Your father," Mom said, "thinks I should have a talk with you."

She spoke with a sort of exasperated amusement as she set the sink to filling and handed me a vegetable peeler.

"Oh?"

"He says you've been seeing a lot of that boy from up the hill lately. William." She raised her eyebrows at me, inviting me to laugh. "He thinks this is a good time to make sure you don't have any *questions*."

I snorted, picking up a potato.

"That's what I said." She slapped the water off. "Personally, I think it's safe to say you've got this. You know you can come and talk to me if you need to, right?"

"Sure." Provided she wasn't on deadline at the time, or absorbed in a project, or handling a Deirdre crisis. Whatever. She was right—everything was fine, everything was going exactly as it should. Even if I wasn't sure what to do with it, I'd manage. I'd dealt with scarier problems on my own.

"The only thing—" She hesitated, and I tensed. There was a certain voice she always used when she was trying to play diplomat between me and Deirdre to get me to include her, to apologize, to extend the olive branch. Of course that was where this was going. God forbid we talk about my life for five minutes at a stretch. "I love that you're making friends, Skye. But maybe spend some time with Deirdre soon. I think she's feeling pretty lonely."

I focused on the potato I was peeling and didn't answer.

"She told me the other day that it's as if you don't even like her anymore."

She was bringing out the big guns. And it worked. My conscience prickled. I dunked the potato in the water filling the sink and let it fall into Mom's bowl. She picked it up and started slicing, but I could feel her watching me. I wasn't going to get away without responding to that one.

"She just always wants to play the same game," I muttered.

"And you're bored of it."

Cue the active listening. I sighed.

"I'm just...*done* with the kingdoms, you know? I'm too old for that stuff. So is she. Why can't she just grow up, like a, a—" *Like a normal human being*, I wanted to say, but I closed my teeth on the words and fell silent, wielding the peeler in savage little strokes. Bits of potato skin flew into the sink.

"Maybe there's something else you could do together?" Mom suggested after a long moment. "Something inside?"

"We're always together," I shot back. "I don't even have a different room anymore. How am I supposed to get away from her?"

There was a telltale sniffle from behind us. I hunched my shoulders and refused to turn around as footsteps thumped away from the kitchen, accelerating toward the end of the hall. A door slammed. Mom closed her eyes and sighed, sagging a little against the counter.

"We'll talk about this later," she said, sounding pained, and hurried after Deirdre, wiping her hands on her jeans.

Deirdre didn't leave the room for the rest of the evening, not even to eat dinner. When I finally gave up and went to bed, she was curled up defensively, facing the wall, and didn't look at me. I changed into pajamas, brushed my teeth, turned out the light. Her silence was as pointed as a stick. I sank back against my pillow and sighed. What was I supposed to say? If she didn't understand why I was leaving my crown behind, how could I possibly explain?

In my dream that night, I was trying to catch up with Mog, following her through Mom's old garden, pushing through the tiger lilies bobbing in her wake, scrambling under the drooping silver limbs of the willow that stood in the corner. Her sleek, gray shape wove through the arches of fern fronds like a dolphin through ocean waves, over knotted roots snaking down past where the road should be. The sidewalk cracked and crumbled as strings of Virginia creeper twined across it, a slowly building tsunami of red-tipped green tendrils climbing the mossy trunks of the trees that pushed their way up through the remains of the concrete. I stumbled to a halt among them, my panic climbing with the vines as Mog ran on ahead through the looming woods toward the bike path, down into the mouth of the ravine. I couldn't follow her. Not there.

"Some champion you are," said a voice. Above and behind me, Deirdre was perched on the garden's stone retaining wall, her legs dangling down into the air.

"You're the Queen of Swords," she told me. "You have to do something."

Panic flashed through me, a lightning strike, with anger boiling up close behind. We'd had this conversation before. I wouldn't listen. Not this time. Not again.

"No," I snapped. Like I should have then. "That's not my job."

I ran past her back up the steps, between the trees that shouldn't have been there. But the creepers snaked over the concrete, and around me leaves and flower stalks whispered and twitched and lengthened, growing, growing. Long coiling vines sprang up around my legs, holding me down. They lashed around my torso, bound my arms, reached for my face. Curling tendrils pried at my lips, whip-thin little fingers. I wanted to scream, to beg Deirdre to help me, but I had to clamp my mouth shut against them. Flowers opened all around me in luminous little moons. *Ipomoea.* Morning glories.

And behind me, Deirdre laughed and laughed.

I woke to the sound of something screaming.

Not a human sound, but the terror in it needed no translation. The jagged shadow of the woods was perfectly still across the star-spattered sky. I sat up, clutching my blanket, as the insect-singing silence washed back into place.

Across the room, Deirdre's eyes were open. Staring at me.

"Deirdre?" I whispered. "Did you hear that?"

She didn't acknowledge I had spoken. Didn't blink.

"Stop it," I said, a little louder. "You're freaking me out."

She sighed and rolled over, away from me, her breath deep and slow. She didn't stir when I whispered her name again. Not actually awake, apparently. But I watched her for a while, anyway, as my dream plucked at me with sharp little fingers, replaying the path of a gray tail through the ferns.

Oh God, was Mog still outside?

I stumbled into the living room, taking in all her favorite spots with a glance. All empty. But there was a *scratch-scratch-squeak* at the balcony door, making me jump all over again. It was just her paws on the glass, scrabbling to be let in.

I hauled the door open, scooped her up, and hugged her close against my chest, letting my heart thud against her warm fur. She permitted it for a moment, then wriggled out of my grasp to thump down onto the kitchen floor, unconcerned.

Stupid cat. I drew a trembling breath and sagged against the patio door. Beyond the faintest outlines of my reflection, the night was moonless, the woods perfectly still. I stood there breathing in the smell of water. Watching for movement that never came.

When I crawled back into bed, Mog was curled up on the pale shadow of Deirdre's hair, licking her paws. It was a long time before I could sleep again.

TEN

THE HELICOPTER BLADES ECHO ACROSS the whole valley, the thin, blue November sky, dogging my steps all the way up the hill. William answers the door still in glasses, squinting a little in the light.

"Hey," he says, closing the door behind me, finally shutting out the sound. "How are you doing?"

"I've been better."

He winces. "Yeah. I imagine. Come sit down. Breakfast is almost ready."

This is the first time I've been inside William's house—weirdly enough, considering all the time we've spent together. It's bright and spacious, a little chilly, with high ceilings, windows ripply with age, floors made of wide golden planks overlaid with plush flowery rugs. It smells like an old house—old books and woodsmoke, overlaid with the warm vanilla scent of cooking.

"How late were you up?"

He shrugs. "Not that late. The police came by and broke up the party not long after you left."

"Oh, shit."

"It wasn't that big a deal. They gave Kevin a warning, you know, for the alcohol. He was pretty pissed, but he'll get over it."

I fold my arms as he pulls plates from the cupboard. I'm not going to say anything about my own encounter with the police. If they were up there because of me, nobody needs to know that.

"They were up here yesterday too," he tells me. "They talked to Christina for a while. Because Deirdre's in her class, I guess."

I nod, slide onto one of the stools standing at the fancy granite peninsula. William flips two thick pancakes onto plates, pushes one at me. I pour syrup over the top of it, avoiding his eyes.

"And she said that Deirdre's a freak, I imagine," I mutter.

"Well," he says, after a telling silence, "she said she doesn't really fit in that well. You know."

"Yeah." Feeling guilty helps nothing, and it doesn't make any sense anyway. It's not like I could have made friends for her, not like I ever managed it before. I take a bite of pancake, but its fluffy golden sweetness might as well be glue in my mouth. "I was supposed to be in charge the other night. When she went missing. My parents were out. And I fell asleep. Mom was in the middle of telling me it's all my fault when I left the house. Maybe I should have stayed, but I…I couldn't stand it anymore. You know?"

"Oh, man."

"I don't understand how it happened. I wasn't even tired. Like, one second I was bumming around on the group chat, and next thing I know it's almost midnight. I've never just…passed out like that. Why did I have to pick that day to fall asleep?" I am not going to cry in front of William. He made pancakes for me. I force myself to take another bite, chew, swallow.

"That's just bad luck, is all," he says. "She's in eighth grade, right? She's old enough to look after herself. There's no way you could have known something was going to happen."

Tempting. But I know better. I put the fork down, grasping for any other direction to take the conversation. "Well. Anyway. Thanks. For breakfast. I was kind of surprised you got my text. I thought you'd be asleep till noon."

"Nah. This is late for me. When Dad's around, I have to get up at oh God o'clock to work out with him."

"Have to?" I echo.

He shrugs. "Well. It's easier to just do it, you know? This is the last day I get the time to myself for a while. He gets home today. Mom and Christina went to pick him up at the airport. They were going to get brunch, I think, so they'll be home in a couple hours."

"That's nice," I say. "That he's coming home, I mean."

"I guess." He pokes at his pancake. "Like, it's nice when he comes home, sure. But it's…kind of a relief when he goes away again too." When I stay silent, watching him, he continues, a few words at a time. "He's gone a lot. So he overcompensates. You know? He's always right here." He puts a hand in front of his nose. "In my face. There's always something. It's like I'm supposed to be this—this clone of him. I'm supposed to fit in exactly the same little box. The name's supposed to be some sort of cookie cutter. William Wright plays hockey. William Wright kills things. I don't *want* to be like him." He pushes the plate away, leans on the counter. "I think my worst fear is that I'll wake up someday and discover that I've become William Wright the fifth. Having to be right all the time. Turning conversations into competitions. I mean, you should get to decide who you're going to be. But did he decide, once upon a time, or did he just—what if I don't have a choice? You know?"

"Yeah. I know exactly what you mean."

I say it with enough feeling that he looks up at me, but when I don't elaborate, he waves a hand with a sheepish smile.

"Anyway. Sorry. I don't mean to go on and on about this. You've got worse problems."

"Except there's nothing I can do about any of them. Trust me, I'd rather talk about basically anything else."

He glances at my plate, which I've barely touched. He's only taken a few bites himself. "Guess my timing could have been better for breakfast, eh?"

"Sorry. It's amazing. I'm just…not very hungry."

"Yeah. Same. Mostly I could use some coffee, to be honest." He gives me a wan smile that makes me suspect he's more hungover than he's letting on. "Want some? And then we'll shoot?"

"Sure."

The back porch, a deep, covered shady space that must be heaven in the summer, houses a wooden swing hanging by heavy chains. It creaks as I settle onto it. William hands me a mug, and then disappears back into the house to return with another one for himself and a woolly blanket. He offers me one side of it, shrugs the other side around his own shoulders. The swing's not that big; our arms rest snug against each other, my thigh against his, the blanket draped around us. We sit in silence for a while as we look out across the scrubby expanse of their backyard, a juniper-dotted field rising into sumac and cloudy white pines to the east. The coffee is hot, the day thin and bright, leaves skittering across the ground when the wind lifts.

"Sophie said you guys went out for a while last year," I say casually.

The mug slips in William's hands, and he almost drops it in his lap. A little wave splashes out to soak into his jeans, and he swears, scrubbing at it. I hide a smile.

"Um. Yeah," he manages. "What did she say, exactly?"

I shrug. "That it was weird."

"Did she tell you why we broke up?"

"The real reason? Yeah."

He slurps at his coffee, frowning. "Huh."

"Were you upset? When you found out?"

"It was kind of a relief, actually. It *was* weird. Like we were both playing parts. And I'm not a very good actor. I didn't know how to talk to her anymore when we were dating, you know?"

"Did you like her, though?"

"I thought I did. It kind of…evaporated on contact. Seemed like a good idea at the time." He shrugs. "It wasn't the real thing."

He looks briefly at me, then away. Silence hums between us. I lean back and watch him over the rim of my mug. I'm tempted to tell him to just say it—almost reckless enough to go there, to see where that conversation leads. Would he back into plausible deniability, pretend not to know what I was talking about?

What if he didn't?

Deirdre would hate it if I went out with William. She'd be incandescent with rage.

The thought shouldn't be so satisfying when she's missing. When I'm the one who turned away from her, when she ran away to drag me back into being her defender. The same old anger comes bubbling up, thick and hot as magma. I should get to have a life. Why shouldn't I have friends? Or a boyfriend?

But the thought chills quickly into ash. Maybe I don't deserve it. Maybe William deserves better than Psycho Skye playing a part.

Suddenly the possibility hanging over us is stifling, and I don't want to face it after all. I shrug the blanket off, sit forward.

"So," I say, with a false brightness that sounds tinny in my ears. "Arrows?"

"Yeah." He clears his throat, sets his mug aside. "For sure. Arrows."

He hauls a target out of the shed—a big block of black foam cut into a many-sided die, fluorescent green targets adorning every surface—and sets it up in the middle of the grass, counting paces back from it. Avoiding my eye, maybe. We take turns using William's bow to fire at it, conversation mercifully not required. We're both off our game—by now I'm usually hitting the target at least half the time, but today we waste a ton of time hunting for the orange-feathered shafts where they've sailed off into the grass. William even misses once; I glance over at him and he makes a face.

"What're you doing," a voice bellows behind us, making us both jump, "trying to let her win?"

William blows his breath out, then puts a smile on and turns around in time for his dad to crush him into a bracing bear hug, thumping him on the back.

"It's the day after Halloween, Dad," he says, sounding natural enough. "Cut me some slack."

"He was at Kevin's all night," Angie calls, leaning out the back door. "He wasn't even up yet when we left this morning—" She catches sight of me and her teasing smile is instantly transmuted into wide-eyed concern. It reminds me of Sophie, that flawless transition. "Skye. Oh, honey. How *are* you? What can we do to help? I've barely slept since I heard about what happened. Is there any news?"

"Not yet," I manage, small and awkward under all their stares. "Thanks for the lasagna."

"Dad, you remember Skye, right? Her sister's—"

"Sure, sure," he says, frowning at me. "Brent Mackenzie's girl. Angie filled me in. I was sorry as hell to hear about everything. How long has she been gone?"

"Since the night before last."

"Two days and they can't find one little kid? What are they doing down there?"

"Well, that's them in the helicopter," William says, "and they were here talking to Mom and Christina yesterday."

Bill harrumphs. "God, I wish I'd been here. I'd have given them an earful. You tell your dad to hold their feet to the fire, okay? They should be going through those woods inch by inch with a fine-toothed comb. Technology's no substitute for knowing the land. If he says the word, I'll have the whole neighborhood down there in five minutes flat."

Behind him, William massages his forehead with one hand. The gesture telegraphs both a headache and terminal embarrassment.

"I'll tell him," I say dutifully. "I'd better go, actually. I don't want to be away too long."

"You let us know if you need anything," Angie says. I duck my head and make my escape. When I glance back from the corner of the house, Bill is drawing William's bow, demonstrating something. William stands there with his arms folded, smiling, smiling. I hadn't noticed how tired he looked before.

I scuff my way home as slowly as I can, kicking rocks into the tall brown cattails that line the ditch beside the road. The helicopter swings past overhead in a long arc, its passage thumping in my ears.

There's no way you could have known. Right. You'd think that. You'd think this would be the sort of thing nobody could predict. Except I know Deirdre better than anybody. There were signs, and if I'd been paying attention, maybe I could have read them. Maybe it wasn't just last night I missed a cry for help.

Have the police found the clearing behind the castle yet? They haven't mentioned it. But there's no reason they should have said anything. It's not like it's evidence of anything other than the extent of her weirdness. The thought of strangers there, poking through her domain, raising their eyebrows, makes my stomach go cold.

The tall dead grass of the empty lot whispers around me as I push through it to the heap of dirt at the far side. Deirdre's influence there is obvious. The ramparts bristle with sticks wedged into the crumbling earth, woven with long spiny thistle stalks, as if she was trying to pen the woods in. Or wall us all out. They cast reaching, spiky shadows in the long slant of the sunlight.

The faintest trace of a trail darts through the brush around to the other side of the hill, less a path than a path of least resistance. It leads under a pair of cedars canted together into a shadowed doorway. The space beyond is almost a room, no bigger than mine at home, a ring of shaggy trees surrounding twists of tall grass and the thin silver whips of saplings, reaching anemically for the sun. The light falls in slivers, shivering gold scraps slicing through the shade. It's colder here.

The rough concentric rings of stones are still there, if you know what you're looking for. The back of my neck prickles in protest as I step gingerly across them, but it's just Deirdre's ritual creepiness, and I won't fall for it. I jerk my shoulders to shrug off the goose bumps.

But aside from the stones, the clearing is empty.

I scuff carefully around the circles to make sure. There are still a few bones left, scattered among the roots of the trees: one long thin skull, maybe a deer's, old and cracked; a femur as long as my forearm; a handful of smaller ones the size of chicken drumsticks. That might be what they are, for all I know. But nothing like I found here before. Nothing worth commenting on. And what was I planning to do if there was?

I stop in the middle of the clearing and let my breath out, hands crammed in my pockets, blinking hard, looking up through the dark combs of cedar branches reaching across the bright sky.

Up there something flutters and ripples in the wind, hooked over a high branch—way out of reach, far over my head. A long streamer of fabric, light and sinuous. Blue as the sky, flecked with silver sparkles. It's one of a dozen or so. All around the clearing, they hang down like sad pennants, torn and fraying, too forlorn to be pretty.

Those shredded scraps used to be a dress. My one dress, the one Sophie insisted I buy. I never even got a chance to wear it. And I knew Deirdre had taken it, though I didn't have any proof until now. I fucking *knew* it. How did she manage to get them all the way up there?

The distant crackle of police radios and the drone of the helicopter have become familiar enough that I've pretty much tuned them out, but one tiny sound cuts through them, yanks my attention back to earth.

The sprightly jingle of a bell.

It's as real as the birds calling overhead, the whisper of the cedar boughs, the rasp of my breath. Unmistakable.

It's somewhere back there, in the tangle of the trees. I push my way through the cedar circle, into the brambles beyond; their claws snag in my coat, my hair. This close, face-to-face with them, you can see it's not really accurate to say the woods are motionless. They're moving constantly, in a thousand tiny ways, reeds sighing, branches trembling under sprinting squirrels. A crow cocks its head to look down at me from high up in a pine tree.

There it is again, that twinkling sound. It's coming closer. I could swear it is. Just like last night.

"Mog," I call, shoving my way through the thicket. "Kitty, kitty, kitty. Come on already."

It's her. It has to be her. I know the sound that bell made as she galloped across the lawn. I press on, ducking branches, ignoring the burrs working themselves into the wool of my jacket.

At first, I think it's a clump of dead grass I'm about to step over, huddled between two fallen logs, but then a scrap of red cloth snags my eye, and the shape makes sense too fast to look away.

Not grass. Fur. Matted into strings. Hanging over bones like wet cloth.

With a collar.

I reel back from the sight with my hand over my mouth, turn away, press my cheek against the rough bark of a tree. I squeeze my eyes shut, but can't unsee it. I won't look closer. I don't want to know how she died.

Deep breaths, deep breaths. This isn't new information. It's just closure. That's all. Closure is supposed to be a good thing, the final word that lets you move on, lets you heal.

I didn't want it. I didn't want to know.

I am not going to think of what closure might mean for Deirdre. She's still out there somewhere. One way or another, she's coming home. Fuck closure. We won't need it.

Slyly, somewhere in the reeds, the bell twinkles out at me. Slinking closer.

I freeze, my neck prickling, listening to it pace restlessly around me. But I'm being ridiculous. So I've been chasing somebody else's cat. No wonder it's not coming when I call.

Still, I'm suddenly aware that the house has disappeared behind me. The sound of the helicopter has vanished.

I'm not panicking. I know the way I came. I slap my way through the underbrush, trying to recognize the shapes of tree trunks, the placement of broken stumps, clumps of moss. Finally, I spot a cluster of cedar trees leaning together—alarmingly, off to my right. Somehow I almost veered off course. Breathless with relief, I hurry out of the clearing, back the way I came. I kick a couple of the stones out of the circles as I pass, hurting my foot.

My parents don't need to know about this. It would just upset them. It isn't anything they don't know already.

It definitely isn't a sign.

ELEVEN

October

SOPHIE WAS TRYING TO FIGURE me out. That was my best guess as to what was going on when one of my attempts at the compliment dance ended in that invitation to go shopping. Maybe I was leveling up. It might have been weird, just the two of us, without William bridging the gap. He was the glue that held our little foursome together. Otherwise the rest of us would probably have bounced off each other, indifferent colliding marbles, without a reason for even speaking. But even so, I'd never had people to hang out with before, not like this, and I was determined. I was learning.

"I'm really glad you asked me," I told her as we strolled through the cool, sunny corridors of the mall. Confidences were part of the game. "You always have the best clothes. I'm totally taking notes."

Sophie gave me a melty smile and hugged my arm.

"Are you kidding? It's so nice to finally have another girl around. And someone who's actually nice."

She bought one pair of slouchy boots for herself, spending her paycheck from working weekends at an ice cream store. But mostly the point of the outing turned out to be for her to dress me up, especially since Mom—depressingly thrilled that I was showing some interest in something as normal as shopping—had given me her debit card.

Sophie steered me through store after store. Basics from Old Navy, skinny jeans and T-shirts that clung so tight, I'd have said they were too small. But Sophie declared them perfect. We spent half an hour tottering around a shoe store in the highest heels we could find, cracking ourselves up, until the saleslady's smile started to look fixed and unhappy. Next came Anthropologie, where she picked things off the rack and held them up to me, piling them into my arms, pushing me into a dressing room.

"I don't even know where to start," I protested.

"With the blue thing," Sophie urged. I made a face.

"I told you, I don't do dresses."

"You have to at least try it on. It's the rules. Come on, just one."

I fished it out of the pile, looked at it doubtfully. It was slinkier than anything I owned, with occasional silver sparkles scattered across the fabric, winking.

"It suits you," she insisted.

"Let me guess. Because of my name."

"No, it's a good color for you. Brings out your eyes. Like, pow. Just try it."

I rolled my eyes and shut myself in, wrestled the dress off the hanger.

"So real talk, Skye," Sophie said through the door, "what do you think of William?"

"William Wright?"

"Of course William Wright."

"He's nice," I said, startled.

"Nice," Sophie echoed.

"Well, yeah. The kind of nice that people take advantage of, you know? He just...*likes* everyone. But everyone seems to like him back. It's weird."

"And what about you?" There was a sly smile in her voice. "Do you like him?"

"Oh, come on—"

"I'm a hundred percent serious here," she protested. "I need to know. I'm the one who's going to have to deal with his broken heart if you don't."

I threw the straps of the dress over my shoulders and leaned out the door.

"Okay, what?"

She gave me a pitying, knowing look, her hands on her hips.

"He really likes you," she said. "Hadn't you noticed?"

I had, actually. It was hard to miss. But I wrinkled my nose and made my eyes pleading. Like I was supposed to.

"Do you really think so?"

"I've known him since I was, like, five. I can tell." She stepped into the fitting room and zipped the dress up the back.

"Do *you* like him?" I ventured, trying to figure out what her agenda was.

"Not like that." She shrugged. "We went out for about thirty seconds last year."

"You did?"

"Yeah. It was weird. I think it mostly happened because everybody expected it to, you know? And maybe because he needed to prove something to his dad. He has a thing about his dad. But with you? Totally different story. Different universe."

"Are...are you okay with that?"

"Aw, Skye," she said, dimpling. "You're so sweet. I'm totally okay with that. Let me put it this way. I broke up with William because I kissed someone else. Her name's Annabelle. Okay?"

"Oh," I said, blinking. "Sure. Okay."

"Not for publication," she said briskly, fluffing my hair forward so it hid my ears. "People are assholes. This is strictly on a need-to-know basis."

"Right." The confidence threw me off-balance. I couldn't figure out why she'd trusted me with it. At a school like ours, that was weapons-grade. But then again, a carefully placed word from her would set a rumor running through the school faster than a virus. Anyone who made the mistake of double-crossing Sophie would be annihilated. "Does Kevin know?"

"Well, obviously. He was the first one I told."

I gave her a look. "We're talking about the same Kevin, right? The one who was talking about you like someone died and made him the world authority on tits?"

She burst out laughing.

"Oh my God, Bethany told me about that." She studied me, her eyes alight. "Holy shit. Is that why you decked him?"

"I barely touched him—"

"Oh my God," Sophie repeated, clapping her hands in delight. "You're amazing. That's, like, the best thing ever. I can't wait to tell him about this."

I eyed her, baffled. "Yeah, I bet he'll be thrilled."

"Seriously." Sophie clasped my arms. Though she kept smiling, her gaze turned searching, like she was willing me to understand something. "I can handle myself, okay? You don't need to protect me. Especially not from Kevin. Look. You don't know about his stepmom, do you?"

"What about her?"

"Well, she's married to his mom. They live in this cute little house in town. I had lots of deep, dramatic conversations with them last year. And Kevin was a total lifesaver. Like, he wasn't even surprised. I think he figured it out before I did. He's got this wicked radar for when people are faking it. It's like bullshit is his superpower or something."

I frowned at my reflection for a second, digesting this.

"That's why he's gone half the time, isn't it? Because he's at his mom's?" It felt like I owed her for confiding in me, so I said out loud, a little nervously: "I figured he was just avoiding me."

"He'll come around. He doesn't trust you yet, is all. That's why you're getting the whole peacock display. It's supposed to be, like, some kind of force field." She tilted her head, considering. "I should figure out some way to get us all together while he's at his moms' place, actually. I bet that'd do it."

"Do what?"

She rolled her eyes. "Convince the two of you to fucking chill already? It'd be hilarious if it wasn't so dumb, the way you set each other off. He's really not an asshole. Seriously. He's just convincing."

"If you say so."

She'd turned the world upside down, like a snow globe, scattering everything I thought I knew about them into the air. After all, if Kevin was the kind of asshole I knew, he'd be making a million stupid raunchy jokes about her behind her back. But for all his ostentatious posturing, he'd never let it slip. Not in front of me. Then again, maybe he was smart enough to get that she'd wipe the floor with him without even messing up her hair.

She'd do the same with me. Why did she tell me? She didn't have to.

"Well, anyway," she said. "I'm going to be after William to actually ask you out so he'll shut up about you for a while. So be prepared."

I was supposed to laugh, but couldn't manage it. "I just...I don't know." I was off script. Sophie arched her brows. "He barely knows me, you know? He might not...like me that much. Up close."

"Now that," she said, "is bullshit. Look. What's not to like?"

She took my shoulders again and pointed me at the mirror, and then I did laugh, blushing with a shyness I didn't have to feign. It was hard to look that girl in the eye, a softer girl draped in shimmering sky-blue fabric that hugged her cleavage and skimmed her bare demure knees. If that was me, anything was possible. Transformation, even.

"You're a wizard," I told Sophie, and gave her an impulsive hug.

"You know it," she said smugly.

When we walked in the door, Deirdre's boots were sitting on the linoleum in a spreading puddle, black mud clinging to them in globs. One mud-streaked sock sat discarded beside them; the other was draped over one of the stairs. Smudged black imprints of toes marked her path from the door, punctuating a trail of pine needles and crumbled leaves.

"Well, looks like my sister's home," I said, and Sophie snorted. I couldn't let it show that I cared, that I'd never wished harder that I could just erase Deirdre from my life. I'd been count-ing on her still being outside. She'd shut herself in our room, at least; maybe she'd stay safely out of sight. But we'd barely set foot in the kitchen when a clatter, a thump, and a muffled growl of frustration echoed down the hall. I exchanged a glance with Sophie, who smothered a giggle under her hand.

When I pushed the door open, Deirdre sat in the middle

of our room, surrounded by dirt and chaos. Bare sticks and cedar boughs were scattered around her on the carpet. She'd shredded one of the flowered sheets from the linen cupboard into long strips. Mom would freak.

She was intent on arranging a handful of the sticks in a tall tripod, frustration twisting her lips as the sticks wobbled and fell from the knot she was trying to tie around them with one of the pieces of the sheet. The room was icy cold—the window was wide open—and it smelled like a gym, stale and sweaty.

"I need some string!" she exclaimed, barely looking at me. "Skye, can you get me some string from the kitchen? This is going to fall apart unless I hold it."

Beside me, Sophie looked at me wide-eyed, putting a hand delicately against her nose. I slung my packages to the floor, my face hot.

"Are you kidding me?" I demanded. Deirdre rolled her eyes in an aggrieved way and ignored me, trying to weave the cloth around the tops of the sticks again. "What are you even doing?"

"I knew you wouldn't understand," she muttered. "If you're going to be like that, you can just—"

"Oh, right. Sure. If *I'm* going to be like that. Like what, exactly?" She glowered at me for a moment, said something under her breath, and my own breath cinched tight in my chest, a knot of rage. "Go ahead and say it! Come on, I'm dying to know!"

She hitched herself around to half turn her back to me, her stringy hair hiding her face. Her shoulder blades poked up around the straps of her spring-green dress—the dress that had to be ruined, probably; there was no way all that mud was coming out. How was she not freezing?

I couldn't do this. Not now. I fought for a grip on my temper, yanking the door shut. Too late. Sophie's smile had vanished into a look I remembered from William's first visit. *Oookay.* I'd crossed a line, cared too much, gotten too intense.

"Sorry," I muttered. "I *hate* sharing a room with her."

"Wow, poor you," Sophie said, looking back over her shoulder as we retreated down the hall. "What a freak show."

She was siding with me, but somehow that made me feel worse than ever. Like a turncoat, a traitor. I couldn't come up with a suitably offhand response.

"Little sisters are embarrassing by nature," Sophie offered as I flopped into a chair at the kitchen table. "It's, like, written in the laws of physics somewhere."

"There's embarrassing," I said, "and then there's fucking creepy. I don't understand what is *up* with her lately. Ever since we moved here, she's just been—I don't know. Off the charts."

"Maybe she needs therapy or something?"

"Probably." Mom and Dad had been muttering about that again lately. For all the good it would do. It wasn't as if it had ever worked before. "Mom thinks she's just lonely. Because I've been spending so much time with you guys. She's…never been very good at making friends, you know?"

"That," Sophie said firmly, jabbing a finger at me for emphasis, "is totally not your problem. She has to sort out her own issues. You can't do it for her. You're allowed to have friends, okay?"

Friends. What a concept. Until Sophie set it there in front of me, I hadn't really dared to think it. It broke over me like the sun—warm, comforting, a little dazzling.

"Okay," I managed.

Even after she left, with a promise to text me later, I kept the thought wrapped around me, bright and buoyant. Insulation against the scuffle and clatter of whatever Deirdre was doing in the bedroom. But it turned hot and withering as I tried to hold on to it. Sophie was right, dammit, she was exactly right. It wasn't fair. Deirdre didn't get to make me tiptoe around her, make me fight to escape her orbit.

I steeled myself and lifted my chin before pushing the door to our room open again. Deirdre threw me a brief, sullen glance and then turned her back on me, rummaging through the sticks on the floor.

"Go away," she muttered.

"It's my room too, Deirdre." I took a deep breath. "Look. Make a mess if you want to. Whatever. But you don't get to humiliate me in front of my friends."

"*She's* your friend?"

The disdain—the disbelief—in those three syllables ignited something.

"Yeah. Sure, she is. Why not?"

"She doesn't even know you. None of them do."

"Right," I snapped. "Because you know me so well."

"Of course I do." She leveled a brief, meaningful glare at me. "I know you better than anyone."

"You do not! That is over!" She was getting to me. She always knew how. "I'm starting over, all right? Why can't you? Why do you have to be like this?"

"You think you've changed so much?" Deirdre snarled. "You think you're all popular now? Because they pat you on the head and let you sit with them at lunch?"

I couldn't breathe. I'd explode in a million pieces. "At least I'm not some spooky, grimy *freak* who's trying to pretend she's all special and magical when she's just a loser no one can stand because she never washes her goddamn hair!"

Deirdre wheeled and threw a handful of sticks at me in a bundle. I flung my hands up to shield my face, automatic as breathing, and they clattered scratchily against my arms, bounced to the floor.

"Shut up!" she yelled. "You don't understand! I'm *making* things!"

"Like what?" I kicked at the sticks on the floor. "What the hell is this supposed to be? You'd better clean it up before Mom gets home, or she'll—"

Deirdre's lip curled in an attempt at a sneer, but tears spilled over to slide down her cheeks, leaving tracks through the smudges of dirt.

"You don't understand. I knew you wouldn't understand. They told me you wouldn't."

"Oh, give me a break, what are you talking about now?"

"I'm not telling you," she hurled at me. "You're just like Tyler. You're just like all the rest of them!"

I didn't think it was possible for me to get any angrier, but I was halfway across the room before I realized it, my hands in fists.

"Get away from me." She folded her arms, hunching her thin shoulders. They were shaking. I forced my hands open, forced myself to breathe.

"It's my room too, remember? And I'm not cleaning up after your little art project, or whatever it—"

This time it was a rock she threw at me, her face twisted up into an awful grimace. It left a mark where it hit the wall, a little dent in the drywall.

"What the *hell*, Deirdre?"

"Get out!" she screamed. "I hate you! You're not my sister, you never were! *Get out!*"

I slammed the door so hard, the sound echoed all over the house. From the thunk and rattle behind it, more rocks followed the first.

"You are going to be in so much trouble," I yelled at the door, and stalked away, making my footsteps as heavy as I could. Her wordless shriek followed me down the hall. It was like she was two years old. Like she was an animal. And worse, I wanted to scream back. She always dragged me down with her.

To my relief and shame, both our parents took my side. It was humiliating, after all this time, going to them for justice. Still, it was surprisingly satisfying to be vindicated. She did cross the line this time. It wasn't just me. Served her right.

Marching Deirdre through cleaning up took more than an hour, but Mom stuck it out, her orders and Deirdre's protests ringing across the whole house. Mom emerged from the battle as I was setting the table for the pasta Dad was making, and collapsed into a chair with a sigh, rubbing her temples. Eventually, it occurred to her to ask about my shopping trip.

"Sophie talked me into buying a dress," I admitted.

"Skye in a dress?" Mom summoned a laugh. "Okay, this I have to see. Go put it on."

I hurried to our room, ignoring Deirdre, who was curled on her bed with her back turned to me. But when I rummaged through my purchases—quickly once, then again, more thoroughly—the slinky blue fabric was nowhere to be found.

I sat back on my heels, reaching for calm, but rage took up a drumbeat in my head, deafening.

"What did you do with it?" I said through my teeth. Deirdre, predictably, didn't answer, just sniffed and swept her hair away from her face. "Goddammit, Deirdre, *what did you do?*"

Mom appeared with a sigh to intervene, to broker peace. "What is it now?"

"I can't find it! The dress I bought! She took it, I know she did! And she had scissors in here before!" I seized Deirdre's shoulder, dragged her around to face me, refusing to let her twist out of my grip. "What did you do with it? Tell me!"

Mom tried to pull me away, but I was adamant, immovable,

shaking Deirdre, yelling in her face, and Mom was yelling too, hauling on my arm until I gave in, threw up my hands, stalked back to my side of the room. Deirdre, her hands over her arms where I'd gripped them, let loose a long, tearful whimper. Great. Now I was in for it.

"Skye, that was unnecessary," Mom snapped.

"Are you even going to ask her? Go ahead, ask her what she did with it!"

Mom leveled a look at Deirdre, who pulled her knees up and buried her face in her arms. The whimper became a wail.

"You hate me! You all do!"

"Oh, Deirdre, for heaven's sake—"

I wasn't staying to listen to the rest; I'd heard it all before. I collected the rest of my bags and left the room.

Mom tried to extract answers, apologies. She finally declared that Deirdre wasn't getting any supper until she talked, but even the next morning, Deirdre wouldn't budge. She just folded her arms and looked away from me, sticking her chin out. Mom grounded her from going outside for the rest of the week, but by then, even she could tell it was a lost cause. She pinched the bridge of her nose for a moment as if to ward off a headache as Deirdre flounced out to catch the school bus—without a fight, for once.

"Mom—" I started, but the words ran aground. I didn't know what to say. This was bad, even for Deirdre. Didn't they notice? Weren't they going to do anything?

"I know, Skye," she sighed. "I'm looking into it. I need

referrals, and the people at her school are useless, and—well, don't worry about it. Okay? It's not your job." She bumped my cheek with a kiss. "I have to get going. I can't keep going in late like this."

Dad got the new window for my basement room installed that Saturday. He let me help him carry sheets of drywall inside, showed me how to score through its paper skin with a box cutter and snap it open to reveal the dusty chalk inside. He held the sheets up while I wielded the drill to fasten them in place, and he didn't say anything when I fumbled and sent screws pinging to the floor. With one wall covered, it actually started to look like a real room, somewhere people could live, instead of the skeletal underworld of the house.

I caught a glimpse of Deirdre once, slouched and scowling in the doorway, watching us. I busied myself filling in the little craters the screws made in the smooth, white expanse of the new wall. I refused to look back that way long after the pressure of her sulky, jealous glare on my back had faded.

Tile, baseboards, paint. Soon the room was finished, fresh and cool and gleaming. A blank slate, just like I wanted.

"We can expand your plant stand, if you like," Dad offered, and I hugged him and said sure, even though I knew it would be months before he thought of it again. When he left to go upstairs, I stretched out on my back in the middle of the floor, threw my arms as wide as I could on the chilly, unyielding tiles. It was mine.

Mine, mine, mine. An oasis. The sun fell over my face and chest like a warm blanket.

But a sharp noise at the window—a bang and a scuffle—made me jump. Outside the glass loomed an impressive black bird. A raven, maybe? Were crows that big? Its shadow stretched across the floor. I stared at it; it cocked its head to stare back at me with one beady eye.

And then it slammed its beak into the window.

Bang. Bang.

"Jesus," I exclaimed, and jumped to my feet. "Shoo, get lost! Get out of here!"

It hopped an unhurried few paces from the glass and took off, into the trees. Its assault on the window had left a mark: a faint scratch that stood out white against the green shadows of the woods beyond.

I was trying to puzzle out math homework on the couch when Deirdre came marching past, looking determined, her arms loaded full of a stack of familiar cardboard boxes. Her dioramas. She hauled them past me into the kitchen, avoiding my stare as studiously as I'd avoided hers. There was a rustle and a crash from around the corner.

"Deirdre?"

She didn't answer, but stalked back to our room—her room now—and returned with another armload. I followed her into the kitchen. She'd smashed the first few, crushed them into the recycling bin, leaving sparkles and feathers scattered over the floor. She set the next stack down beside it, ruthlessly squashing the pile together.

"Deirdre, what are you doing?"

"Starting over," she said coldly.

"But—"

She wasn't listening, had already disappeared back into the living room. I pulled the Queen of Wands from the wreckage, smoothing her bent limbs. Her tinfoil crown was gone. *Isn't this what you wanted?* she asked, looking up at me through lidded eyes. Isn't this what I'd said she should do? Move on? Grow up?

There was no taking this back, anyway. The smashed dioramas made a crunching rattle when I nudged them. Well, I hoped she wasn't going to decide this was a mistake and have some sort of meltdown later.

She took one last box overflowing with paper downstairs. When I caught up, she was pushing it into the woodstove, snapping a match against the carton until it flared to life.

"Deirdre," I blurted, unable to bear the thought any longer. "Deirdre, you're not doing this because I said—"

"Don't be stupid," she said flatly, and poked the match into the paper, which curled and blackened and sprang into flames. We watched for a few moments as the fire leapt up, and then she pulled the screen closed and looked around at me. Amazingly, she smiled. Maybe a little mockingly. *Aww*, the smile said. I'd have been annoyed if it wasn't so disconcerting. If she hadn't suddenly seemed so much older than me.

"Seriously, Skye. You should see your face. Don't worry. You were right. So I'm working on something new. Something real this time. You'll see."

She reclaimed the Queen of Wands from my nerveless fingers, pulled the screen aside, and threw her into the fire.

TWELVE

I'M IN MY ROOM, LEAFING half-heartedly through a garden
magazine without really seeing it, when Mom yells my name.
The urgency in it sends shock waves through my chest. I drop the
magazine and run for the stairs. They've found something; they
must have found something.

"What?" I call, breathless, as I hurry up to the landing.
"What is it?"

But when I get to the top of the stairs, Mom, Dad, and
Officer Leduc are all looking at me with closed, serious faces. And
Officer Leduc is holding my sword.

Disappointment washes over me, a crushing weight settling
back into place.

"Oh," I manage. "That."

I open my mouth to say more, but Mom's voice lashes across the space between us.

"You owe us an explanation, Skye!"

The words scatter from my head. I stare at her, bewildered, but she doesn't give me a chance to blunder through an answer.

"You could have compromised the search! You could have gotten lost too—or hurt, or—or—" She chokes to a stop, and Dad puts an arm around her.

"We talked about this," he says to me, darkly.

"But—" I look helplessly from Mom's tearful face to Dad's stern one. "I didn't—"

"And especially going so deep in the woods. That was *dangerous*, Skye."

It's like they've parachuted in from some alternate universe. I stare at the sword in Officer Leduc's hands and struggle to piece together what they're saying.

"You mean—you found that—"

"We almost didn't." Officer Leduc holds the sword out to me, hilt first. "It was at the very edge of our search area today. The guys who found it were pretty excited at first; they thought your sister might have left it there. Until I told them you had it yesterday."

It takes me a second to figure out that I'm supposed to take it from him. The wood is cool and smooth in my hand. The room seems to fall dizzily away from me as I watch the light gleam from its polished golden surface.

"But—" I can't get any further than that. This doesn't make sense. He said they were working their way down the block,

searching through the woods piece by piece. He said they'd probably get out past the end of the street today. They found it all the
way out there? *Especially going so deep in the woods.* But it was
under the apple tree. I threw it; I saw it land.

My first electric thought is that it was Deirdre. That she
picked it up after I went back inside. But how could she have been
literally a stone's throw from the house, how could she make her
way all the way over there—without boots on, without a coat—
and leave no trail? They would have found her.

"I know it's hard, feeling like there's nothing you can do,"
Officer Leduc says quietly. "But this is a race against the clock,
a case like this. We can't afford to waste time. And your parents
need you safe. Understand?"

I nod dumbly, because they're all glaring at me. But the sword
draws my eyes, heavy, solid, impossible. Undisputable. Maybe an
animal picked it up. It's the only other explanation.

So why do I suddenly feel exposed, as if something is watching me, wondering idly if I'll rise to the bait?

Afternoon slides into evening by slow degrees, and I can't sit still.
I throw myself on my bed, and nameless jitters prod me up again,
across the room and back. Snapping a kick at the air doesn't help.
It just leads me to memories of Deirdre. Everything does.

I shoved the sword under my bed, where I couldn't see it.
The harder I ignore it, the more its presence chafes at me, striking

little sparks of fear too ridiculous to contemplate. I will not let them set me alight. I will not freak out.

I'm not like her.

But what if? the sparks whisper, flying up around me. *What if—?*

It's as if the kingdoms are haunting me. As if Deirdre's using them, somehow, to reach out to me, pull me in. Which makes no goddamn sense. That was a game. I've never thought very hard about the line between real and make-believe. It's obvious as gravity. Or the difference between awake and dreaming. You might move back and forth between them, but you can always tell them apart. Once you're back on the side that's real, anyway.

But I'm not dreaming now. The sword was under the apple tree. And I've never fallen asleep like I did the day she disappeared. What the hell is this? What if—?

No. What if nothing. It's nothing. It's not worth explaining. I'm not thinking about this.

I'm not thinking as I pull Mom's rain boots from the closet, not thinking as I slam through the door into the deepening evening. Shadows and chilly silence pool among the trees as I march across the yard toward the empty lot. Browning lawn gives way to tall rustling grass and thistles that catch at my legs. I wade through them up to the bank of the creek, where the water gets deep enough to slice through the reeds in a shining ribbon. I stop there to comb through the grass for a stick. A nice straight one with a witchy fork at the end.

Stupid. God, this is stupid. I hope she's good and pleased with herself, wherever she is. I hope she's satisfied.

I stab the end of the stick into the muddy bottom of the creek. Twist it around, like a key, as far as my wrist will go. This was how we always opened the gate to the kingdoms. But it's weird without her. All wrong. I could swear Deirdre is standing right behind me, looking over my shoulder.

The cop in the nearest car is frowning at me. Wondering what the hell I'm doing. I don't know what I'll tell him if he asks.

I shuffle in a hurried circle, splashing in and out of the water. Three times around the stick in the mud. I'm supposed to say something; I'm supposed to use that oath of hers. Words I haven't spoken since the spring. I almost turn back to the house, but somehow doing this halfway is worse than trying it in the first place. I close my eyes and inhale slowly.

"Give her back," I mutter. "Give her back. I demand it. By… by wood, stone, water, and bone." There. I pace around the stick again, making it a chant. "Wood, stone, water, bone."

I repeat it one more time, walking faster. I lose track of how many circles I've made and keep going until I have to stagger to a dizzy halt, the woods tilting in front of me. The wind rustles in the grass. A crow caws somewhere far away. Nothing moves.

Well, obviously. What was I expecting?

I yank the "key" free from the mud and throw it away into the grass. I storm back the way I came, and my idiot tears make the house dim and blurry before me. I don't look back. I won't.

THIRTEEN

October

M OM SENT ME OUT LOOKING for Deirdre once, a few
weeks ago now. I yanked my coat on and stomped outside,
scowling. Like I'd even know where to look. The leaves were
turning, and the sullen maze of the trees was ablaze in red and gold.

She didn't answer me when I yelled, predictably enough. I
crunched through the browning grass through the garden, to the
edge of the woods. Past the twiggy remains of the rosebushes
Mom tried to plant. They'd drooped and wilted within days. It
was like the ground had rejected them. I heard somewhere that
when they transplant an organ, sometimes the body attacks it,
defends itself as if it's being invaded.

I teetered down along the tree roots into the shallows of the swamp, branches snagging at my clothes and hair. I pulled my sleeve loose from a clinging branch, and Deirdre's words to William popped into my mind, as clearly as if she'd spoken them beside me. *You're not welcome here.*

I shivered, folded my arms. The afternoon was tilting into evening, golden light slicing through the leaves. Crows cawed in the treetops, wheeling and swirling in the air, black rags against the rosy clouds.

I made a full circuit of the yard, hopping awkwardly over the ragged ditch where the creek had sunk to a sluggish brown trickle, pushed through the tall dead grass to the castle, threaded my way around the back. Through the leaning cedar doorway, into the chilly shade of the clearing.

"Deirdre?" I shouted, turning around and around. "Deirdre, you have to come home!"

Stepping backward, I nudged something with my foot, something that rattled away with a hollow sound.

A bone, broken and cracked. Worn to a silver gray, almost like driftwood. It was one in a pile. Carefully stacked, thigh-high.

I shied away from them. There was no telling what animals they belonged to. Here the thin comb of a rib cage, there a long leg bone topped with a blackened knob. I thought I might have seen an eye socket staring out at me—or maybe the hollow of a pelvis—but I wasn't looking any closer to find out. I just about tripped over the row of stones in my haste to get away from them, hurried back out into the fading daylight.

It was obviously Deirdre who'd put them there. Who else? The stone circles were Deirdre all over. The bones, though—that was a whole new level of creepy, even for her. The thought of what Mom would say about it settled over me, cold and sickening.

Whatever. That wasn't my problem. I was done. I'd done my job. It would be dark soon, anyway. Gray twilight pooled under the eaves of the forest, in the hollows and the depths, slowly rising.

"Mom," I yelled, slamming into the house and kicking off my boots, "Mom, I can't—"

"Can't what?" Deirdre asked coolly, passing the stairs on her way to the kitchen.

"There you are," I sighed, and scowled at her. "Mom sent me out looking for you."

"Well, I've been home for, like, ten minutes," she shot back, tossing her hair.

"You could have at least answered me," I snapped. "I know you heard me calling."

"Sorry," she said, clearly not sorry.

"Yeah, well, I went stomping all over the yard looking for you." I glared at her pointedly. "Like behind the castle? In the trees there?"

Her face went blank and still, though her eyes didn't leave my face. I shrugged off the memory of her staring at me in the dark, unblinking.

"Yeah." The light from the kitchen made her half a silhouette, unreadable. "And?"

It was a challenge. A dare. Whatever she was trying to drag

me into—again—I refused. I pushed past her. Our shoulders clashed, each of us refusing to cede the space.

Then came the night Mog didn't come home.

It was the first time Deirdre knocked on the door of my new room, asking if I'd seen her. But none of us had. There had been no squeaking paws at the balcony doors—or at my new window. We called her from the balcony, over and over again; we pulled out a bag of her favorite treats to rattle enticingly. But no lithe shadow came bounding out of the dark to greet us; we stood side by side at the rail, listening, but the twinkling sound of the bell on her collar never came.

The sound of the back door closing pulled me from dreams of our old street, dark and icy, the lights of the houses shining down from higher hills than I remembered, gleaming secretively between trembling evergreen boughs. I lay in bed, muddled and dizzy for a moment, trying to figure out if the sound had been part of my dream somehow. But then a shadow slipped across the pale wash of the neighbor's far-off porch light, a thin fleeting silhouette.

I started upright, but it was only Deirdre. The ghost of her voice carried through the glass, crying out.

I threw my sweater on and hurried upstairs, through the garage, to lean out the back door. The light from the garage spilled out into the yard, catching Deirdre standing under the apple tree, facing into the woods. Her long nightshirt flapped around her bare legs, a pale flag.

"Deirdre?" I called.

"Mog," she wailed. "Mog! Here, kitty! Here, kitty, kitty!"

I hugged my sweater close and hurried out toward her.

"Deirdre! Deir, come inside!"

I tried to put an arm around her bare shoulders. Her skin was icy under my hand. But she pulled away, sniffled, went back to calling for the cat.

"Deirdre, come inside," I repeated helplessly. "You're going to freeze out here. She'll come back eventually."

"You don't understand," Deirdre said tearfully. "There are *things* out there. We have to find her before they do!"

"Mog has cattitude," I tried to reassure her, but her panic pinched my heart. "She's always made it back before."

"You don't understand." She stormed away from me, her arms folded over her chest. "This is my fault. I have to find her. I should never have let her out—"

When I caught up to her again, grabbed her arm, she started to sob, sagging in place like a broken doll. I hugged her, holding her up, bewildered.

"Deirdre, that doesn't even make any sense," I protested. "Mog goes out all the time. She's a cat. It's not like you can give her a curfew."

Deirdre buried her face in her hands.

"I wish we'd never come here," she moaned. "I wish we'd never left. I'll never see her again, never, never."

"Oh, Deirdre, you don't know that—"

But she just pushed away from me, ran back to the house, leaving me behind. Inside the garage, the door opened and closed with a bang.

I sighed, shivered, pulled my sweater close around my neck. Behind me, the leaves on the reaching branches fluttered and murmured speculatively. I turned to look up at their pale undersides flickering in the light from the garage. I stood there peering into the dark, every hair alert to the feeling of being watched. Evaluated.

"Go away," I snapped, as much to hear my own voice as anything else, and I hurried back to the house, refusing to look over my shoulder. I pulled the garage door closed behind me with a bang and only then, let my breath out in a trembling rush, waiting for my jumping heartbeat to slow.

I was as bad as Deirdre. At least nobody had been around to see it.

The first few mornings after Mog disappeared, I came upstairs to find Deirdre asleep on the kitchen floor, waiting by the patio doors for the sound of paws on the glass, her head pillowed on a couch cushion. Mom woke her up while I retreated to the bathroom, cranking the water on to drown out the sound of her crying.

She spent more time than ever outside after that. Most days, she was gone when I got home, her backpack and sneakers left forgotten in a heap inside the front door. She came back just when it was getting dark, never quite late enough for Mom to worry, sticks tangled in her hair, her face smudged with dirt. Mom made a big deal over that, hauling Deirdre into the bathroom, growling all the while about her deadlines.

"You're thirteen, Deirdre, for heaven's sake," she snapped, jerking the brush through a snarl in Deirdre's hair. "I shouldn't have to do this! I don't have time!"

Deirdre just let her head yank back, expressionless, and said nothing. She seemed calm, at least. Preoccupied.

"Are you working on another kingdom?" I asked her at dinner that night, feeling like I should ask. She looked at me suspiciously.

"Kind of," she muttered, but didn't elaborate. I focused on cutting my chicken into little pieces to hide my relief and guilt. I didn't ask for details.

The night she disappeared, before Mom came barging through my door, I'd been dreaming about the valley, the path an asphalt ribbon winding down the bottom of the ravine toward the river. I couldn't do it again. I'd changed my mind. I had to turn back before I reached the dry streambed, the tumbled rocks leading into green shadow between the trees. But the tangled trees of the swamp had closed over the path behind me like gathering clouds.

"Hurry," Deirdre demanded, crouching down at the crest of the castle to reach out to me, beckoning for me to take her hand. "I'm waiting."

FOURTEEN

M<small>Y SLEEP IS SHALLOW, FULL</small> of scurrying dreams, and my eyes snap open at the sound of something scratching at the window.

Not like Mog did, with her soft, scrabbling paws. It's a slow, stuttering squeak, something pressing hard against the window-pane in a long, stiff stroke. It clicks against the glass on contact like it's pointed. Sharp.

I clutch the blankets in the dark. I'm not imagining it. The sound is clumsy, dogged. Painful. Repeated over and over again.

I don't want to look. But what if it's Deirdre, trying to get my attention, trying to get me to let her in? If it was Deirdre, she'd knock, wouldn't she? What if she's hurt?

When I finally twist around, a looming shadow lurches

away from the glass, making me shrink back in my bed with a little shriek. The porch light leaves it in shadow, no more than a silhouette, but it has a corner that lifts and falls. Like a knee or an elbow. Under cloth.

I throw the covers off and jump up to look out the window, but the twitching lump of movement steals around the corner of the house and disappears. I run upstairs to the long windows overlooking the yard. Something's out there, skirting the spill of light from the house. Something upright and faintly paler than the night, making swaying, staggering progress toward the edge of the woods.

Icy prickles sweep my skin as I watch it shamble across the lawn, but it's too tall to be anything but a person.

A person in a dress.

I cast frantically around for a flashlight. My phone is sitting on the kitchen table, and I grab it and flick on the light, cram my feet into my sneakers, fling myself down the stairs and out the front door. My breath smokes in the pale wash of the LED light. The grass is slick with rain that soaks through my shoes, icy patches blooming against my toes. My circle of light swings wildly over the ruins of the garden, the bare trunks of the trees, as I pelt around the house.

"Deirdre!" I cry. "Deirdre, wait!"

The slight figure of hanging white stands still at the edge of the yard, glowing brighter in the approaching light of my phone. I stumble to a halt at the corner of the house, panting, peering out at it. Is it Deirdre? It's definitely white cloth I'm looking at. It lifts sluggishly, soddenly, in the wind.

"Deirdre?" I pant. "Deirdre?"

The white shape doesn't move. Fumbling, trying not to take my eyes off it, I bend down to pick up one of the long scraps of two-by-four Dad left lying in the grass. It's an awkward weapon, too wide to grip properly. I wish I had my sword. It's only wood, but I know I can do some damage with it.

Clutching the phone, holding the two-by-four out defensively, I creep closer. Closer. "Deirdre, is that you?" It doesn't move. Not a twitch, not a turn, not a hesitation. Is it her? It has to be her.

"Deirdre, please," I whimper. Please let it be her. "I'm sorry. Please, please—"

But in the brightening circle of light from my phone, the cloth is tattered, mud-streaked, trailing on the ground. It hangs strangely, lopsided and shapeless, and what I thought was an arm is a wizened silver branch draped with a scrap of shimmering blue cloth, and a stiff claw of a hand isn't a hand at all, it's an antler. Pale bone.

It's turning to face me, with a rustle and creak like a tree bending in the wind, like something stalking through the woods.

And its face is bone too. A long, white skull, an animal skull. Sockets emptier than the sky.

My scream is breathless, choked, and I drop the phone to swing the two-by-four in a flailing arc. The nightmare figure collapses in pieces with a thunk and clatter, the wet cloth slaps onto the ground. And something glittering flies from the tines of its hands—antlers—hands—to land in the grass at my feet. A gleaming gold medallion, a familiar tree twining roots and branches in a knotted circle around its edge.

I stand there panting, trying to look everywhere at once. The wind in my ears is the only sound. I snatch the necklace from the grass and run like I've never run before. I run for my life. I run for the safety of the house.

When I slam the back door behind me, my legs turn to jelly, and I sink dizzily down to sit on the gritty tiles, my breath sobbing in my throat, the necklace a cold hard edge against my palm. For a minute, I'm afraid I might throw up. The bright silence of the house presses down around me. The furnace clicks on, making me jump.

I don't go back to my room. I don't wake my parents. I yank the blinds closed with a rattle on all the living room windows, shutting out the night, and throw myself on the couch.

I've been clutching the pendant so hard, my fingers are stiff and painful when I unfold them. The tree and its spreading roots and branches are etched in black in its gleaming gold face, forming a swirling, knotted circle.

I bought it for her. This past Christmas, before we moved. Her mouth fell open when she lifted it from the box. I will remember the look on her face forever. The utter disbelief that it was really for her. Mom helped her with the clasp, and she ran to look in the mirror, then ran back and threw her arms around me so hard, she almost knocked us both over.

"It's beautiful," she breathed. "It's *magic*. You're the best champion ever."

"I thought you'd like it," I said.

I hold it up by the chain, watching it twist back and forth.

Over and over again, I see the monster in the yard turning to face me, the empty hollows of its eyes. I know the difference between awake and dreaming. It can't have happened. Is this me losing my mind? This is what nightmares feel like—the pulsing, unreal fear you can't shake. It's chemical. Something pouring through your brain. You can't trust it.

But I can still feel the two-by-four in my hands, the reverberation of the wood at the impact, see my breath hanging in a cloud in the air. The sodden, dirty cloth that shrouded the thing. The sprigs of little flowers on it. The sky-blue fabric looped around its arms, fraying, familiar. Slinkier than anything I own.

Was *that* what Deirdre was making in our room that day? With the bones in the clearing, the shreds of Mom's sheets, of my dress? That thing?

She's been making monsters since we were kids. None of them ever came to life. But she never made them here before, in the shadow of those woods. And she's been getting weirder and weirder ever since arrived. I think of her shoulders standing out white against the dark, bare despite the cold. What if—what if there's something out there, in the forest? Something that took over one of her monsters, brought it to life?

What if something took her?

The thought crushes the air from my lungs. What if the necklace—like the sword, like the bell—is a message? A cry for help, for rescue?

Or a dare?

In my room, I kneel to reach under my bed, fumble across

the tiles until my fingers meet wood, and drag the sword out into the light.

I sweep through a couple of experimental slashes, a lunge. It's so familiar in my hand. Once upon a time, it was everything. Once upon a time, I was a queen. My wrath was legendary, and nothing could stand before me. And I stood between Deirdre and anything that dared to challenge her.

I vanquished all her enemies. At any cost.

But it was never once upon a time. Not really. Once upon a time was a lie. In the real world, people are fragile. Even Tyler, large as he loomed, was just a person. No more than human. Breakable.

If I go with this, if I let myself believe it's real…if it's real, it means there are monsters, real monsters, out there in the dark. And I'm just Skye. The new Skye, who has friends and wears expensive jeans. I'm the one who's breakable, a thin fluttering sapling. I've never felt it so clearly, how defenseless I am. How useless. It screams at me in the pathetic bristling of my skin, the sweat trickling down my side, the sour taste at the back of my mouth. It was taller than me, that thing. Was it the only one? What am I going to do against reanimated sticks and bones?

But the Queen of Swords—that's exactly where she belongs. Waging war. Riding to the rescue.

I've done my best to bury that person, to forget the roots winding down into the dark. I don't want to follow them. I'm afraid to find out how far down they go. But they were there all along, underneath.

If this is real, so is the Queen of Swords. Who might have

a chance to save Deirdre. And if she can save Deirdre, maybe the Queen of Swords isn't a monster. Maybe she never was. Maybe she just needed monsters to fight.

I don't want William to see the Queen of Swords. I don't want any of them to know she exists. But they don't need to. This is between me and Deirdre. All William will know, if I manage this, is that I saved her. That I found her in the woods. That's all anybody needs to know.

There's no question, no debate. Not really. There's no choice. The Queen of Swords never does have choices. Her path is straight and narrow as her blade.

You can't just walk away when someone needs a hero.

As the darkness ebbs away, the fog settles in, and the woods are ghostly, spindly shadows sinking into gradations of emptiness, thin gray lines of tree trunks fading with distance.

Wisps of vapor swirl around my feet as I walk. My sneakers are still wet. The sword is heavy in my hand, but I keep the point outstretched as long as I can, swinging it every now and again to rest my arm. There's nothing left where the creature fell last night, of course. Just the two-by-four lying in the grass.

Well, this will be the test. Real or not. If nothing happens now, it was just a dream. I'll forget all about it. I press forward until the house is a faint suggestion behind me, threatening to disappear. The air is still, clammy as cold hands against my face.

Deirdre's necklace dangles from my hand. If this is real, then there's a way in. There's a way to find her. I'm past caring if it's ridiculous to try this. It's what Deirdre would do. And for once, that's exactly what I need. To follow her footsteps.

If I'm the Queen of Swords, even a kingdom that's turned rogue, grown wild, has to answer to me.

I stalk to the very edge of the woods, through the border where the grass gets tall, the ground uneven, riddled with hidden animal holes. You could break your ankle back here if you tried to go too fast. Dad said once that we'd have to add more dirt someday; the water doesn't look like it's moving, but the swamp is eating away at the dirt they used to fill it in, bit by bit, absorbing it too slowly to see.

I edge my way onto the jutting shelf of rock that overhangs the tangled maze a few feet below. The dripping silence closes around me. The shadowy trees lean twisted branches overhead, shedding wet leaves in a slow but continuous trickle. They're the only movement.

I hold the necklace out and shout raggedly into the woods.

"You have to take me to her," I demand. "I'm her champion. I'm the Queen of Swords. You have to give her back!"

My voice sinks into the swamp without an echo, but behind me there's a rustle and the soft crunch of a footfall. I whirl to face the same monster from last night—a long, white skull perched atop a misshapen bundle of sticks and cloth, pointed antler-fingers reaching out for me. I raise the sword like I can ward it off, but it trembles in my hand. The creature stops just out of my reach, half turns, like a bird or a deer, as if to see me better from the pit of its eye.

And—oh God—there's another one. It lurches out of the trees on my other side as if it was waiting there. It's shorter than the first, mantled with a bristling pelt that looks like it might be a porcupine's, feathered with long, white spikes. Its torso is armored in strips of rough bark. Another one hobbles behind it on a tripod of long wooden legs, bound with long, fluttering strips of dirty cotton. It has one hand. Too many fingers made of thin bones— something's ribs. Above its blunt fanged muzzle and the gaping hollow of its nose, two mismatched rotten wings fan out like the crest of a fantasy warrior's helm.

I stand there, wheeling from one to the next as they close around me. Was this Deirdre's mistake? Thinking she could control them?

"Stay back!" I make a desperate feint like I'm about to lunge at them, swiping the air with the sword. "I'm the Queen of Swords, goddammit! You have to tell me what you've done with her! Stay back and answer me! By wood, stone, water, and bone!"

They jerk to a reluctant halt, just out of my reach, and stand in place, swaying, leaning toward me like hungry dogs outside a fence. They smell dank and rotten. The faintest whiff of spoiling meat is a nauseating thread through layers of cold water and decaying leaves.

And with a creak and groan of bending wood, they all sink into a low bow, with a twitchy unison flourish like a suppressed smirk.

I open my mouth to reiterate my demands, but all through the branches behind me there's a rustle and a flutter of something like birds' wings or overlapping leaves. There's no wind to stir the fog, and the leaves still clinging to the branches hang wet and silent. The sound continues, spirals around me, trailing over my skin, and in it there are words.

Look look look who's here

A papery cackling washes over me, layers of delighted voices twined together to coil around me. I heft my sword, but there's nothing to threaten with it, just the stick-and-bone monsters, still bent over the ground.

Who is it? Look look it's the Queen of Swords, the Queen of Swords coming back for her kingdom, look look look

"So what?" I demand. "I came back for my sister. Tell me where she is!"

Or what? the voices breathe gleefully. *OR WHAT? You can tell us, Queen of Swords*

"Shut up!" I smack the sword against the nearest tree, making it quiver. The voices moan like a low wind, laughing.

Oooooh scary, so scary Queen of Swords, we're scared now yes so scary

"Who are you supposed to be, anyway?" I yell. Giggles make the trees clack and shiver in the breathless air, stirring the fog into ragged swirls.

Maybe we're the Queen of Winds. The whispers twine around me, still laughing. *Maybe we're the Queen of Bones, maybe we're the Queen of Broken Promises—*

"That's just a game! That was *our* game and you've stolen it! You've stolen my sister!"

Your game, Queen of Swords, now it's yours? The laughter in the air dies as suddenly as a snuffed flame. *Now you want her back? You walked away, she's gone, she's never coming back to you, go home, she's never coming back, you already walked away, walk away, go on*

"She's my sister," I say through clenched teeth. "I'm not walking away. Not without her."

So noble, so braaaaave, look look at the Queen of Swords trying to win her honor back, look at the Queen of Swords who fell asleep on her watch, who fell asleep and let the wolves in

"And what do you know about that?" No response, but the laughter boils up around me again. Desperately, I brandish the necklace at the trees. "Look, you came after me, remember? Fine! Here I am! What do you *want?*"

Walk away, Queen of Swords, walk away, she's ours, you don't love her, you never did, you walked away, walk away, walk away

"She's my sister!" I wail. "Of course I love her!"

She's ours, we love her more than you do, ours forever, walk away

"That's not true! You don't even know what that means!"

Prove it then. The words pour over me, an icy river of contempt. *Prove it. Prove it. Prove it.*

"Well—but—!" I let the point of the sword drop to the ground, bereft, bewildered, thinking frantically. "How? What do you want?" There's a silence, and then I see where this is going. "There's something you want me to do, isn't there? Stop playing games and tell me what it is!"

The branches of the trees shiver. The voices drawl.

Oh let's see, let's see, let's give the Queen of Swords some tasks for us, some trials, yes let's see her prove it, yes prove it

"Fine," I snap. "Fine. And if I pass, you let us go. Both of us. And never bother us again."

Yes, yes, if you pass, the voices sigh, sounding bored, and then they sharpen again, like pointed bone on glass. *And if you lose, if you lose, we keep you both, just for us, for always*

For a moment I can't speak; I'll choke on the words. This is a terrible idea. Horror-movie-level bad idea. But there's nothing else to do. The monsters are looking up at me now, eager and horrible, flexing their bony hands. I stuff the necklace in my pocket, so I can hold my sword out with both hands, but there's no way I could keep them at bay all at once. They took Deirdre. I bet they took Mog too.

I'm next.

Could I walk away, could I really walk away, knowing this was up to me? I'd prove them right.

They've got me already. There's no way out or away from this. Only through.

And I *will* win. I have to. I'm the Queen of fucking Swords.

"All right." I'm shaking so hard, it comes out in a stutter. "Okay. I'll do it."

The voices seethe in wordless triumph, like a kettle hissing.

Yes, yes you will, oh you will, they bubble. *This will be perfect, yes we will have so much FUN*

"Whatever," I snap. "What am I supposed to do already?"

Oh let's think what will we ask of the Queen of Swords, she should make us a gift, yes the Queen of Swords can give us a present

"A present?" I echo warily. "Like what?"

Let's start with a secret, yes, a secret, a secret, they hiss. And then they laugh like mad.

"What do you mean?" I shout. They don't listen to me. "That doesn't make any sense! What secret?"

Your secrets, Queen of Swords, your secrets of course

"My—?"

She's so dense, she's so dull! Queen of Swords, you're supposed to be shhharp!

"You want me to tell you a secret."

No no no not us, she already told us, we already know, we KNOW all your secrets, what good would that do? We want you to GIVE UP a secret, make a present of it, give it up, sacrifice, we want you to PAY FOR IT

The last three words are like slaps, delivered with such venom that I reel back a few steps.

Lay it out in the sun, they purr, *the best secret, let the invaders know who they're dealing with, Queen of Swords, make them understand, make them hate you, make them bow and scurry, spread your secret far and wide where we can see, where everyone can see. We are watching you, we are watching, we will know. Make them hate you, hate you, hate*

Invaders. That's what Deirdre kept calling William. She hated him before she even set eyes on him. A memory flashes through my head: her crouched over a collection of bones, glancing sullenly up at me. *I've heard all about them.*

"What's so different about me and Deirdre?" I demand. "How come we're not invaders too?"

Did we say you're no invader, Queen of Swords? We said no such thing, no, this is how you prove it, your sister proved she loved us, now you have to prove it, prove you're no invader. Make them hate you or you're one of them and your sister is ours forever, ours to love and keep

"Right," I manage. I feel sick. "Sure."

We'll give you till the full moon. The words have gone faint, but they're distinct as a breath in my ear. *Prove it by the full moon, we are watching.*

The monsters cross their stick arms over their torsos and hobble back into the woods, disappearing into the fog until they're only the faintest trace of lurching movement, until they vanish altogether. As if they were never here. I stagger backward, my heart thundering in my ears, and slowly turn toward the house. It swims up out of the gray blankness as I stumble across the lawn.

That was real. Was that real? Oh God, what am I doing?

FIFTEEN

A SECRET. THERE'S ONLY ONE secret. Deirdre was the only one who knew.

In my room I shove the sword out of sight under my bed, drop the necklace into an empty pot, and push it into a space between the plants on the shelves. And then I don't know what to do with myself, with the hissing, laughing voices replaying in my head. I stand paralyzed in the cool, broadening light, listening to my breath rattling in my ears. Overhead, ordinary footsteps creak into the kitchen.

Denying it is a reflex, well-honed. *It can't have happened. I won't think about it.* It made about as much sense as nightmares ever do. And anyway, what they're asking is impossible. I'm not throwing away everything I've built here because of some sort of fever dream. But it nags at me, belief—and fear—taking root, mushrooming up no matter how many times I try to cut it down.

I don't have any choice. They have Deirdre. I'm the only one who can save her.

It takes me a couple of tries to make my fingers cooperate enough to manage a Google search on my phone. It's three days until the full moon. I should have guessed. I have three days to burn everything down.

I want to tell myself I don't know what they mean, that they're messing with me. I keep looking for a loophole, some alternate interpretation. But I always knew that the Skye I'd started to create was a sunny falsehood, one I'd have to cut down. *Make them understand. Make them hate you.*

Some things you just can't escape. Deirdre's dragging me down into the mud again, like she always does, even from wherever they're keeping her. It's not fair.

I watch my parents moving like robots through the day, staring out the windows, fielding sad phone calls. They argue, once, dispiritedly, over Dad opening a can of beer. After that, Mom doesn't stop him, and the empties clank into the recycling one by one. The police mill in and out of the driveway. None of it is as real as the certainty perched on my shoulders, digging in its claws. I know exactly what I have to do.

But day one bleeds into day two as I pace around my room, as I stare into the inane abyss of my notifications, as I clutch my phone with the contacts pulled up. But eventually I have to admit that I'm just procrastinating. Why would texts or a post even count? It's not like the monsters follow me on Twitter. No, I have to do it face-to-face. March up the hill and start knocking on doors.

And I can't.

I drag myself up the stairs in answer to Mom's summons, and I almost jump when I find Sophie waiting for me in the foyer.

"Get your coat," she says, with determined good cheer. "We're going to Kevin's place."

"We're—but I can't," I stammer, looking from her to Mom, but Mom turns an indifferent hand out and trudges wearily back up the stairs. Sophie's perky tone only falters a little.

"It's okay. Really. I cleared it with her already. I thought maybe you could use some company. While you wait. It's a good night for a fire. I told William to bring some stuff for s'mores."

"You thought—" The words lodge in my throat.

"You don't have to. I mean, maybe you'd rather stay with your family. I don't want to—God, I'm sorry, I'm being so awkward about this. I just thought…I'd want my friends with me, if it were me. You know?"

My friends.

It levels all my defenses in a single strike. TKO. I have to turn away with a hand over my mouth. Sophie puts a hesitant arm around my shoulders as I gulp for control.

"I'm sorry. I'll go if you want. The last thing I want to do is make things worse."

"No, no, it's okay. I just—nobody's ever—"

I'm making it worse. I press the heels of my hands to my eyes, fight for a breath that's not a sob.

"Here." She pulls my coat from the closet and tosses it to me. "Come on, let's get out of here."

The last of the light is seeping from the sky, leaving the woods a silent, ragged silhouette. The silver peal of a bell twinkles somewhere at the feet of the trees.

"Is that your cat?" Sophie asks, looking around for its source. I shake my head and walk as fast as I can, not looking into the gathering dark.

After that, she's silent, stealing worried glances at me as I struggle to collect the scattered pieces of my armor. I don't want her to care. It'll eat me alive. It's like she's poisoned me. The gleaming, untouchable gossip queen I've always envied is shrinking at my side, turning into something I can hardly bear to look at: a girl who told me a secret. Who will never forgive me for mine.

"This is…this is really nice of you." I scrub at my eyes with the sleeve of my coat. "Sorry I'm such a mess."

"Don't be ridiculous. She's your sister."

I can't explain. But I'll have to. And soon.

We find them on the weedy patio just behind Kevin's house: William crouched in front of a round-bellied decorative stove, poking at a smoking heap of kindling, with Kevin offering helpful commentary. "Seriously, how can you suck so bad at this?"

"Shut up and wait thirty seconds," William says equably, not looking up.

"I thought we were going out to the party rock," Sophie says.

"We were." William sets a couple of logs against the kindling, knocking some of it over. A tongue of flame smolders reluctantly to life, then flickers out again. "It's just—I don't know, it's creepy out there tonight."

Kevin rolls his eyes. "Just as well, since we're apparently doomed to freeze to death in the dark."

William gives him a look, and he actually winces.

"And also, I'm an idiot," Kevin says to the paving stones. "Sorry."

"I'm used to you." I meant it as a joke, but it comes out weird and harsh. Too awkward to take back. I swallow.

"Anyway," William says, after a painful silence, "his dad's out on a date, so it's not like we're going to bother anyone if we stay close to the house."

Perfect. "Is there anything to drink?"

"Hot chocolate?" William offers.

"No. I mean, is there anything to *drink?*"

"On a school night?" A few days ago that tone from Sophie—skeptical, but light enough not to invite confrontation—would have had me backpedaling. Tonight, I ignore it.

"*I* don't have school tomorrow." If I drink enough, maybe I can tell them. If I drink enough, maybe I won't care. Anesthesia. "Seriously. I could really use a drink. Please?"

They exchange glances. Kevin shrugs and disappears into the house.

"I just don't want us to get in trouble with your parents," Sophie says. She actually sounds anxious.

"Don't worry." I sweep the leaves off one of the long lounge chairs, sink down into it. "It's not like they'll notice."

Kevin emerges with a thermos and a stack of plastic cups, pours me one full of something dark and fizzy that smells faintly like lighter fluid. It's pop, but mixed with something fiery and medicinal tasting. I take a long drink, as long as I can, and surface coughing and grimacing. Kevin lifts his own cup in salute, eyebrows raised, and takes a more conservative swallow. William pours himself one too. Sophie reluctantly accepts another.

"Well—fine, I guess," she sighs. "Just one, though."

The kindling in the stove collapses, letting out a fresh billow of smoke.

"Okay, this is pathetic," Kevin declares, setting his drink aside. He disappears around the corner of the house and returns carting a leaf blower. "Out of the way, peons. Let's get this party started."

He aims the leaf blower at the bottom of the stove and switches it on. Flames gutter into life, flicker higher and higher, lashing in the onslaught, until fire spouts out of the top by two feet, and we're all laughing and cheering.

"See?" He sets the machine aside, lifts his cup. "That's how it's done."

"You're a genuine man of the woods, Kev," William snorts.

"Hashtag zombie apocalypse skills," Kevin returns, and holds the cup out for a toast.

We knock our cups together, and I toss the rest of my drink back, pour another before anyone can object. I still have time, a little bit of time. I can forget for a while. Pretend it's not real. For a while, I can pretend everything is normal, here in the firelight with warmth stealing through my veins. With my friends, laughing under the gibbous moon.

The lounge chair becomes a gravity well. Soon, I'm flattened into it, my head fuzzy and sloshing, the stars reeling overhead in a slow waltz.

"You guys didn't have to do this," I tell them.

"Shut up with that already." Sophie swats my arm. "Of course we did."

"I'm serious," I protest. "You don't know me. You don't know anything about me." I take a deep breath. "I never had friends before. There's a reason."

Sophie talks over me. "Look, Skye, who cares? Seriously. That was then. It doesn't matter. *Now* matters. And now, you're a total badass. C'mon."

I heave a sigh, look out into the dark. The firelight spills over the grass in a wide semicircle that doesn't reach the woods. "You don't understand."

"We like you," Sophie insists. "Just deal."

She hauls herself out of her seat before I can argue, heads into the house. I hide my face behind my cup to find it empty. Again. I have to tell them. This was supposed to make it easier. I thought it was working. The hurt was melting, turning blunt and shapeless, but now it's rising all around me. Overflowing.

"It was okay that I didn't have friends before," I say, "when there was Deirdre. When there was just me and Deirdre."

William watches me, and Kevin studies the ground, both

silent. The fire snaps and settles. The trees loom over us, slicing across the moon.

"I didn't think you guys really got along," William says eventually.

"You don't understand," I repeat, and laugh brokenly at my own slurring syllables. *You donunnerstan.* My lips feel numb. "She wasn't always like that. Not with me. She was…she could be magic. You know? She could halfway convince you anything was real because she believed it so hard." And now my voice is going wobbly. I don't care. "Deirdre wasn't the problem. It was everyone *else*. We'd have been fine if they could have just left her alone."

"You need some water," William says firmly, and takes my cup, disappears with it inside. That leaves me and Kevin, which means the end of conversation for a little while. Just as well. I settle back in my chair, stuffing my icy hands in my pockets, marshaling my courage. But Kevin breaks the silence.

"I don't get you."

I let my head drop back against the cushion.

"Whatever, Kevin. I'm an open book."

"What you are is kind of mean," he says, startling me into looking around at him. He's watching me, frowning, his knuckles at his mouth. "And, I don't know—judgy."

"Aw." I make it a sneer, but I'm stung despite myself. "What, are you saying I hurt your feelings?"

"Look, I don't like you either," he shoots back. "But my friends are telling you all their secrets for some reason, so I'm at least trying. And you take a shot at me every chance you get. Like, what the hell? Am I missing something?"

"And what kind of friend are you?" I snap. "A friend wouldn't talk about Sophie like she's a piece of meat. William doesn't."

"That was one time! See? Judgy!"

"Yeah, maybe people might judge you when you spout bullshit! What a concept! Do you ever mean *anything* you say?"

"Do you?" he challenges. "Your whole voice changes when you talk to Sophie! It's so fake, it's fucking creepy! And I know William's all dazzled by your Wonder Woman act, but—"

"And you're interrogating me about this now." Playing this card feels like losing, but suddenly I don't care anymore. Whatever will shut this conversation down. "*Tonight*. God, they keep telling *me* you're not an asshole."

It works; he falls silent and sits back a little, frowning. I glare at the fire so I won't have to look at him. He thinks he sees right through me, does he? Well, the joke's on him. Mean and judgy barely scratches the surface.

"Look," he says finally, "I didn't mean to—" He stops, tries again. "Look. I'm drunk. So're you. This is a good time to call a truce, isn't it? Live and let live? I mean, maybe they're right about both of us. You know?"

Above me the moon goes blurry. The moon that's almost full. I squeeze my eyes shut, but the misery closes over my head.

"Yeah," I manage. "And maybe they're wrong."

"Here," William says, pulling the patio door closed behind him. "Rehydrate. You're going to have a hell of a morning tomorrow otherwise." I put my hands over my face, turn away, trying to hold the pieces together. "Skye?"

"It's fine. I'm fine. Forget it." This was a mistake. I flounder off the deck chair, hear my knees collide with the patio stones
before the pain sparks reluctantly through to my swimming head.
William leans over the chair, trying to help me up.

I pull away, stumble to my feet. Sophie's voice rises behind me.

"Skye? What's wrong? Kevin, what the hell?"

"Don't look at me," Kevin protests. "She's the one who—"

"Honestly, you guys, I was inside for five minutes!" She
sounds like my mom. "Skye, where are you going?"

I don't answer, pushing forward into the dark, away from
them. The night dissolves into fragments: footsteps catching up with
me halfway down the driveway. William's hand on my arm, his arm
around my shoulders, half holding me up as we stumble down the hill.
The moon glaring down at us, watching. The windows of the house
swimming up out of the night, bright and empty. The pale tiles of my
bedroom floor, blue in the moonlight, cold against my cheek. The
shadow of the sword waiting under my bed, the one thing that seems
to stand unmoved as the room spins around me, rocks me to sleep.

A hand on my shoulder drags me back to the surface with
a rough shake.

"Skye. Skye! Wake up!"

The spinning hasn't stopped, but it's turned nauseating,
keeping time with a stabbing pulse in my head. Dad is a silhouette
above me, framed by golden light spilling in through the door. I
pull away from his hand and curl up on my side with a groan.

"You scared me," he says. And then, more sharply, "You've
been drinking."

"Leave me alone," I mutter. "I don't feel so good."

"Yeah, I bet," he says darkly. "You're practically giving off fumes."

"Leave me alone." I cover my face with my hands.

"I thought you were more responsible than this, Skye! We can't deal with you acting out now, with your sister—"

"I just wanted to forget for a while," I cry. "Isn't that why *you* do this? To forget?"

There's a silence.

"Let's get you into bed," he says gruffly. "We'll discuss this in the morning."

He helps me to my feet, tucks me fully dressed under the covers. A few minutes later, he returns with a couple of Tylenols and a tall glass of water.

"Let's not mention this to your mother," he says. "Okay?"

I swallow the pills, set the rest of the water down on the night table. The clock says it's 1:07. I close my eyes and turn away from it, bracing myself against the sickening merry-go-round swoop of the darkness around me.

This is it. When I get up again, it will be the last day. And I still have to tell.

SIXTEEN

THE DISCUSSION DAD PROMISED, PREDICTABLY, doesn't happen. When I wake up, close to noon, the nausea has dulled to a dizzy, hollow feeling that's almost hunger. But eating seems like an idea from another lifetime. I stay in bed the whole day, and my parents, mercifully, don't intrude.

When William texts—asking how I'm doing, offering to come over and watch a movie after school—I type *sure* without letting myself think about it. This time I'll do it, I tell myself. It will be easier if it's just William, if I don't have to face all of them at once. I can tell him. I'll work up to it. If it's the end of the world, it doesn't make any difference if I watch a movie first. I can take two or three more hours for myself, can't I, before letting the nukes fly?

When I open the door, he steps inside, sets down the grocery bag he's carrying—a bag of chips crinkles at the top—and wraps his arms around me in a careful, gentle hug, as if I'm any of the normal people he cares about, as if it's natural as breathing. And I hug him back, because why the hell not. It shouldn't be comforting, the breadth of his shoulders under my arms, the warm fabric of his shirt against my nose. He smells good—like his kitchen, that morning a million years ago. Sun. Vanilla.

Two or three hours. I can do this.

"You look terrible," he says.

"Thanks," I return, and his mouth tilts into an embarrassed smile.

"You know what I mean."

"Yeah. Rough morning."

"Well, cheese fries are supposed to be the best hangover food, so I brought the closest I could get." He empties the bag onto the couch: potato chips and shrink-wrapped cheese sticks.

I make him pick the movie. He shuffles through Netflix for a few minutes before starting *Pride and Prejudice and Zombies*. "It reminds me of you," he explains, "with your ninja skills and everything."

We sit side by side in silence, watching busty Regency ladies trade haughty dialogue and whip swords from improbable hiding places to splatter zombie blood across the battlefield. I crunch through a handful of chips to be polite. The screen burns into my eyes. When I look away, I find him watching me instead of the movie; he gives me a little smile, guileless.

He won't look at me like that once he knows.

When the world is ending, everything is permitted. I sink slowly down on the couch to curl up on my side, pillowing my head against his thigh. After a moment, a long moment, he brushes my hair away from my face with warm fingers, rests his hand very carefully on my arm.

The afternoon slides away from me like sand through my fingers. And eventually the credits roll, and he squeezes my shoulder and tells me he has to go.

Here we are. I push myself upright, let my head hang, wait for deep breaths to steady me. This is it, this is my last chance. I have to tell him. If I tell him, he'll tell everyone else, won't he? Doesn't that count as telling everyone? I trail helplessly after him as he makes his way to the door. I don't know where to start. I don't know what to say.

"We can do this again," he offers, a little too casually. "You know, if it helps."

"William?"

He stops with his hand on the doorknob, alert to the choke in my voice. Do it, I tell myself. Say it. Go on.

"Yeah?" he says slowly.

But the words are dying, dry leaves filling my mouth. He's waiting for me to say something so different. It's the end of the world, and he has no idea. I shake my head, mop my eyes. All I can get out is "Thanks."

When I dream that night, it's of Deirdre, crouched in the garden with her back turned to me. Under the skinny straps of her dress, her shoulders rise and fall, rhythmic—she's digging, tossing the dirt away into black heaps. I push my way toward her, but branches whip across my path, catch at my legs; my progress is slow, as if I'm floundering through deep water.

I try to call her name, but my mouth is full of leaves. I spit them out clumsily, and they turn into gold coins, gleaming as they fall, thumping to the ground at my feet.

Rage boils through me, a helpless fury at being thwarted, enchanted, and I thrash against the grip of the greenery closing over my head, the leaves slowly eclipsing my sister from my sight. I have to warn her. About that thing in the yard. About the voices waiting for her in the woods. I have to warn her not to follow the bell.

But when Deirdre turns, there's only carved white hollows where her face should be, a grinning skull, and her hands are antlers, ending in wicked points. At her feet is a gaping pit. A grave.

"You'll grow fine roots," she says meditatively. And the million hands binding me carry me forward, choking, and give me a shove. Topple me into darkness.

I jerk back into consciousness, sputtering into my pillow, my mouth dry and gritty as if it really was filled with leaves. It takes a long moment to sort out that the floodlight beaming cold light over my face is just the moon.

The full moon.

The house is silent. There's a line of light glowing under the door, all the lights still on, keeping watch for Deirdre. But there's a chilly edge to the air, a taste of cold, green water standing in deep shade, and my heartbeat doesn't slow.

I've left it too long. Are they looking for me? Could they get into the house?

Hugging my blankets, I sit up, scanning the room. No pale lurching creatures. Nothing, nothing.

Except that one of the doors that hides the crawl space—the doors I helped Dad cut down and install over that creepy cavern of bare concrete—one of them is a little ajar, the latch gleaming.

I slap the light on, but it's still true. The door doesn't move, doesn't even quiver. I lean cautiously out over the edge of the bed to get a closer look, and find that something pushed it open: some sort of sinuous tentacles. They've spilled out over the tiles, little rivulets of darkness against the gleaming squares.

I fumble to pull my sword from under the bed, almost fall. Are they moving, those tendrils? I don't think they are. I pad closer, step by step, the tiles icy under my feet, and prod one with the tip of my sword, then smack it. It doesn't move, but it doesn't yield.

They're made of wood. Roots.

When I pry the door open, the crawl space is full of them: a thicket of them, knotted into and over one another in a tightly coiled snarl, like a nest of snakes. I let the point of the sword drop to the tiles.

"All right," I whisper. The sound is harsh in my ears, unnatural. "All right. Fine. Message received."

It takes fifteen minutes to track down Dad's little utility saw, buried in the heap of tools on the workbench in the laundry room. It takes me an hour to saw through all the ropy coils that have crept over the threshold, so I can close the door again. It doesn't help that I keep imagining the twitch of ragged white cloth at the window. Every click and creak of the house settling in the night is pointed bone on glass, unwelcome footsteps staggering overhead.

I pull Deirdre's necklace from the pot on the shelf and put it around my neck. It's cold and heavy, gleaming hard-edged and bright as a sword. Or a coin.

None of it matters. I don't care. I can't afford to care. I'm the Queen of Swords on a mission, and I'll do whatever it takes, I'll deal with whatever ruin I have to call down on us. On me. I suppose I deserve it, anyway.

SEVENTEEN

I'M AWAKE BEFORE MY ALARM, opening my eyes to gray dawn from a shifty, ashen sleep. Determination is a cold rock in my belly. I remember this feeling. It means that today I'm going to do something terrible. Today I'm wearing an iron crown.

Mom stands at the window, looking out into the woods, hugging a mug of coffee, tapping her nails against it without drinking. She doesn't turn around when I come into the room. The computer's open on the table, the screen crowded with red-lined graphs.

"It's been a week," she says, without inflection. Like a ghost. "Almost a week."

"She's still out there, Mom."

The quiet strength of my voice surprises me. But after

all—after everything—that's one thing I know, now. One thing to cling to. Even if I can't explain it. Mom presses a hand to her face.

"They said we have to—we have to prepare ourselves for the possibility—"

"She *is*." Mom looks around at me, finally, her eyes brimming with wanting to believe me. "I just know it, okay? She's out there, and she'll be fine. It'll be okay." I swallow. "I promise."

She sets the coffee down on the table, sloshing a little bit over the side, and wraps her arms tight around me.

"You always looked after her," she says into my shoulder. "I shouldn't have blamed you, Skye. You—you've been really brave, you know that?"

The words burn. "I have to go," I mutter. "I'm going to miss the bus."

She pulls away, frowning.

"You're going to school?"

"You're writing code."

"It just—helps take my mind off things. Well. Not really. But it's something to do. And it supports our family. It's my job. Anyway, the social worker said she'd come by again today, and you should really spend some more time with her."

"There's some things I have to do." I pick up her coffee from the table—it's cold—and down half of it in a long gulp. It's black and bitter and does nothing to chase the taste of leaves from my mouth. "I'll talk to her later, okay? I have to go."

I flee from the house without even bothering to put on a coat. The morning is wet and roaring, with a wind that knifes through my sweater and lashes the bare branches. A white sun sifts through the clouds, a pale and ineffectual circle, and vanishes again. It's one of those drowned end-of-fall days that promises ice and winter following close behind.

I duck my head, fold my arms, and soldier up the hill. My ears are already aching from the knives in the wind. I will not falter. I will not doubt myself. I will not listen to the voice in my head still crying out that none of this can be real, that I'm about to spill my guts for no reason.

A flash of black feathers bursts across the road—a crow, riding the wild wind. It swoops down among the branches that lean out over the creek, a thicket of silver birch and fuzzy branching sumac, and comes to rest on a bare branch.

A branch that moves. A branch connected to a torso of rough bark. A spiky fur cloak. A long, skeletal face.

The ground seems to tilt beneath my feet, sending me stumbling back, fear sending tingling runners through my chest and arms. But the monster makes no move toward me. It stands there, immobile as the bones of the forest, utterly silent. After a long moment, it jerks into a bow, the crow still clutching its outstretched twiggy arm, flapping a wing for balance. Watching me.

The monster straightens again and twitches its arm skyward, launching the crow back into the air to alight in the trees just down the road. And when I look back to the creek, the figure has vanished.

I draw long, shaky breaths, darting glances into the shifting labyrinth of the woods on either side of the street, pulling my hands inside my sleeves. The crow hangs ahead of me in the trees, a silent scrap of black. Finally, I haul my gaze back to my feet and keep moving.

So they're watching. They said they would be.

The whole thing seems more and more impossible the farther I walk. This can't be real. This can't be happening. Maybe I imagined everything. Maybe I should go home and tell my parents I'm seeing things. Tell them Deirdre's been kidnapped by monsters. They'd summon the social worker. Call the psychiatrist. Ship me off to the hospital, even. They'd take all of this out of my hands.

I could still do it. I don't have to tell. Do I?

Voices drift through the air as I trudge around the last corner. Talking, laughing. They fall silent as I approach: Kevin, Sophie. William.

"Hey," Sophie says, all concern. "How are you doing? Did they find her?"

Awkward silence falls when I shake my head. They exchange glances.

"Are your parents seriously making you go to school today?" William says. I can't look at him. I clench my teeth.

"No. I just—I have to."

Sophie winces in sympathy. Kevin shifts a little, looks at his feet. William shuffles over on the rail beside the mailbox to make room for me to perch beside him in my usual spot. I shrug my backpack to the ground so I have something to look at besides them, so my brittle shell won't crack and betray me. When I hop up and settle myself on the rail, William actually puts an arm around me, as if to keep me warm, and I just about come undone.

I can't do it. There has to be some future where they don't hate me.

But with an explosive snap and ruffle of black wings, a crow sweeps down in front of us, its feet meeting the rail across from us with a clang. Everyone jumps.

"That," Kevin says with a nervous laugh, "is a big fucking bird."

He feints a lunge at it, trying to scare it off; it flaps one wing and stays put, eyeing him. I edge away from it, remembering the one that attacked my window.

"Leave it alone, Kev." Sophie tugs at his arm, looking uneasily at the crow. "What if there's something wrong with it?"

"What's it going to do," Kevin counters, smirking, "peck me to death?"

The crow cocks its head, studies us. Studies me. As if it's waiting.

Kevin picks up a rock and pitches it, despite Sophie's protest—"don't!"—and the bird stands stone still, unfazed, as if to prove it doesn't care, before it gives us a last disdainful look and takes off. It doesn't go far, though, just flutters up into the branches of the huge willow drooping over the eaves of William's stone house across the street.

"Did you ever hear that crows can recognize people's faces?" William says into the silence. "There were these researchers catching crows to put bands on their feet, and they had to wear masks because otherwise the crows would dive-bomb them for weeks afterward."

Sophie looks up at the crow, tugging her hat down lower over her ears. "Nice job, Kevin. Now you've probably pissed it off."

"Oh come on, it didn't even do anything," he scoffs.

"That was creepy, though," Sophie insists.

Round and round they go, back and forth. Their voices rattle down around me without meaning. That was real. They saw it too. It's not just me. I can't pretend. My teeth are clenched so hard, my jaw aches. I'm running out of time; the bus will be here soon. What I have to say is a weight crushing down on me. They used to execute people like that, piling heavy stones on their chests until they broke.

I just have to start talking. I just have to start somewhere. Anywhere. Get it over with.

"I almost drowned somebody once," I say loudly.

Put like that, it sounds weirdly casual. Like it was an accident; like it was no big deal. But it gets their attention. They all turn to frown at me, the conversation shattered like a reflection in a pool.

"What?" Sophie says, like she's not sure she heard me right.

"Uh—" William begins, his eyebrows up in a baffled line. I shrug my way out from under his arm.

"His name was Tyler," I bite out. "He was in my year. And he wouldn't leave Deirdre alone. She said I had to do something, I had to make him stop. I always had to make them stop. It was practically my job. But with Tyler around, nothing I did made any difference anymore. I gave this one guy a black eye once." I whip a punch at the air to demonstrate. William twitches away from me, startled. "It just got me suspended."

"Um," Kevin interrupts, looking uncomfortable, "I don't know what your point is here, but—"

"Shut up, Kev," William says.

"Skye," Sophie puts in uneasily, "maybe this should wait until—"

"No!" My voice cracks. "No. I have to do this. I have to do it now."

They exchange glances. I breathe in, breathe out, my head pounding with adrenaline.

"Tyler was the ringleader. If I got to him, everyone else would back off. And he knew I could have kicked his ass anytime. But I'd have gotten expelled. And then it would have been open season. She wouldn't have had anyone left to defend her. So." Breathe in. Breathe out. "I took it outside of school.

"I spent a while following him. Figuring him out. He didn't live that far from us. There was…this valley." I have to stop and swallow, close my eyes. "He cut through it on the way home. He was so fucking cocky; it never occurred to him it might be danger-ous to be out there alone. Boys never worry about that. But I was out there too. And I knew where to wait for him."

"Look," William interrupts. "You were protecting your sister. You don't think we get that?"

"You don't understand!" I push his hand away from my shoulder; my fingers are white and numb from clutching the railing. "There's a river at the bottom of that valley. It's fast, and cold, and people drown in it all the time." The words are tumbling out faster now, a machine set in motion, nothing left to lose, no point in stopping. "I waited for him by the river. And I hauled him down to the water, and I held his head under. Again and again. I told him I was going to drown him. I told him nobody would ever know the difference, nobody would ever know he hadn't just fallen in. You should have heard him. He cried so hard, he could barely talk."

Silence. The wind whistles around us. My heartbeat pulses behind my eyes. I wait for it to sink in, for them to back away, for the mutters of revulsion to start. But all that happens is a touch on my hand that makes me jump: William's fingers closing over mine.

"What are you doing?" I demand raggedly. "Did you hear a word I said?"

Above our heads, the crow gives a warning caw. I'm running out of time. Isn't this enough? *Make them hate you.* Haven't I tried? Is it my fault they can't take a hint?

"Skye—" Sophie trades a look with William. "Look, that's… pretty not okay, but…"

"I have a sister too," William says. "I get it."

His grip is gentle, but he won't let me pull away, and my desperate resolve crystallizes into a spike of rage. I seize his hand, twist his arm around so that his shoulder has to follow. He stumbles off the rail with a yelp of pain and surprise.

"Hey," Kevin protests, but I ignore him.

"You don't get it!" I shout. "You don't get it at all!"

"Okay, hang on," William tries again, massaging his shoulder, one hand out, placating. I jump down off the rail and slap it away.

"Have you ever hurt somebody, William? On purpose?" He's backing away from me now, but I stalk closer, my hands in fists, raising my voice to drown out his shaky attempts to talk me down. "It's easy. You barely need to know what you're doing. Want me to show you?" Grab, twist, turn, and I've shoved him face-first against the mailbox, his arm pinned behind his back. "Another few degrees and I could break your arm. I could do it! Right here! If I wanted to choke you out I could do it in *ten seconds*. Less! How about it? Is that what it's going to take?"

I push his arm a little higher, a little harder, mashing his cheek against the mailbox's metal face.

"Ow, *ow*," he gasps, "let go, shit, ow—"

"You think he didn't beg? You think he didn't apologize a million times?" Behind me somewhere, Sophie is shouting something, shrill, random sounds that I can't string together into words. "Imagine if someone was hurting you, and they didn't want anything from you at all except to see you suffer! To see you pay! That's what I did, *William!* Do you think he believed me when I said I'd kill him if he told anybody? You bet he fucking believed it!"

Kevin pushes his way between us, his eyes wide, his mouth moving, and somewhere far away his voice says things like *what the fuck, calm down already,* and though I let William scramble away out of reach, I grab the arm Kevin's put across my chest and twist and heave, sending him sprawling to the asphalt. He doesn't know how to land, goes down with a cry and a wicked smack of bone against pavement. It's so easy.

"Are we done yet?" I demand, panting, as William helps Kevin stagger to his feet, blood streaming down his face. I scream it up into the trees, to the watchers waiting there. "*Are we fucking done? Is that enough yet? Are you satisfied?*"

Sophie's still babbling—into a phone, her face drawn with panic. Summoning help. One long lunge and I snatch it from her hand, hurl it to the pavement as hard as I can. She shrinks away from me as it bounces once, crunching, and tumbles to a stop in the middle of the road.

Silence falls after that. We stare at each other, me and them. Kevin and William draw protectively around Sophie, pulling her away from me. In another world, the bus is wheezing down the road toward us.

"What is wrong with you?" Kevin demands, trying to stem his nosebleed with one hand. "That was completely fucking psycho!"

And there it is. I fold my hands over my head, let my shoulders slump.

"I know," I say.

I throw my bag over my shoulder and run back down the hill, their bewildered, outraged voices following me like arrows.

EIGHTEEN

THE CROW SWEEPS PAST ME into the sumac branches over the creek. The water makes a narrow gray corridor into the brush, and I storm right into it, ignoring its icy bite soaking through my jeans, after the bird. It startles into flight as I approach but doesn't go far—just enough to keep me following as it hops from branch to branch, with a guttural clucking like low-voiced laughter. Soon I'm knee-deep in the water, my feet and calves in screaming knots from the cold, and the street is lost behind me, the house vanished from sight. Civilization disappears so fast, and so silently.

"Well?" I yell up at the crow, into the treetops.

You took your time, Queen of Swords. The whisper buzzes past my ear like an insect. I almost put up a hand to swat it away.

"So what? You got what you wanted. I told them. That was my secret." I falter. "And now they hate me. Now everybody will hate me."

Did we really get what we want now, did we?

"You know you did!" Can they hear the frantic rabbit racing of my heartbeat? They can't tell me now that I misunderstood. There's nothing else they could have meant.

You can't cheat us, Queen of Swords, we know you, that wasn't the real *secret, not the one that really costs, it's cheap, barely any flavor*

"What do you mean? That was the only secret I've got! It just cost me all my friends. I made sure it did! You were watching, you saw it!"

A shiver goes through the brush. The crow twitches its wings, flashing black feathers somehow reminding me of hair flipped over a shoulder.

"You don't get to change the rules!" I shout. "You got your fucking present! Where's my sister?"

So hasty, they murmur, *so rude, you drag your feet till the moon is full and now you're so hasty, is that any way to give a gift? Have some manners, show some respect*

I want to scream. I want to hit something. But what am I going to fight, the crow? The trees? I don't even have my sword. I can't fuck this up, not now. I take a deep breath, fold my arms.

"Sorry."

What do you say, come on now, what's the magic word?

I grit my teeth. My feet are numb, my jeans clinging icily to my thighs.

"Please," I grate out finally. "Please. I did what you told me to. Please give me my sister back."

Giggles flutter down around me.

Aww, look at the Queen of Swords all alone without her friends, should we have pity on her? Let's think about this, let's consider

"Come on," I cry. "I did my part! I did what you asked! Isn't that enough?"

Ohhhh it's a start. There's a smile in the words, a predatory glee. *It's certainly a start.*

"Fine." My teeth are rattling now. "Great. So what is it I'm supposed to do next?"

Meet us in the castle, you'll need to find the way, of course, you'll need a guide

"What do you mean, a guide? What guide?"

So dull, Queen of Swords, sharpen up if you're going to play this game, you already know how your sister did it

I open my mouth to protest, because that isn't remotely true. I have no idea what Deirdre did to get us into this mess. Except for—

"So I…have to make one of those monsters. Is that it? How?"

Sharpen up, Queen of Swords, you'll figure it out and you'll have to pay for it, of course, everything has a price

"Like what, exactly, in this case?"

You'll figure it out, they drawl. *You should know what we like by now, you'll figure it out, go figure it out now, go*

"Perfect," I mutter. The crow's throaty chuckle rises up behind me as I turn and splash back the way I came, stumbling.

I'm not going home, not yet. My parents think I'm at school. I should have the whole day to deal with this, to put it behind me, and I'm not going to think about what will happen after that. My soaking jeans feel like they're made of molded ice, but I'm not stopping to change, to risk getting mired in questions the second I walk in the door.

I push my way through the grass in the empty lot, around the looming heap of dirt, and through the slanting cedar doorway. Those last few bones haven't moved from their hiding places in the grass. A skull, a long thighbone, little random bones. I line them up on the ground and crouch over them, hugging my knees to hold the warmth in, trying to think.

A few orange sprigs of fallen cedar make an impressive, feathery crest when threaded through the crack in the skull. Twinkling from the ground here and there are bits of broken glass, blue and green and dirt-smudged. I collect them, polish them with a corner of my sweater, spread them out on a rock. Two of them look about the same size as the eye sockets, which gives me an idea; I wedge them in place, grinding the sharp points against the bone, so that two mismatched eyes gleam up at me.

They ought to like that.

I scour the clearing for possibilities: pebbles, mud, long twiggy branches, and stouter pieces that might be good for building something. Pale, reaching mushrooms. Dead fern fronds. Wet, rocky clay dug from the ground.

But the clay proves ineffective at holding any but the smallest pieces together. I wince at the memory of Deirdre demanding I fetch her some string. String would be perfect right about now. After another flash of insight, I wrestle my sweater off, yank my T-shirt over my head—one of the ones I bought with Sophie—and pull the sweater back on by itself, shivering. There's a hole starting in one of the shirt's underarm seams. Cheap crap. But that makes it perfect. I dig my fingers into it and yank until it rips.

It takes a surprising amount of time and effort to tear the shirt up further, but between the sharp points on the remaining bits of glass and a desperate strength, I manage it eventually. Still, getting the component pieces lashed together in some configuration that will stand turns out to be a serious pain in the ass. When I think about Deirdre's creations, though, I can't imagine they're especially sturdy. The one I hit collapsed easily enough. Whatever's animating them must be holding them together too. I resort to leaning my creature against a tree, hoping the woods will do me the same favor.

I'm trying to figure out how to get the skull mounted as its head when it dawns on me that the voices yelling in the distance are familiar. They're shouting my name. When I pull my phone from my bag, I have thirty-five missed calls. All from home.

It's not even noon. Sophie's frightened face flashes through my mind. She was calling her parents. Who must have marched right down the hill to demand justice from *my* parents. And the police are still camped out in our driveway.

Shit. *Shit.*

I take a last, hurried stab at hanging the skull from the long, zigzaggy branch I propped up as the creature's spine, and the whole thing falls over with a crash. I smack my fist into the nearest tree in frustration, but I can't stay here any longer. They can't find this place. God knows what they'll think if they see this. I shoulder my bag and duck out through the cedars, running through the grass to the road.

I've reached the driveway when Mom comes around the corner of the house, catches sight of me. She staggers a little, like I've hit her. And then she comes running toward me, flings her arms around me so tightly, I can barely move my arms. For a moment, the only sound is her shaky breathing.

"You," she says, in a leaden voice that promises the direst consequences, "had better get inside."

It's bad enough that my friends—my former friends—reported my transformation into a raving lunatic, my unprovoked attack at the bus stop. But then I went and disappeared. And surfaced again soaked and filthy, my lips blue-tinged with cold, and my shoes caked in mud and pine needles. It doesn't take a detective to surmise that I'd gone looking for Deirdre again.

Not only am I confined to the house, I'm confined to my room.

"I can't go out at all?" Dad, standing over me, shakes his head. "But—I'm working on—I have to! It's important! I won't go far, I promise!"

He just looks at me with a beaten, incredulous expression that says *Really?* "Forget it, Skye."

"You don't understand." I can't keep the tremor out of my voice. "I—it's *important*. What about school?"

"With everything that's going on? Are you kidding? You're obviously not coping as it is." His voice goes oddly pointed, his lips thin. "It can wait. *Some* things are more important."

Mom, standing behind him, lifts her chin. They don't look at each other, but tension quivers between them. If I got up and left, would they come after me, or would they just start yelling at each other?

Dad's weary lecture is followed by one from Mom that's ranting and tearful—I have to pay for Sophie's phone; they're never signing me up for martial arts again—and a brief, stern one from Officer Leduc. I'm lucky I didn't seriously hurt someone. I'm lucky I'm not facing charges.

I nod through it, staring at my feet, waiting for the killing blow. But it never falls.

There's not a word about Tyler.

They don't bother taking my phone away, so in the bright quiet of my room, with muffled voices arguing overhead, I sift through the online wreckage of my attempt at being someone else. A raft of people I barely know are suddenly invisible, having blocked me. Sophie has disavowed me with capitals and exclamation marks, though not by name.

TFW someone you TRUSTED shows you what they're REALLY like!!!

Kevin has chimed in too.

uh yeah! told u so, maybe listen to me next time!

His response is followed by a clamour of exclamations and questions from Sophie's handmaidens and ominous replies of *DMing you!!* And William, absurdly, is trying to play peacekeeper.

Come on guys her sisters missing of course shes
    freaking out
JFC William I know you like her but WAKE UP this
    is NOT OK.
I didnt say it was ok, just saying theres context is all
in denial much
sucks that yr gf is a crazy bitch but srsly
  ^This. You're TOO NICE you can do better!!!

I puff out my breath in a ghost of a laugh. I'm tempted to post a comment agreeing with her. I scan the exchange again. *I know you like her. Yr gf.* Well. Whatever. That's all about a different person. I'm the Queen of Swords. I'm steel inside. The words bounce off me without impact.

Why the hell is he still defending me? It's either sad or hilarious, I can't decide which. But they haven't told anyone about Tyler yet. How is that possible? Why wouldn't they?

A text message flashes across the top of the screen. It's from William—three letters: *wtf?????*

I toss the phone aside. WTF indeed. Welcome to my life. If he has any sense, he'll stay out of it from now on.

NINETEEN

THEY ONLY LET ME OUT of my room for long enough to sit through a painfully silent dinner, all of us picking at our food—meatballs, this time, and potatoes—while evening seeps into the room. I don't know why they even bother. I pass the hours alternately pacing and staring at the ceiling, trying to formulate some sort of plan. I'll have to sneak out tonight, after they go to bed. I'm not looking forward to doing this little arts-and-crafts project in the dark. But it's not like I have a choice.

I wait, and I wait, and I wait. I can't jump too early and give myself away. Three o'clock ought to do it. Surely that will leave me with an hour or two. I grab Mom's good sharp scissors, the ones we're forbidden to use in case we ruin their edge, which are stowed in a drawer beneath the sewing machine, waiting patiently in the laundry room for her to come back around to that particular project. I take safety pins too. Embroidery floss. Contact cement. A roll of copper wire and cutters from Dad's workbench. I go back to my room and pull the sheet from my bed, use the scissors to slice it into hasty, uneven strips. I yank on an extra sweater—I can't risk the creak of the front hall closet opening to get my coat. Finally, I pull the sword out from under the bed. It doesn't really make sense to take it; I'm pretty sure the woods won't try to hurt me if I'm working for them. Still, the weight of it in my hand makes me feel better.

The rasp of my bag zipping up slices through the night. The furnace clicks on and whirs to life. In the merciless light— every room stays lit up all night since Deirdre disappeared—the house will never feel truly asleep. Now is as good a time as any. I have to try.

I creep up the stairs as soundlessly as possible and pad through the front hall, the silence straining in my ears.

"Where do you think you're going?"

I startle so badly that I stumble, clutch the railing to keep myself from falling. Mom is sitting on the stairs going up to the living room, hunched over an empty coffee cup, glaring at me.

"Jesus, Mom."

"I asked you a question."

"I'm—I'm going—" Sudden inspiration strikes. "I'm going to see William."

"At three in the morning."

"I have to apologize. He probably hates me now." I make my

mouth go thin. It's not hard to summon tears when they're not all fake. "Please just let me go tell him I'm sorry."

Mom's expression softens at the edges, but her eyes travel to the sword.

"It's for protection." I sniffle. "I'm not going to walk around in the dark without some way to defend myself. Not after Deirdre—"

I let the tears rise up, and Mom sighs, capitulates, sets the mug down to hug me wearily. I'm no different than Deirdre at all, in the end. I'm as good at this as she is.

"I was so happy to see you making friends," she whispers. "Go back to bed, Skye. You can invite William over to talk in the morning. Okay?"

That's as far as I'm going to get. I nod, wipe my eyes, and retreat for now.

It wasn't wasted. That gives me my opening. An excuse they'll accept, because they want to believe it so bad. *I was so happy to see you making friends.* They'll bend their rules if they think I'm trying to undo the damage, make nice, piece the new me back together.

IOU an apology, I text William. Three a.m. is a good time for a text like this. *Please come over tmrw so we can talk.*

There's no response, but I'm not expecting one, not really. He'd be stupid to show up. I mostly hope he doesn't. But if he doesn't... I won't think about what I'll do if he doesn't. I'll figure it out.

I lie in bed with the phone in my hand. It stays still, inert, like the bones waiting for me in the woods. Waiting to be brought to life.

"What do you mean?" Mom's voice starts dangerous, grows shrill. "You can't call off the search! You can't do that!"

Officer Leduc, leaning earnestly across the table, draws a breath like he's bracing for her to scream or hit him.

"I know," he says, "I wish there was——"

"My little girl is still out there! She's still in those woods somewhere! You haven't found a single sign of her, and you're just going to *leave?*"

"I can't tell you how sorry I am," he says. "I wish I had answers for you. We stayed out here longer than we usually do in this sort of situation. The amount of water back there makes it a challenge, but still…honestly, it's strange as hell we haven't found more leads. We just don't have anything left to go on. Given the temperature, and how far she could have gone barefoot…I promise you, we have done everything, *everything* in our power to find her."

To one side of her, Dad sinks forward, props his forehead up on his hand. On the other side, Janelle, the social worker, clasps Mom's hand, glances up at me to measure how I'm doing. I look back at her without blinking, regal, unassailable. You'd never know my crown is grinding into my temples with every heartbeat.

"You think she's dead," Mom says flatly. "You're giving up."

"We're not assuming anything. The file's still open. I mean, if we were looking at a kidnapping or something…it doesn't really add up that way, with her boots back there where we found them, but we can't totally rule it out either. We've talked to people all through the neighborhood, and we'll do it again, just to be completely sure we don't miss anything. The second there's any new information, we'll be all over it. But right now, from the woods? We just don't have any answers. Sometimes there aren't any. That's the truth, and it's terrible, and I'm just…so sorry. Truly."

That's when Dad starts to cry, his rugged reserve crumbling, his shoulders jerking with silent sobs as he buries his face in his hands, and I shove my chair back and wheel from the room, my own hands in fists at my sides.

Sometimes there aren't any answers. Sure. But this isn't one of them. The Queen of Swords makes a bad enemy. I will find a way out of the game they're playing, the trap they think they've set for me. I will smash their bony faces in. I will make this stop.

I glance up in the middle of thumping down the stairs and find I'm looking right at William, who's standing outside the front door, one hand lifted to knock. I freeze, and we stand there staring at each other through the glass. Behind me, Mom is brokenly trying to comfort Dad, and their tearful voices drive me forward, outside, slamming the door to block them out. It works, mostly.

William, shaken, looks at me in alarm. "Is there news?"

"They're calling off the search."

"Oh. Wow. I'm—oh my God. I'm really sorry."

I shrug, fold my arms. The silence stretches. His arms are folded too. He keeps a safe distance between us, but he watches me in obvious consternation. If he had a script prepared, this wasn't in it.

"Look," William says eventually, "this is obviously a bad time. I should—"

"No." The word escapes more desperately than I meant it to. "Please. Please stay."

He doesn't answer, just looks at me. But he doesn't leave.

"I wanted to tell you I'm sorry." The words are wooden, dead as leaves in my mouth. "For freaking out on you. On everyone."

He acknowledges this, the inadequacy of it, with a twist of his lips. "It's Kev and Sophie you should apologize to. I mean, all you did to me was twist my arm."

"I don't think they'd listen."

"That's not really the point."

"Well. You're listening. You're here. I…I appreciate that." He shrugs, studiously neutral, and I lift my chin. "I get that you don't want to be friends with me anymore. That's okay. That's probably smart of you."

He shifts a little, as if he wants to say something, but instead he just looks out toward the road, then meets my eyes again. Still silent.

"Listen. I'll leave you alone forever after this if that's what you want, but I…I need your help with something. Please." He opens his mouth to reply, but I push forward. "I know, I *know*—I know I can't ask you for anything after the other day—"

"Are you going to tell me what that was, exactly?" he interrupts, a glow of anger in the words. "I mean, aside from fucking scary. Was that true, all that stuff you said?"

I sink onto one of the garden stones, rest my head on my knees, and nod.

"You get that we kind of have to tell someone. I mean, I

convinced Kev and Sophie not to. It's not like we have a ton of information. But that's probably assault, what you were talking about. At least."

"Yeah. Probably. Do you know what he was like afterward? Tyler, I mean." The words come marching out. "He was a mess. I didn't need to defend Deirdre any more after that. He took over the job. Because I told him to." He took it up, in fact, with a fervor that bordered on hysteria. I swallow. "But a little while later—people were saying—well, he was on a swim team. And he couldn't even do laps anymore. He had these...total panic attacks anytime his face was in the water."

"Jesus—" William says, looking sickened.

"He quit, obviously," I continue in a heavy monotone. "He quit a lot of sports. People said that started happening, all of a sudden, any time he was out of breath."

"God, enough!" William holds his hands up in surrender, turns away from me and then back again, a helpless little circle. "Why would you tell me that? I mean, that's a hell of a secret to keep, I get that, but—what the fuck, Skye? Why? You know I have to tell someone!"

"What good do you think that would do?" I snap. "He never reported it. It was months ago. And what evidence is there, besides your say-so?"

"I don't know, okay? It's the right thing to do!"

"Sure it is." Right. Because everything's that simple. "Go ahead. You totally should. Just...not yet. Okay? Please. I had no choice. She's my sister."

"That's a pretty big fucking favor," he says tightly. And then, "Look. I'll give you a week, all right? A week. And if you haven't said anything about it by then, I'm going to have to."

"That's fair," I say faintly. He sighs. "But that's not what I need your help with."

"You—*seriously*? You can't be serious."

"I can't explain this to you, okay?" My voice is fraying. That's fine. That's great. "There's something I have to do. I don't want to. I don't have a choice. It's the same thing all over again. She *always* does this to me. And I mean, if you hate me now, that's fine, you're supposed to. But I really, really need your help. I wouldn't ask if I weren't desperate, all right? I don't have a choice. I don't—"

His hand on my arm startles me, a brief, warm, awkward clasp, quickly withdrawn. He sits beside me.

"I don't hate you," he says.

"Oh," I manage. And then I burst into tears. I do it right on cue, my face hidden against my knees. I cry for Deirdre, I cry for my family, I cry for all my awful manipulative bullshit.

It's so easy. And I don't have a choice.

All I have to tell them is that William came by. That we talked. That we're going for a walk tomorrow, after school.

"I can do that, right?" I plead, and Mom hesitates, but Dad shrugs, brokenly, all resistance gone.

"Sure," he says. "Fine. Take your phone with you, is all."

"Brent," Mom protests, but he's already disappeared down the hall. She rubs her eyes, gives a little huff of a sigh. "You tell us when you're going to be home. Got that? If you're thirty seconds late, I will call the police back here so fast—"

"I won't be."

Even now I'm still the reliable one, the one they trust. After that, all I have to do is smuggle my backpack and the sword out to the garage. And then I wait.

TWENTY

MAYBE THEY'VE MANAGED TO DO something to the time, out there. It funnels by so slowly. Piece by piece, the circus packs up and rolls out of our driveway, leaving nothing but churned-up gravel. In my room, I stalk through steps and combinations, whipping my fists and feet out at invisible enemies. Upstairs, Mom and Dad are arguing again. "It's my *job*," Mom yells at one point.

The hours tick past through a restless night into a thin gray day with stray bits of snow fluttering from the sky. Mom rattles away on the computer at the kitchen table, intense and hollow in the wash of light from the screen; at the opposite end of the house, Dad stays slumped in bed in front of the TV. Neither of them look up when I pass. It's like the house has fractured into three separate worlds, with splintered edges that cut when they collide.

Four o'clock snails past. Five o'clock. Maybe William changed his mind, maybe he's not coming. I could hardly blame him. I could just leave, say I'm meeting him somewhere. Would they buy that?

But finally, there's a knock on the door. William stands looking warily at me, hands in his coat pockets. I shout up the stairs to let my parents know I'm leaving, that I'll be back by eight. I hurry out into the leaden evening without waiting for a response, pulling the door closed.

"It'll be dark soon," I mutter.

"Not that soon. Why? I thought you said we were just going—"

"It doesn't matter. Come on."

I lead him around the garage to the back door, where I shoulder the backpack. He raises his eyebrows at the sword in my hand, but doesn't comment. He falls into step beside me as we crunch down the driveway. When I glance at him, his face is closed and worried, and he's looking anywhere but at me. The house recedes behind us. With the windows all lit up, it's easy to tell they're empty. No one's watching.

I veer off the road into the tall brown grass of the empty lot.

"What exactly are we doing?" William asks finally.

"Not we. I. There's something I have to do." I stop in the shadow of the castle. It looms over us, craggy, inert. "You wait here. But sit down, so they can't see you from the house."

"Okay, what?" He steps back, frowning. "Just a minute."

"I'm not going far," I insist. "I promise. I'll just be over there. See? In those trees. Just wait for me. Please?"

"I—no! What the hell? Skye—!"

"I'll be fine. Really. I just need a couple of hours to myself, okay? Out here. I won't go anywhere. I'll be in earshot. I'll call over every now and again to prove it. Please, William."

"I'll go with you," he says firmly, but I shake my head.

"No. No! Just wait here. Don't follow me, and don't spy on me. This is…this is personal. Private. It's between me and my sister. I don't want to get into it. It's just something I have to do. Okay?"

He peers at me for a moment, then swipes his hands over his hair and sighs.

"This is bullshit," he says, but sits on a gray piece of fallen log, clasps his hands, bouncing his heels unhappily.

"Tell me about it. I'll be back in a bit. I promise. Don't follow me."

He spreads his hands in an *all right, all right* gesture and pulls out his phone. I push past him through the grass, casting a glance over my shoulder to make sure, but he's hunched over the screen, not looking at me. I hurry around the back of the castle, through the cedars, and kneel beside the tumbled remains of the creature I was making, slinging the backpack to the ground.

"Okay, this is where I'll be," I call over my shoulder. "I'm not far, see?"

"Whatever," William calls back, plainly annoyed, but cooperating. At least for now. I let my breath out and get to work.

It takes some experimenting, but the wire turns out to be

perfect; it works much better than the cloth to bind the pieces together. I use the pliers to twist the loose ends into little spirals, a touch Deirdre would approve of.

"Skye?" William calls.

"Still here," I return, not looking up.

After a few tries, I even manage to get the whole thing to stand upright, balancing on large stone feet. Threading wire through the skull lets me fasten it in place at the top. It sags to one side, but it stays.

By the time I toss the wire into my bag again, trying to think of what else I could add, daylight is seeping away, the bones turned faint and luminous, the trees silhouetted against the sky.

An all-too-familiar skeletal face stares out at me from among the trunks, hanging ghostly above a swath of white cloth.

I scramble away from it, fumbling in the grass for my sword, and it hobbles after me, spreading pointed antler-hands wide in a low bow.

We underestimated you. The voices teem with pure delight. *Oh we did not give you enough credit, Queen of Swords, how magnificent you are, more stern and pointy than we ever thought*

"Thanks," I say cautiously, remembering just in time to keep my voice down. "This is…going to work for you, then?"

Oh yes. Oh yessss. We know him of old. Poor jester, poor lovesick puppy, give him here, serve him up, give him to us, call him over, call

"What?" The world takes a sickening plunge sideways as I figure out what they're talking about. "No. Oh no. No! That wasn't part of the deal!"

You promised to pay, they hiss. *We told you there would be payment, we warned you, and you've brought us sssssuch a nice gift, oh yes, we've longed to feast on the bones of William Wright*

"No! Shut up!" The voices twine around me, giggling, though I toss my head and shrug and swat at the air, trying to shake them off. "That's not fair. That's not why he's here!"

So then we can keep you instead, they purr. In the twilight, the leaning shape of the monster looms closer, bony hands reaching out to tap my sword mockingly, a sound that echoes, wood on bone. *This is the payment we demand, and if you won't pay, you lose, and we keep you forever, we keep the Queen of Swords for always*

"No! Stay back!" It comes out a squeak. I have to warn William. I have to tell him to run. But when I turn to shout over my shoulder, my lips already forming his name, he's right there. A shadow crouched frozen among the shadows of the trees, one hand holding up a rock, ready to throw it. He meets my eyes, his face pale and horrified.

"Goddammit—!" I stumble backward, grab his coat, pull him behind me, keeping the sword up. The monster shambles after us a few paces, its hands outstretched, head turned to look at us from one bottomless eye socket.

"What the fuck!" William wheezes, his voice cracking. "What the *fuck*, Skye, what is that thing?"

"Shut up and stay behind me," I tell him.

Here you are, the voices bubble. *We know YOU hiding on the hilltop in your stone fortress, you think you're so safe, you think you can take and take and TAKE. You'll be sorry you crossed paths with the Queen of Swords, she's the enemy of invaders everywhere*

"What?" William yelps. "What do you—what did I take? I didn't do anything!"

"Leave him alone." My voice wobbles. I make it stern. "This has nothing to do with him!"

We know him of old. There's a grinding, snapping sound from deeper in the woods, like gnashing teeth. *Thief in a long line of thieves, give him to us, his blood runs so hot, so delicious, give him to ussss*

"He's harmless! Leave him alone!"

Harmless. HARMLESS. Nothing is HARMLESS, Queen of Swords, least of all William Wright, and you owe us a gift, you owe us payment

"I could give you something else," William tosses out.

"Shut up!" I hiss. William pushes past me, stands in front of the monster, looking up at it.

Oh delicious, the voices chortle. The creature reaches out to trace his cheek with the point of one antler. He flinches away from it, bumping into me. *Delicious, go on, go on*

"Would that help?" he demands, his voice quaking. "Would you let us go, if I gave you something else instead?"

Well, let's see, they muse. The monster leans over him, twitching, like it's barely reined in. *How harmless are you, puppy dog? Do you have teeth? If you're harmless, then you're prey, you're a rabbit, you're blood and meat and guts. Do you bite?*

"I—" William chokes on a response. "I—"

We'll let you show us, the voices sigh magnanimously, *we'll let you prove it, after all you're not the only William Wright now, are you? You can do it instead*

"What?" William says. In bewilderment and dawning horror.

You've wanted to prove you have teeth for a long time now, poor puppy, here's your chance to show your teeth, sink your teeth into William Wright, you're not the only one, if you have teeth, you can do that

"What do you mean? You want me to *kill* him? That's not—"

Oh poor puppy, poor frightened puppy, let's start with blood, that should be easy, use your teeth

"No, wait!"

Either bring us his blood or we take more than yours, puppy. Which will it be?

"But I can't just—"

Are you harmless, William Wright? The antler draws back, held high like a knife, pointing down at him. *Are you prey?*

"He'll do it!" I shout, shoving my way in front of him again. "Back off!"

Manners, Queen of Swords, manners please, remember your royal ETIQUETTE. The last word clatters down around us like little bones. *Let your jester speak for himself, let's hear it, let's hear him say it*

William is a gray-faced shadow behind me. His gaze skitters over to mine before returning to the monster.

"Sure," he says faintly. "Fine."

Do you know the words, puppy, did she teach you to speak the words? Say the words, now, say it

He looks at me with fresh panic, but I'm already hissing them at him. "By wood, stone, water, and bone. Wood, stone, water, bone. Just say it!"

He parrots them after me, and the monster gives a little shiver of delight or hunger as the voices cackle around us.

"Can we get back to the point?" I demand. "I made my guide, didn't I? Does it work for you or not?"

So close so close, the blood your jester fetches can pay for the guide, he volunteered, didn't he? Blood of William Wright for a living guide. Aren't we merciful, aren't we kind?

I grit my teeth. "How much blood are we talking about?"

Bring your hands together, make a bowl of your hands, that's it, that should do, don't you think, aren't we generous?

I keep my eyes on the monster, not wanting to see William's reaction. "All right, great, and then?"

The voices drop to a coy, knowing mutter.

For the key and the bell, Queen of Swords, you know what the price is, you know what we want now, you've already been down that path after all, so let's see if you'll go back, let's see how far you'll go

I want to refuse to understand, insist I have no idea what they mean. But there's no point. I know the path they're talking about. There's only one. And I won't go there again. I can't.

"No." The sword wavers in my hands. "No way."

It's not much farther, they return sweetly. *You can go a little farther, let's see how far you'll go, you decide, Queen of Swords, you decide if you'll pay the price. You'll make your choice.*

"Too goddamn right I will." I throw my bag over my

shoulder and grab William's sleeve, pull him back with me toward the gap in the cedars.

You decide, Queen of Swords. The monster's long skull is a pale shadow receding into the trees. *We can wait.*

PART THREE
SKYE

But the dark pines of your mind dip deeper
And you are sinking, sinking, sleeper
In an elementary world;
There is something down there and you want it told.

—GWENDOLYN MACEWEN, "DARK PINES UNDER WATER"

TWENTY-ONE

WE RUN, STUMBLING THROUGH THE long grass in the twilight, toward the bright island of the house, the windows beacons calling us in from the dark. The creek is a twist of silver reflecting the sky, a leap just wide enough to be awkward. William lurches across it and staggers, sinks down into the grass.

"Come on!" I tug at his arm, but he pulls it away.

"I just"—he gasps—"I need a minute. Just give me a minute."

"I don't want to be out here in the dark," I snap. "For obvious reasons."

He nods, keeps nodding, heaving breath after ragged breath.

"I know. I—just a minute." He sags over his knees. "Oh, Jesus. Jesus Christ."

"Yeah," I sigh. "I know."

I watch the darkening silhouette of the forest, clutching my sword, as he struggles to pull himself together. Nothing moves. A bell sounds briefly in the shadows. I wheel around to point the sword at it, but it bounds away, going quiet.

"They took your sister," he comes out with, finally. "That's what happened to her. Isn't it? That's what you're doing, you're trying to get her back. That's why you told us all of that, the other day. They made you." I nod, and he laughs a little, helplessly. "Oh my God, all of a sudden this week makes so much more sense."

"You shouldn't have followed me." I tug at his arm, urging him to his feet, and this time he pulls himself upright and throws off my hand.

"What the hell was I supposed to do? Just sit there like an idiot? You could have been getting rid of a body for all I knew!"

"You thought—!"

"That you killed her? That was Kevin's theory, *actually*, but yeah, I have to admit it kind of crossed my mind!"

I close my teeth on my outrage, swallow it. Of course that's what he thought. What they all thought. I would have too, proba-bly, in their place. "Well. Now you know better. Can we get inside already? Please?"

I slam the front door to announce my arrival home and lead William downstairs to my room, yanking the door shut behind us—never mind that Dad will flip if he finds I've got a boy in here with the door closed. Let him think we're in here making out. That's fine. That's a problem normal people have.

William collapses onto my bed, his head in his hands. I sit

next to him, dropping the sword to the tiles with a clatter and kicking it under the bed.

"That was real, wasn't it?" he says to the floor. "That really happened."

It seems like it shouldn't be true, in here, in the light, facing the serene tapestry of my plants. Night presses up against the windowpanes. For the first time, I wish I had curtains to block it out.

"At least now I know other people can see them," I say.

"How are you so calm about this?"

"If screaming would help, I'd do it."

He waves one defeated hand, accepting the point, and doesn't look up. Somewhere deep down, though, far removed and faint, his question leaves a bloom of satisfaction. Calm. That's fitting for the Queen of Swords. That's something.

"Deirdre made them," I tell him at last. "The monsters. Or their bodies, anyway."

"Seriously?"

"Don't ask me. Monsters are her thing. She used to make up these whole civilizations for them. Usually they're just, like, weird little clay statues. Or things made out of felt."

William makes a face. "Or mouse bones?"

"Ugh. No, that was—she was never *that* weird. Until we moved here. I don't know. Maybe she just never had bones to work with before."

I think of her bare, hunched shoulders, turned away from me. I should have known something was wrong. Something was getting to her. Something was pulling her in. And I rolled my eyes at her, went to parties, went shopping.

"I think something must have been…controlling her somehow. Maybe she was under some sort of spell. Or maybe she thought those things were her friends, and then they turned on her."

"This wasn't the first time you saw them," William says.

I shake my head. "They came looking for me, a few nights back. Scratching at the window."

He glances apprehensively up at the glass, then to me, finally.

"What was it they kept calling you?"

"Queen of Swords." I fold my arms. "Long story. It's from a game we used to play. Sort of like Deirdre's version of a knight in shining armor."

A rueful smile ghosts across his face. "It suits you."

I shrug this off. "It was just a game. They're making fun of me or something. Trying to get to me. I don't know."

"What were you even doing back there? What was—you said something about a guide?"

"They wanted me to build another monster. Like Deirdre did. I guess it's supposed to take me somewhere? They said I had to go to the castle."

"Castle? What castle?"

"I have no idea. Deirdre called the dirt pile there a castle, maybe that's what they were talking about."

"But it's…a pile of dirt."

"I don't know. None of this makes any sense. I guess I'll find out eventually. I mean, I made the thing for them, they said I was close. I just…have to pay for it."

"No," says William, looking away again. "I do."

There's an awful, weighted silence after that. I can't bring myself to break it.

"They don't like me," he says. "Whatever they are. Why? What did I do?"

"I have no clue." I say it automatically, but then a possibility drifts reluctantly up through my thoughts. "But you're not the first William Wright. Maybe your name's been around here long enough for the woods to remember it. Deirdre kept calling you an invader."

"How is that fair?" he cries.

"It's just an idea, okay? They know me, and I've been here for less than six months. For all I know, they were yanking your chain because you were there."

"No." He pushes himself to his feet, paces back and forth across the tiles. "No. I think you're right. It makes sense. I think that's it." But then he pauses, puts his hands to his forehead again. "But my dad goes hunting in the woods all the time! If they wanted—why wouldn't they—why now? Why *me?*"

"Look, it really doesn't matter. Okay? *Why* doesn't change anything. We have to figure out what to do."

"We," he echoes, like he doesn't like the taste of the word.

"Don't look at me like that. This wasn't my decision. You're the one who followed me."

"And you're the one who dragged me over there!" He

straightens up, all accusation. "You used me to get out of the house, and now—"

"I told you, I didn't have any choice! What was I going to do, explain this to my parents? 'Oh, sorry, Mom, I can't be grounded right now. I have to go do the bidding of the monsters in the woods.' You've seen them now; you know I didn't have any choice! They have my sister!"

He returns my glare for a few heartbeats before he caves.

"I know," he says helplessly. "I know."

"All I wanted was a way out of the house. I swear that's as involved as you were supposed to get. Believe me, I'm not exactly thrilled about this either."

"So that's it? You're just—playing along? Doing what they want?"

"All we have to do is get through it. Right?"

"But what if we don't?" He clenches his fists. "What if I can't?"

"Look," I sigh. "Let me show you something."

I unfold myself from the bed and stalk across the room to pull open the doors to the crawl space. The light slides over the reaching, tangled tendrils of the roots. He recoils from them, bumps into the shelves.

"This wasn't there before, okay? I had three days to tell you guys about Tyler. And then—this. So I finally did it on day four." I close the door, shutting them out again.

"But they want me to—they said I had to—" He can't even finish the sentence, looks at me wild-eyed, a cornered animal. "I can't do that!"

"I don't think *can't* is an option here! If you don't, they'll come after both of us. You told them you'd do it!"

"*You* told them I'd do it!"

"Jesus, William, do you not understand what would have happened otherwise? I was protecting you!"

He puts his hands up, fending off the words, his teeth clenched like he's gripping calm between them.

"Look," he says. "Look. We shouldn't talk about this here." He jerks his chin toward the crawl space. "Right? Let's go to my place. It must be pretty safe there, if they haven't gotten inside in two hundred years."

"That's nice for you and everything, but some of us—"

"We just need somewhere to talk." He lowers his voice. "We need a plan."

My parents, slouched at the kitchen table, hesitate when I tell them we're going to William's house, maybe reading something in our faces. There's only so much shifty anxiety you can hide.

"We're just going to watch the game," William says. He's passably casual. Good. "There's a really big screen at my place."

Mom and Dad exchange a glance.

"Your parents are around tonight, I assume?" Dad manages casual too. I'd have been mortified by that question, ordinarily. The thought drifts past from somewhere far away, an observation on a surreal pantomime.

"Oh—yeah. Yeah, of course." He even manages a sheepish smile. He's better at this than I'd expected. He can get us through this. He has to.

"Just don't be too late," Mom puts in, only a little shaky. It hurts, how hard they're trying to be normal. How hard they're pretending they're okay. I'll get Deirdre back. I will. I'll fix this. "You've got your phone, right?"

I nod, accept her kiss on my cheek. And we're free to go.

Angie, washing dishes at the sink, goes stiff and wary as she spots me following William through the kitchen. Bet she's been talking to Kevin and Sophie's parents.

"William?" she calls after him, looking at me.

"It's fine, Mom." He doesn't even turn around, and I quicken my step to catch up.

William flicks on the TV—and it is impressive, a screen so wide it practically belongs in a theater—and turns the volume way up, hunkering down right in front of it, leaning back against the coffee table. I crouch beside him.

"We need a plan," he says, keeping his voice low. I have to lean in to hear him over the roaring of the game. "Some way to fight back."

I dig my fingers through the plushy carpet, reaching for patience. "We have to be realistic here, William."

"Well, have you tried it?" he demands. "Fighting?"

"No," I mutter, "I've got better sense."

The floor creaks behind us, and we both whip around. Bill Wright, looking startled, raises his hands apologetically and bows out of the room again. William settles back, blowing stray bits of hair away from his face. The light of the TV makes him look haggard, hollow-eyed.

"There has to be some other way out of this," he says. "Some way around them, you know? Help me think!"

"William—"

"Let's start with what we've got already, okay? What do you know about them?"

"Not much. Not more than you do. They have Deirdre. They live out there. They're fucking scary."

"Come on, there has to be something. Like—what about your sword? They paid attention to that."

"It's nothing special. It's a toy. My dad made it for me."

He frowns. "So why does it work, then? Is it because it's made of wood, do you think?"

"No, it's just something to knock them over with."

"So maybe we need better weapons," he says, "like axes or something. We need something they're afraid of."

I fold my arms over my knees, rest my head against them. "I don't think they're afraid of axes."

"Aren't they all mad at my family for cutting down trees or something?"

"Have you seen how huge that forest is? Even if we had a chainsaw, how much damage do you think we could do? Do you really want to piss them off even more?"

"What about fire, then?"

"Right, burn down the neighborhood. Great plan. A-plus."

"We just need some sort of leverage," he insists, doggedly ignoring my tone. "Something we can use against them. We need to level the playing field, you know? So we're not the only ones with something to lose."

"What makes you think that's even possible?"

"Just—help me out here!" He glances quickly over his shoulder at the doorway, then slumps down, lowering his voice again. "Seriously. Work with me for a minute. Please? There has to be another way."

On the screen, lines of blue and green uniforms erupt into knots of motion, particles breaking off and colliding with each other.

"We're wasting time," I tell him.

"Great. Thanks for that." He scrubs his hands over his face. "Come on, help me think. There must be rules. Things they can't do. Places they can't go. Like here. Why?"

"I don't know, because it's made of stone? Are you planning to never set foot outside again? Or convince your family to do the same? I don't see that working out very well, somehow."

"For fuck's sake, Skye—" He draws a deep breath, sits back. "You don't understand."

I just look at him, and he throws up his hands.

"All right, fine. I know you do. Sorry. But haven't you thought that we shouldn't be giving in to them on this? They'll just ask for more and more! You're showing them they have power over you!"

"That would be because they do," I snap. "I don't have a choice. She's my sister."

"And he's my dad," William says. It's a plea. A puppy dog whimper. It cuts, and I falter. He's looking at me like I'm withholding some answer, some way out.

"I would tell you if I had any ideas. I really would. Let's just…focus on getting through this. Okay? I need that guide, and they said that's the payment. There's no other way."

He shakes his head, his mouth a thin line, and we watch the game in silence for a while. Athletes crash into each other in slow motion. A referee in black and white makes a series of arcane gestures, announcing a penalty declined.

"We should warn Sophie and Kevin," William says.

"What?" He can't want to do that. My stomach twists at the thought. "Why?"

"There's fucking monsters in the woods, Skye! Wouldn't you want a heads-up?"

"Do you want them getting dragged into this too? You think they'd thank you for that?"

"But they could help," he insists. "Maybe they'd have some ideas. Maybe they could think of something we can't, you know?"

"That's assuming they believe you. Which they won't, until it's too late."

"And you know that how?"

"Think about it. What would you have said? If I'd tried to warn you?"

He opens his mouth like he wants to argue, but hesitates and subsides, turning back to the screen.

"I should have bargained with them," William says. "I should have argued more."

"I don't think that's how it works."

"But there must be something they want! What are they trying to—"

"William," I interrupt, "look. Here's what I know. What they want is to hurt you. Do you get that? You can't bargain with something when that's all it wants from you. Whatever they ask you for, it's going to hurt. That's the point. Do mice get to bargain with cats?"

He stares at me.

"We just have to survive. Okay? They'll have their fun, and they'll let us go. It's—it's just blood. It's not like they're asking us to kill anybody."

"Not yet," he says darkly, and I don't know what to say to that. The memory of voices uncoils in my head. *It's not much farther.*

It doesn't matter. That's not what they meant, can't be what they meant. I'm not going to think about it. Not now.

"I'm not doing this." William folds his arms, hunches his shoulders. "I won't. There has to be another way."

"What part of this is unclear to you, exactly? It's not complicated!"

He cuts me off before I can get any further. "You don't want me to be right about this, do you? You want it to be true, that you have to play along! So you didn't tell your secret for nothing!"

"What I want is my sister back! I want my family safe!

And—" I stumble over it, but I force the words out, in case they'll mean something. In case they'll work. "And I want you safe. William, you have to do this. You have to."

But he withdraws from me, shaking his head over and over, his face half in shadow.

"No," he whispers.

"You don't have a choice!"

"I do!" He takes a deep breath, settles into resolution. "Look, I'm sorry. About your sister. But I was up against the wall back there. I—I have to take it back. I'm not doing this for you, okay? I can't."

I push myself to my feet. For a bottomless moment, standing over him, I'm tempted to tell him what I'm facing, what they wanted from me first—what they still want from me. But I can't risk making him even more determined to abandon me.

"I'm going home," I say instead. "When you're ready to make plans for real, you let me know."

Panic snaps at my heels the whole way back, with fury close behind. He's not going to do it. He has to. This is the only way through. He's putting us both in danger. Why can't he see that? What's it going to take?

And how could they do this, how could they put this all on him and take it so entirely out of my hands? I thump my fists uselessly against my thighs. Haven't I cooperated? I need to make him understand. I need him back on my side. He is not hunkering down in his stone house and leaving me and my sister outside to face the monsters alone. I will not allow them to turn him against me.

In that version of the game, he doesn't stand a chance.

TWENTY-TWO

MY DREAMS DRAG ME DOWN a familiar street half obscured by blinding, howling snow. I know the footsteps crunching toward me. They're not Deirdre's.

But some rational part of my mind argues that it wasn't snowing the last time I lay in wait for him. Which means it's not the same; I don't have to do it again. I can choose, I can change what happened. I cross the street, turn my back on the entrance to the bike path, and struggle homeward, hope a terrible staccato in my chest. But as I flounder through the snow, the houses on either side recede from me, perched on high hills, on the plunging sides of the ravine.

I'm on the bike path anyway, and he's right behind me.

When I turn, bracing to face him, it's not Tyler standing

behind me in the snow. It's William. Massaging his shoulder, reaching out a pleading hand. Behind him, the woods loom all in shadows, and one of the shadows breaks off, leans close, towering over us. Deirdre's monster. Plunging the wicked point of an antler down toward us as I haul William out of the way—

I fling myself out of sleep and sit up in the dark, my hand flying to my chest where I could swear I felt the blow strike home. And something's there. Something that tumbles into my lap, crumbling, leaving wet, gritty residue between my fingers.

I snap the light on. My lap is full of brittle gray clumps, some of them still held together with wet paper.

Drywall.

When I look up, the wall and ceiling are buckling, sagging, the paint blistering, cracks zigzagging through it under the onslaught of something pushing its way through. Even as I stare at it, another little shower patters down around me.

I scramble out of bed with a scream that I can't seem to stop once it comes spilling out of me, a long, ringing noise that brings my parents running.

"Skye? Skye, what on earth—"

I huddle against Mom's shoulder as they gape at the damage.

"What the hell?" Dad says.

"Don't touch it!" I cry, but he's already digging his fingers into one of the cracks, yanking crumbling chunks away.

"It's soaking," he says. "The drywall, the insulation, every-thing. What the *hell*—"

Then he uncovers the black roots knifing through the clear

plastic layer between the drywall and the insulation. It's strained and shiny under coils of wood trying to press their way through, little beads of water running down the inside of the surface. I shrink back from the sight, but I can't look away. I knew it. It doesn't matter that they wanted William to pay the price. If he doesn't, they're coming after me too. I told him.

"But that doesn't make any sense," Dad says. "That doesn't *happen.*"

"What do you mean, it doesn't happen?" Mom's voice rises dangerously. "Apparently it does!"

"No! Honestly, Sarah, this isn't the way tree roots work! They follow water. They can't live in concrete, there's nothing to draw them into the house. I'd have noticed if there was water down here, you'd see the condensation on the plastic, or—"

"Oh, condensation? You mean like that?" Mom throws a hand out at the trickling drops. Her voice has an acid edge. "Did you even look? Or did you just slap drywall over the insulation and call it a day? This didn't happen overnight, Brent! Tree roots don't grow that fast!"

"No, they don't! That's what I mean. Can you trust me to know what I'm talking about for a second? For *once?*"

"How could you miss this?" Mom cries. "You said we didn't need a home inspector! You said you had it covered! You said everything was *fine!*"

"It was!" Dad rakes his hands through his hair, staring up at the frozen tangle heaving against the plastic. "I don't understand how this is possible! What tree could they even be coming from?"

Mom shepherds me out of the room, not bothering to answer, and leads me upstairs. Dad's voice drifts after us in escalating dismay. "Oh my God…oh my *God*…"

"You can sleep in Deirdre's room for now. Is that okay?"

I shrug. It doesn't matter. Deirdre's not coming home on her own.

"You can sleep on the couch if you want. But…I have a feeling it's going to take a while to fix this." She sniffs. "And who knows how much money. What a nightmare. Sometimes it's like something doesn't even want us here. You know? Like—it's trying to push us out, or swallow us up, or—"

"Do you think there's something out there, Mom?" I whisper. She blinks in surprise, then takes a deep breath, forces a smile.

"No! No, of course not." The smile slips. "Oh, Skye, honey, you must be having a terrible time if my nonsense is getting to you like that."

"I just had a bad dream," I mutter. I've never been the one with the runaway imagination, the one sitting up clutching the blankets.

She tucks me in, kisses my forehead. Her eyes are full of tears, though she blinks and turns quickly away, thinking I won't see. Not because of the basement—because it should be Deirdre in this bed, needing reassurance in the middle of the night. The pillow smells like her, despite the fresh linens. It's like wearing her clothes. I'm tempted to retreat to the couch after all, but I can't bring myself to twist the knife.

My parents' arguing voices echo up to me through the basement for a while, then drop to fierce whispers as they come back upstairs to their room. The door closes behind them. Above me, beyond the eaves, the stars wink in and out between shifting clouds. Cold clarity wells up in me as I watch them—a calm. The icy logic of the Queen of Swords, the narrow path, the cutting edge of what must be done.

I tried to push him out of the way. I tried to protect him. And he's not cooperating. If he's not going to act, I'll have to make him. I have to make him see. I have to show him just how much there is to lose.

Outside, the night shifts and rattles in irregular sighs, like something breathing. I hurry across the lawn, my shadow a long-limbed giant in the light from the windows. I clutch the phone and the bundle of white cloth I yanked from my backpack in my coat pockets to keep my hands from feeling so empty. But my skin still buzzes with an icy, naked vulnerability. Without my sword, I'm insubstantial. Breakable. Prey. But I'm knocking on my enemy's front door as a supplicant; it wouldn't do to go armed. If I really wanted to make nice, I'd bring them something. But the way they were talking last time, I'm not sure anything less than blood would do.

At the edge of the yard, I pull the phone out and switch on the flashlight. The circle of white light shivering across the ground is almost worse than no light at all. The darkness seems thicker beyond it, and peering into it just makes my vision swim with ghostly sparks and pinwheels. I fumble through the long grass until I find a fallen branch and tie a scrap of the cloth around it with shaking fingers.

I edge across the threshold of the clearing, my flag of truce held out before me. My own monster's glass eyes twinkle in the light, but it's unmoved, leaning drunkenly in its corner. There's no other sign of them. I step over Deirdre's stone circles and wedge the flag upright between some rocks in the very middle, prop the phone against it so the light washes upward into the cedars. Deirdre would have some sort of gesture you're supposed to make, some invocation.

"Hi," I say. The word is flat, absurd. "It's me."

Silence. Something flutters over my head, but when I look up, it's just one of the strips of cloth, twisting in the wind.

"Look, I need to talk to you. By, um, wood, stone, water, and bone. Are...are you around?"

The answer rises with the wind, a long hissing sigh that flutters in my ears.

Always.

I shrink back into a half crouch without meaning to, lifting my hands, but manage to stop myself short of curling them into fists. I have to be respectful. I have to be polite. I spread them wide instead, to show they're empty, trying to look everywhere at once, into the shadows between every tree, searching for a glimpse of bone.

"Look, we need to talk. Please."

Is she surrendering? The voices murmur speculatively. *Has she had enough already? Disappointing, Queen of Swords.*

"You know me better than that." Giggles rain down on me. "I'm here to talk. That's all. You're asking too much from him. William. There's no way he'll go through with it."

That was the wrong way to start. Snapping, rustling movement fills the darkness all around me, and the voices have a hungry edge when they speak again.

You're getting soft, Queen of Swords, you're not made of steel plates at all, are you? Shall we find out how soft you are?

"No, wait!" Long, pale shadows lurch into visibility all around me. Long twiggy limbs step out from between the trees, hands made of antler, bone, wood crossed over torsos wound with cloth or fur. This time there's more than three. "Dammit, hear me out! Please!"

You came to us, Queen of Swords, you came to us unarmed, unarmored, now that was foolish, that's not like you at all

"I'm cooperating!" I cry. "Listen, we can help each other out here. I know a way to get you what you want, all right? So I can get what I want. We all win. Come on!"

The monsters pause, looking at me sideways, considering. Interested?

"You can't reach him, can you? Not up there on the hill. But I know how to get to him. I need you to help me. All he needs is a push in the right direction. Okay?"

Silence, broken only by the mutter of the wind, the creak and clack of the swaying creatures that ring in the clearing. Their smell creeps over me, wet and rotten. I swallow my rabbit-racing heart, swallow again.

"All I need is some time." Here we are. I'm really doing this. I can't turn back. I have no choice. "And…and something dead. Something messy. Can you manage that?"

Something leans invisibly closer, some presence that stands stooping over me, contemplating whether or not to pounce. Every stirring of the wind is its breath in my hair.

Will it work, you think this will work?

"I know it will. And…and if not, just…bring me more. Tomorrow night. He'll get the message." Just like I did. "I promise."

Oh, that's more like it, the voices purr, and I scrub my hands over the back of my neck to erase the feeling of the words crawling over my skin, unable to help myself. *That's so much more fun, so full of surprises, Queen of Swords*

"Is it a deal or not?"

This was never a deal, it's a game, the best game, you're better at it than we thought

"Whatever! Are we on?"

Go home, Queen of Swords, you'll find our contribution, yes, go give him a push, oh delicious, go give him a push, let's see if you can give your puppy dog a taste for blood

The monsters give that same maddening bow and part to one side, leaving me a path out of the clearing. I snatch my phone from the ground and stalk past them. I won't run. I won't let them see my fear.

This has to work. This has to be the right thing to do. Someone tell me I'm not just fighting the inevitable, thrashing in the spider's web, getting myself more tangled than ever.

When I push the back door open, waiting for me at the very edge of the pale wash of the porch light is the green reflective gleam of unblinking eyes. They don't move. When I edge my way closer, rubber gloves creaking as I flex my fingers, a heap of gray-brown fur becomes visible against the night, a masked face.

Well. There we go. This is good. I can do this. It's dead. It's just meat, right? I can handle meat.

I shake out a black plastic garbage bag, as quietly as I can, and crouch over the raccoon, trying to shimmy the plastic around and underneath it. But it's no good. There's no avoiding it; if this is going to work, I have to lift it. I turn away, take a deep breath of clean, cold air, and then reluctantly slide my gloved hands under its front legs. Like I would have lifted Mog.

I was expecting it to be rigid. Isn't that what happens to dead bodies? But it's limp and soft—warm, even—in a horribly lifelike way. Not at all like meat. Meat is clean, anonymous, without history. But in the drooping head, the staring eyes, the slack little clawed hands, there's a personhood. An absence. Which makes the faintest wet sound, the red-gray spill of intestines—a tangle my eye can't help but follow—even worse.

I clench my teeth, focus on the unstained fur of its flank, ruffling a little in the wind, the fuzzy rounded triangle of its ear. I will not think about Mog. Nausea squirms through me, but I wall it off. It's like the acid burn of aching muscles, the dizziness at the beginning of a run—it's just one more messy trick your body pulls on you. I can ignore it.

I push the body over, roll it onto the plastic, briefly exposing the wreckage of its belly and a terrible smell. I will not, *will not* throw up. I reel back, wait for it to dissipate. And then I gather the ends of the bag, heft it, its slack, soft contents bumping against my leg.

The walk up the hill has never been longer. The bag is heavy as I hold it out in front of me, but I'm not slinging it over my shoulder. My hands are hot and sweaty in the rubber gloves.

William's house is dark, other than a light on over the garage. I stand there, trembling, for a long minute, trying to will myself back into motion, into doing what I came to do. I keep to the shadows, at the edge of the circle of light, and set my burden down on the sandy cut stones of the front walk, tug at the plastic until the body comes tumbling out with a spatter of fluid.

I do gag at that, at the mushrooming smell, and stagger back with my face pressed against my arm. Once I've forced the wall back up, I edge close enough again to grab one foot, roll the raccoon over so the ragged chasm of its body gapes wetly open. Above me, the windows are still empty and sightless.

Then I snatch the plastic bag and run—like a criminal, like a scavenger—back into the dark.

At home, I bury the plastic, the gore-smeared gloves, in the garbage. I strip down to my underwear, pitch my clothes—though they're unstained, I think—into the wash, splash soap into the machine with a shaking hand, set the water as hot as it will go. And then I scrub my hands at the sink, over and over, trying to erase the smell of rubber. Eventually, I have to crawl back into Deirdre's bed, afraid the running water will wake my parents. I lie there staring up at the sky through the window, but the stars are hidden again behind a blank, flat wall of cloud, a shade paler with the beginnings of dawn. The iron certainty that's been driving me has turned brittle and flaky, a shell between me and what I've just done.

I should have known better than to trust that certainty. I should have remembered that it doesn't last.

I turn away from the window, pull the blankets up around my ears. This isn't the same; it's not that big a deal. It's just a raccoon. It was already dead. I moved it, is all. It won't hurt anyone. All it will do to William is freak him out. That's all I need it to do.

When the knock comes at the door, I let Mom run to answer it, waiting rigid in the rocking chair by the window, where I was staring out at the woods. It might not be him. It's probably not him. It could be the police, or a neighbor. But Mom's uncertain call drifts up to me from the foyer, and I take a deep breath, fighting the dizzy, premature swoop of hope in my stomach. Did it work? It has to have worked.

But it's not William waiting for me at the foot of the stairs. It's Sophie, flipping her hair over her shoulder, golden hoop earrings swinging, her polished lips pressed into a grim line.

"Hi," I say carefully, but she obviously hasn't come here to build bridges. Even in front of my mom, her expression is distant and pitiless.

"We need to talk," she says.

Mom, looking back and forth between us, clears her throat.

"Well. I'll just give you girls a minute, then." She retreats up the stairs, into the kitchen. I watch her go, unable to return the death stare Sophie's giving me any longer.

"Come on." Sophie pulls the door open. Reluctantly, I kick my shoes on and follow her outside. She nods toward the empty lot. "Over there."

The wind lifts pieces of her hair off her shoulders as I follow her through the tall grass. Pinpricks of rain scatter across my face. I hug myself, wishing I'd brought my coat. The sky hangs low and sullen over the cedars behind the dirt pile. In the shelter of the hill, Sophie finally turns to face me.

"I don't know what's going on with you guys," she says, "but you need to stay the fuck away from William."

I close my eyes. Stay away from William. If only.

"It's none of your business," I manage.

"When my best friend's in pieces? I'd say that's my business. I went over this morning and he'd been *crying*, Skye."

Hope unfurls after all, a coil of nausea and uncertainty. I'm getting through to him, then. I must be. And he can't have told Sophie what's going on. I give her my best Queen of Swords look, turn my face to stone.

"Why are you assuming that has anything to do with me?"

The look she gives me could cut glass.

"I don't have to assume. He admitted it. And he was afraid to tell me any more than that. Well, *I'm* not afraid of you. If you think your little show the other day is going to intimidate me, you're dead wrong."

"Look, I'm sorry. Okay? I didn't—"

"Yeah. Sure. Are you sorry about that other kid? The one you were talking about?" When I stay silent, clenching my teeth, Sophie's lip curls. "That's what I thought."

"You don't understand. I didn't have any *choice*."

"Uh-huh. And what happens when William pisses you off? When he figures you out? When he tries to get away from you? Is that what you'll say then?"

I want to respond, to defend myself, but the unblinking shine of green eyes in the dark flashes through my mind, a small bloody body tumbling onto the stones. What I've already done to make William cooperate. But that was different. That was life or death. What else was I supposed to do?

"I'm not having this conversation." I turn my back on her, start toward the house.

"Maybe you should be afraid of *me*, Skye," she yells after me. "I've got leverage on you. And I'll use it!"

I can't walk away from that. And she knows it.

"Yeah, that got your attention, didn't it? Who else knows about all that shit you told us?" She watches me through narrowed eyes, considering. "Do your parents?"

My voice locks in my throat. My parents. My clueless, grieving parents.

"They don't, do they?" Sophie takes a step closer, sensing weakness. "Want to find out what they'd do with that information? Want to find out what they'd think?"

"Leave them alone. They're falling apart as it is."

"Sure, go on lying to them, I don't care. As long as you leave William alone."

"But I *can't!*" I can't explain. I have to try. I refuse to turn around, to scan the woods, though the faint silver sound of a bell dances out from between the trees. "Look, I had reasons for telling you. I'm...I'm in over my head here, okay?"

"What the hell are you talking about?"

A hundred responses flicker through my head. All of them impossible. I know exactly how it'll sound if I make any mention of *them*, and *they* won't hesitate to stop her. "I can't control what happens if you try to get in my way, Sophie. Do you get that?" I draw a long breath, force the words out. I have to try. "You're my friend. They could—you could get hurt."

"Is that supposed to be scary?" Sophie sneers. "What kind of friend are you supposed to be, exactly? Don't think this is some sort of mutually assured destruction. I trusted you with something. And that was stupid of me, apparently. But sure, go ahead. Spread it around. See if anyone believes you. I can survive a few rumors. I think you have more to lose than I do."

"That's not what I meant. My sister's already in danger. So is William. I—"

"Oh, right. Your sister. Boo-hoo, poor Skye, her sister's missing. William fell for that all over again, didn't he? Don't you *dare* threaten him."

"I'm not." The words tremble; my heartbeat fills my head. "I'm trying to warn you. I never wanted—"

"You don't visit him, you don't call him, you don't text." She counts the conditions off her fingers. "You don't talk to him at school. Leave him alone. The second I hear otherwise, I'll be on your doorstep, and your whole act comes crashing down. Got it?"

"What are you going to do?" I cry. "Bug his phone? Read his messages?"

She doesn't answer. She doesn't have to. Her house is right down the hill from William's. She's lived here her whole life, the whole neighborhood is eyes and ears for her. But how am I going to do this without anyone seeing me and William together, now that he's gotten dragged into it too? Panic snakes over me like twining vines. I need William to make this work. But God, if my parents find out about Tyler... My heart goes cold and small, flinching from the thought. But the only way to avoid it is to break my deal with the monsters and let the woods come after us through the walls.

The Queen of Swords never has choices.

"Got it?" Sophie repeats, louder this time. It doesn't matter what I say. At my back, the trees creak and mutter in the wind.

"Kevin was right about you," she says when I stay silent, shaking her head in slow disgust. "I should have fucking known. You're just as creepy as your sister."

When she walks away, she knows she's won. I can see it in her long steps, the toss of her hair. She reaches the road without looking back once. She'll be out of sight soon, behind the screen of trees.

My chest is full of stones again, a crushing, choking weight. I have to apologize. I have to scream, or cry, or tackle her, anything to claw my way out of this impossible trap I've landed myself in.

This is why William broke down and talked to her in the first place. He was desperate. Just not desperate enough to give in.

Wingbeats over my head make me jump. A crow, two crows, go sailing out over the treetops. Following her. And the sound of the bell darts away, across the lot, in their wake.

It could be coincidence. It could be nothing.

"Don't." It comes out a squeak, a plea. They won't listen. I sound like prey. "Come on. I'll figure this out. Leave her alone."

How many of them can you protect, Queen of Swords? comes the mocking answer, a flicker of a touch against my ear. Like a snake's tongue. *Whose champion are you?*

I jerk away from it and head for the house. Not running. I fumble for my phone in my pocket. But just like every other time I've looked at it today, nothing has changed: no calls, no messages. I dial William's number with shaking fingers. I wait with my teeth clenched for the call to go through. It rings twice before going to voice mail. Blocked.

If he keeps ignoring me, I'll lose. All this will be for nothing if I lose.

I can't lose.

TWENTY-THREE

A RATTLING BUZZ YANKS ME out of sleep the next morning—my phone, vibrating on the night table, again and again. It's barely light out. But William's been texting me. Sending pictures, a whole series of them, flash-lit and bloody, of two corpses heaped side by side on his front walk. I grit my teeth and flick past them, not looking too closely at the fur matted with red, the white flash of brain and bone.

It was easier this time, hauling dead things around. Would anyone get used to it this fast? Maybe I just knew what to expect now. The porcupine was a pain in the ass because I didn't dare touch it; I had to heft it into Mom's wheelbarrow with a shovel. At least it wasn't too hard to keep the red, runny mess that was left of its head out of sight. Without the two long, yellow teeth jutting out of the lower jaw, it wouldn't even have been recognizable. The rabbit with its throat torn out was almost easy, though its head flopping at an unnatural angle—held on only by gristle—made me swallow hard. At least it didn't smell like the raccoon did.

I had to take the wheelbarrow right up onto the Wrights' lawn. Thankfully there was no frost to leave tracks in. I couldn't just leave them there in a heap, though. I had to make it impossible to ignore. So I lined them up carefully, shoving the porcupine around with a branch, so they lay prone side by side, pointing at the door. Like Mog's offerings used to be. Just bigger.

Maybe it worked.

The phone buzzes again, and William's number eclipses the photos. Reluctantly, I swipe at the screen to pick up.

"Did you see?" he demands without preamble, his voice half an octave higher than usual. "What is this? What the *actual fuck* is this?"

There. That's more like it. I lean back against the headboard, gone shaky under the waterfall of relief. If it takes me a second to come up with an answer, that only makes sense, right?

"It's supposed to scare you, I guess."

"Well, it's fucking working! There was a dead raccoon here yesterday. That could have been a coincidence, right? That wasn't necessarily—but now—"

"William—"

"The big one's a porcupine. Something ate its fucking *face*, Skye, it doesn't have a *face* anymore!"

"William. Calm down. You're going to hyperventilate or something."

"I am calm! I am. I'm fine. I just—oh my God—it was *them*, wasn't it? Obviously it was them. What is this supposed to be, some sort of message?"

"I don't know what you want me to tell you."

"Listen, I know I said—"

"William. You know why they're doing this. All right? They already told you what they want. It's like—it's like the roots in my basement. You know?"

There's a long pause; his rapid breathing is the only sound. That's enough. Surely that's enough. What more can it take?

"I had three days," I say, finally, when he still doesn't speak. "Maybe they're counting for you."

"Oh my God," he says, the words choked. "This can't be happening. Look. I need—I need your help. Can you come over? Please?"

"I shouldn't even be talking to you. Sophie's blackmailing me into cutting you off."

"What? What do you mean?"

"She said she'd tell my parents about Tyler if I didn't. You must have really freaked her out when she came over yesterday."

A silence. "Look. No one's up. No one needs to know, okay? She won't find out from me. I promise."

"William."

"Ten minutes." His voice is fraying. "That's all I'm asking for. Please. I can't do this by myself."

I shouldn't risk it. Not for this. But when I close my eyes, the creak of the wheelbarrow echoes in my head. And I need him to trust me.

"Ten minutes," I sigh. "I'm on my way."

"Okay," he whispers. "Just—hurry. Please."

William, in sweatpants and a ragged T-shirt, is sitting on the front step with his head in his hands. Partway down the walk, a faded sheet is spread over two humped shapes.

"I couldn't look anymore," he says as I skirt around it, through the grass.

"Yeah," I manage. "Understandable."

"They didn't leave anything at your place, did they?"

"No. But the roots…they're all through the wall. They came right through it, the night before last. My parents are freaking out. Tree roots aren't supposed to do that."

"The night before last?" The glasses make his face rounder, somehow unguarded. "You didn't tell me."

"I tried to call. Yesterday."

I speak gently, but the words are arrows. He folds his arms across his stomach, sinks forward a little, and doesn't answer.

"Come on." I pick up the edge of the sheet. "Let's get this over with. We can use this to carry them, right?"

Neither of us wants to look too closely, much less touch them. In the end, I pull a shovel from the shed and roll the bodies onto the sheet. We haul them across the yard that way, in a long sling. I assign William to take the lead, so he can keep his eyes forward. We tip them into the brush at the back of the lot, and I drop the bloodstained sheet, stuck through with porcupine quills, carefully into the trash.

When I come back out of the garage, William is leaning on the shovel, staring down at the dark stains on the stone. *That* was me. That heartsick look he's wearing—that's what I've done. What I had to do. Before I can think better of it, I put an arm around him. He doesn't shrug it off.

"They're not going to let this go," he says, not looking up. "Are they."

"Everything okay?"

The call comes from behind us. Bill Wright steps out the front door in slippers, a mug of coffee steaming in one hand, frowning at us.

"You look like somebody died," he says.

Under my hand, William's shoulder goes rigid. "It's fine, Dad."

"We just…we found a dead animal." I let my hand drop. Try to speak naturally. Shit. I knew it, I knew this was a bad idea. It's not like I can tell Bill not to mention my visit. "On the steps. We took care of it."

"Again?" He comes over to look at the blood on the stones. "Huh. That must have been a hell of a mess."

William nods, his eyes fixed on the ground again. His dad breaks into a smile, claps a hand over his shoulder.

"Well, as long as you kept your breakfast down, eh?" He

leans toward me. "He's got a bleeding heart, our William. We used to have to have funerals for dead snakes on the road."

William doesn't speak. A muscle jumps in his jaw. Bill laughs.

"Don't worry, I won't stick around and embarrass you. Just letting Skye know she doesn't need to beat up on you to get her way." He actually winks at me. "Eh?"

"Right," I say faintly, "I'll remember that."

A honk from the road makes me jump, and I turn to see Sophie leaning out the window of a silver SUV.

"Well, good *morning*," she calls. I flinch, and hate myself for it.

Bill nudges William. "Look at that, son. You've got all the pretty girls coming out of the woodwork." Sophie laughs, on cue as always. She's even convincing.

"I just stopped to tell Skye I'll be over later today," she says sweetly, her smile bright as the glint of keys clutched between knuckles. "We have a lot to talk about. Don't we?"

I lift my chin and return her pointed look.

"I'll be there." My voice is even, at least. This is my own goddamn fault. I should never have come up here.

"Good," Bill says, as Sophie waves and pulls away. "Excellent. I told your mom this would blow over, son, didn't I?"

William takes a long, slow breath before answering. "Yup."

"Exactly." If Bill notices the tension in William's voice, he ignores it, raising his mug in a sardonic salute. "You're lucky someone around here remembers what it's like to be a teenager."

The door swings closed behind him. After an endless few

heartbeats of thrumming silence, William hurls the shovel aside. It hits the rocks with a clang.

When the doorbell rings, it punches my breath from my lungs. So this is it. At least it'll be over soon. What's worse, having to bring the sky crashing down on yourself or waiting for it to fall?

Voices drift down the hall as I shuffle from Deirdre's room. Mom's sounds full of hopeful surprise at first, but gradually turns worried and wary.

"Skye, do you want to join us?" Mom calls from the kitchen. Her voice is dangerous but civil; she's already on high alert.

"Not really," I mutter, but I slide into the chair she's pointing at. Sophie perches on the seat across from me, her composure flawless.

"Anything you want to say, Skye?" Sophie asks softly. Like an executioner allowing their victim a few last words.

"There's no point," I tell the floor. My heart is a wingbeat in my ears. "Knock yourself out."

"I would really like to know what this is about, please," Mom says.

"Well." Sophie speaks carefully, like she's choosing her words. "The other day, when Skye…lost her temper on us. She told us something that we've been talking about, and we thought you should probably hear."

Mom doesn't look at me. "And that is?"

Sophie opens her mouth, but she's interrupted by the frantic, rapid-fire chime of the doorbell being mashed several times in quick succession. All three of us sit frozen for a moment before Mom pushes herself up from the table and hurries down the stairs to answer it.

"Mrs. Mackenzie?" a familiar voice pants. "Is Sophie here?"

"She is, actually," Mom says, "we were just sitting down to talk about something. Is everything—"

"It's fine, it's great," William says. "Mind if I join you?"

He comes springing up the stairs, taking them two at a time, his cheeks and nose bright red from the cold, still breathing hard. He meets my stare, then Sophie's. He looks like he ran the whole way here.

"All right," Mom says, sitting again while William braces himself against his knees, catching his breath, "someone really needs to explain what's going on here."

"I was just saying," Sophie picks up after exchanging a look with William, "that before she attacked us, Skye was telling us about this guy from her old school." I close my eyes. Waiting for the axe to fall. "Someone who was bothering her sister. It sounded like she hurt him pretty bad, and we thought—"

Then William's voice slices quietly through hers, through the scream building in my chest.

"That's not true."

There's an endless, crushing silence. I can't breathe. Mom looks back and forth between the two of them with a stone face that could rival mine.

"Excuse me?" Sophie says, with a winded half laugh, a sound of utter, furious disbelief.

"I said, it's not true. I'm really sorry, Mrs. Mackenzie, but she's making this up. I was there. That's not what happened."

"Are you kidding me?" Sophie doesn't raise her voice, but anyone at school would have scurried from it like bugs hiding from the light. "You're trying to cover for her now? What the *hell*, William?"

"Back off, Sophie. I mean it."

"You're seriously doing this. You're seriously going to do this after I came over yesterday and—"

"She's jealous," William says grimly, raising his voice a little to cut her off. "That's all this is. I don't know if Skye mentioned it, but Sophie and I went out for a while last year. She's been trying to blackmail Skye into staying away from me. And now she's mad that it didn't work."

Mom's eyebrows climb higher and higher as this exchange goes on, but otherwise her expression doesn't change.

"You did not just say that," Sophie breathes.

"Prove me wrong, Soph," William returns bleakly.

"My daughter is missing." Mom's words are quiet, heavy as stones. "She might be dead. Whatever drama you three are trying to dump in my lap, I'm really not interested in sorting it out."

The quiet turns glacial, miles thick. Impossible to break. Even the clock is silent; it hasn't occurred to anybody to wind it, these past few days.

"You need to leave," Mom says, in her very best manager voice. "Both of you."

"Mrs. Mackenzie, I don't know what his problem is, but I would *never*—"

"I said leave. *Now.*"

Sophie gets to her feet, face flushed. She doesn't look at me; only William.

"You," she tells him, "are making such an *epic* mistake."

She pushes past him, heading for the stairs.

"Sophie, wait," William says, and when she doesn't pause, he follows her, thumping down the stairs. "Sophie!"

Mom is slouched in place, massaging her temples, not even looking at me. So I run after them. William is just catching up to Sophie as I come outside. He tries to grab her arm, but she wheels and shoves both hands into his chest, sending him stumbling back.

"Fuck off!" she yells. "How could you say that? How could you *humiliate* me like that? And for what? For *her*? You think it's even going to work? Kevin was there too, you idiot! Whose side do you think he's going to take?"

"Sophie, wait. Please. You don't understand!"

"Don't even talk to me! And you—" She sputters to a halt for a second, glaring at me like she's struggling to find words vile enough. "I hope it's worth it. Everything you're destroying. I hope you're fucking happy."

She turns her back on us, storms toward the road, almost running. William stares after her with his hands raked into his hair.

My voice doesn't want to work; I have to clear my throat before I can speak. "You didn't have to do that."

"It was my fault." He doesn't look at me. "For asking you to come over this morning."

Silence. I scan his face desperately, waiting for something to change. For him to crack.

"William." It feels cruel to say it. Ungrateful. But that doesn't make it any less true. "We're running really short on time here."

He jerks his chin in a nod. Still not looking at me. "I know."

"Okay." Nothing left to say. No other buttons left to push. Please, let it be enough. "Well. I'll see you."

There's nothing left to do but turn back to the house. I make my steps small and slow, hoping for him to call my name, tell me to wait.

He doesn't. When I close the door behind me, he's still standing in the driveway.

My phone buzzes a few hours later as the afternoon is turning into evening, dull and gray. A text. It's from William.

ok let's talk.

When I get to the clearing, he's already there, sitting as far away as he can get from the glass-eyed monster, but staring intently at it, chin resting on his folded hands, jogging his knees up and down.

"Hey," I say, when he doesn't seem to see me. Even then, he doesn't look up. His face is pale and set.

"You were right," he says.

It's snowed since this morning, leaving a thin, patchy crust not deep enough for boots. The wind drives flecks of ice like little needles. Even the cedars don't do much to break it. I hug my coat tighter and crunch across the clearing to perch on William's log. The tension radiating from him keeps an automatic distance between us. We're like magnets pushing each other away.

"Sophie's in the hospital," he says at last.

The words are lightning, striking home. I sit transfixed, unable to speak, unable to move.

"She was on her way to work. Right? She takes Old Almonte Road to get to work. So she doesn't have to deal with the left turn onto the highway."

Old Almonte Road. The one that cuts across the swamp.

"She crashed her mom's car. Totaled it, pretty much. Broke her knee. Her mom said she's going to need surgery. Her mom said"—he pauses, forces the words out between his teeth—"that something wandered out in front of them. Something weird."

There should be a word for this, for a problem suddenly, horribly erased, bringing no relief, no satisfaction. I refuse to be reminded of those empty, ashy days after Tyler, the quiet that set in as the rumors spread. This time it wasn't me; this wasn't my fault.

"You were right," William repeats. His voice teeters on the edge of breaking. "I should have listened."

Across the clearing, my monster's mismatched eyes glint out at us, its cedar crest trembling in the wind. I bet they're laughing. I can almost hear it in the ringing that fills my ears.

"My dad's going hunting this weekend," William says beside me. Still not looking at me. "It's the last weekend before gun season, you know. He goes with Kevin and his dad every year. He said I could come too, this time, if I wanted to." His lips twist. "If I could handle it."

This is what I wanted. What I was pushing for. This is what it took. "Oh," is all I can say.

"Yeah. Oh." He drags his hands down his face, closes his eyes. "Bow hunting's pretty safe, you know? But still. Anything could happen out there. All kinds of accidents."

"Listen—"

"Don't." He jerks his arm away from my touch like it burns. "Just—don't. Okay?"

I swallow and pocket my hand again. *Sorry* is a small, stupid word, and I won't voice it. Either he knows or he doesn't. Saying anything will just scatter broken glass for us both to walk on.

As if my presence propels him to his feet, he gets up to pace back and forth along Deirdre's stone circles, arms folded, eyes fixed on the ground.

"I thought about telling her," he says. "Her and Kev. We were always going to band together for the apocalypse, you know?"

"They'd never believe you."

"I know. I *know*." He scrubs his hands through his hair, pulling pieces of it loose around his face. "This whole thing sounds like a bad trip. But what if they go after Kevin? I should warn him, shouldn't I?"

God, bringing Kevin into this is the last thing I need. "We already talked about this."

"Yeah, yeah." His shoulders slump. "How do you even stand it? Not telling people. Are you just...planning to tough it out through the end of the world alone?"

"I think maybe you're always alone for the apocalypse." I kick at a crust of snow. "That's how you find out who you really are. Survivor or zombie."

"Sure." He looks out through the trees, his mouth a thin line. "And I'm the guy who'd turn on anyone to save himself, apparently."

"That's what survivor means, William. It means you do what it takes."

"But you're trying to save your sister," he counters. "What does that make you?"

It makes me the Queen of Swords. He has no idea what I've done to save my sister—what I've done to save myself. I rest my head on my knees so I don't have to look at him. The wind flutters through my hair, trailing icy fingers across the back of my neck.

"They're not even done with you, after this, are they?" he says. "They still want you to do something. What is it? Do I have to...do you need my help?"

I don't want to think about the price that's coming due next. It's a train bearing down on us, a meteor. I can't think about it. At the end of the world, you learn how far you'll go. Whether there's anything you won't do.

"I don't know." My mouth is so dry, it's a rasp, barely more than a whisper. "I guess we'll find out."

"Well. I had an idea. I should have thought of it before. Something that might bring your guide to life, instead of...instead of what they want from me. And you have to be here too, right? In case it works."

"What are you talking about?" When I look up again, he's

holding one hand out. He shifts his weight, shakes his head, blows out a breath as if he's bracing himself. It takes me a second to parse the gleam in his other hand, something held ready over his arm. The flash of an edge.

"Jesus Christ, William!"

He steps back, away from me, still holding the razor blade poised.

"They said they wanted the blood of William Wright." Something wild has crept into his voice. "So I have to try this first. I have to."

"William. Don't. Give it here."

But when I lurch to my feet, he sucks in a breath and drags the blade down his arm, his lips skinned back from his teeth in a horrible grimace.

"Fuck!" he gasps. He drops the razor, clenches his hand over the wound. "There! It has to hurt, right? That hurts like a mother-fucker!" He holds his arm out to me, blood seeping up between his fingers in little red lines, welling over them to drip onto the ground. "That should be enough, shouldn't it? Isn't that enough?"

The words ring away into the trees, into silence. Somewhere a crow calls. Laughing. Between us, the figure I built stands empty as ever, the skull hanging slightly askew, ridiculous, a parody of something that was ever alive.

"Come on," William pleads. He wipes his bloody fingers on it, leaving red smears across its long face. I count the seconds past. One, one thousand. Two, one thousand. Three. "You've got what you wanted. That's the blood of William Wright. Come on already."

But a minute slides by. Another. And we're the only things that move.

William sinks onto the ground, sitting hard in the snow, curled over his injured arm. The blood runs in jagged lines toward his elbow. I come unfrozen enough to yank a strip of cloth from my coat pocket; he doesn't resist when I take his fingers, pull his hand toward me. The wound is like a mouth, not that long, a clean red slice edged in pink-white. I will not think about the ragged edges of the raccoon's belly, the wet red inside of rabbit skin. I tie the cloth around it, cinch it tight, wind it round and round. Red blooms through the fabric in rusty patches.

"It doesn't matter," he says through his teeth. They're chattering with cold or nerves, his face gone oatmeal-pale. "It doesn't make a difference. I'm not like you. I can't do this."

"Don't be an idiot." My voice won't stay firm, has slipped off its foundations. "You don't want to be like me. I'm psycho, remember?"

"And I'm harmless. It's true, isn't it? I really am. I'm pathetic."

"The only thing wrong with being harmless is that it makes you a target. You're just a decent human being. Unlike some of us. And you might need stitches or something."

He shakes his head, his hair falling around his face.

"I can't do it," he cries. "I have to. And I can't. I don't want to hurt anybody. I don't want to hurt my dad."

There's nothing left to say to that, nothing to do except put my arms around his shoulders and lean my head against his while he struggles to choke down tears. The woods stand over us, watching.

TWENTY-FOUR

S KYE?"
Mom's touch on my shoulder jerks me awake. I only
sat down for a minute, in the rocking chair beside the window,
but after so many broken nights, sleep sneaks up on me. The
only warning was my carefully controlled panic loosening,
breaking up into something raw and screaming, something I
could sink into.

"I made you some tea," Mom says, setting a steaming mug
on the side table.

"Thanks," I manage, rubbing my eyes with the heels of my
hands. I clutch my phone, but the lock screen is blank. No texts.
No calls.

Mom settles onto the footstool, her hand on my knee. "I thought we could talk, maybe," she says. "About everything."

I close my eyes, close my teeth on the first words that spring to mind. *Do we have to?*

"I know I've been kind of preoccupied," Mom persists. "I know I came down hard on you. I just…I know I can count on you, Skye. You're my rock. I always know you're going to be okay. You're the one person in this house I never have to worry about."

I can't listen to this. "Mom—"

"We're all hurting right now. But that doesn't mean the world has stopped turning, right? I get that. There's something going on with you lately, isn't there? I don't want to pry. I really don't. I'm just worried about you."

"Nothing's—"

"Skye. Come on. Even if we forget about that scene Sophie pulled, you're glued to your phone. You're obviously not sleeping. You look like you're in the middle of a high-wire act. Without a net."

I'm standing in a floodlight. I'm on the road with headlights bearing down on me. They can't start asking me questions. Not now. Every time I turn around, there are more eyes on my back, more ways this whole thing could go straight to hell.

"I heard about her accident," Mom ventures, more gently. "That's an awful thing to have happen to a friend."

"We're not friends." Not anymore.

"Yeah. Things are obviously pretty tough right now with all of them. With William." I pull away, protesting, but she's not giving up on this. "I'm only seeing the tip of the iceberg here. I could tell, yesterday. I'm here to help. Don't you want to talk about it?"

My face is going hot, my eyes blurry. Great. I'm so tired. Sooner or later, I'll stumble. I'll make a mistake. I have to keep it together.

"It's complicated," I quaver, scrubbing a hand across my face. "Okay? It's just...complicated."

"Of course it is," Mom murmurs, squeezing my knee. "Love always is."

I sob a laugh. Love. Like that's what this is about. Like there's any such thing. Like there's anything to any of us beyond our private stews of guilt and fear and obligation.

My phone's placid chime saves me from having to answer, but the screen lights up with William's number. Oh God, now what?

"Go ahead," Mom urges, sitting back, but not budging from her seat. "You obviously need to talk."

I push myself out of the chair and swipe at the screen.

"Hi." My voice is unmistakably stuffy, but it'll have to do.

"Can you come to Kevin's place?" William sounds as tired and strung out as I am. "Like, now?"

"I...guess so?" I hesitate, bracing for the roller-coaster plunge. I know it's coming. "Why?"

"I'm telling him. Kevin. I'm telling him everything."

"*What?*" It's a sucker punch, stealing my breath. Mom bites her lip, watching me, and I turn away from her. "You can't do that!"

"It's not up for debate. He's my friend. This is my decision.

Just like going on this fucking hunting trip. He'll be there too, you know. He should know what's going on."

"William, listen to me—"

"I'm telling him. Right now. And I need you to come over and back me up. So it's not just me."

How did this get so far out of control? The room reels around me. I have to convince him. I have to stop him. But even if I run the whole way there, I'll still be too late.

"If you don't show up," William says, his voice a little stronger, a little more desperate, "he'll think I've had some sort of mental break. That's what I'd have thought, if you'd tried to tell me, right? You think they'd let me anywhere near a bow after that? I'm telling him, Skye! You decide how you want this to turn out!"

"Fine," I choke out. "Fine. I'll be right there."

I stab the end button and press my hands to my face. I can't believe this.

"Skye?" Mom's hand closes on my shoulder. "What's going on?"

"Nothing! I'm going out. I'm going to Kevin's."

"You are not! Sit back down. Right now. You need to tell me what this is about."

"It's about William! That's all. Okay? This is between him and me. I have to go!"

"Skye—"

"No! You don't get to ask me about this now. If you wanted to know what was going on, maybe you could have looked up from the computer screen for five minutes. Any time this *whole year* would have been great!"

My aim is as good as ever. She wilts, shrinks into herself, just like I knew she would. When I turn away, she doesn't stop me.

"I'll be back in a bit," I mutter. I hurry down the stairs, out the front door. And then I run.

It's a long, ridiculous story, even leaving out the parts I have to keep to myself. It comes out in clipped, awkward sentences that still manage to sound like absurd rambling. When I finish, Kevin—sitting in the big leather armchair in the corner of his living room, his arms folded—looks back and forth between me and William standing over him, his jaw working.

"This is not fucking funny, you guys," he declares.

"Why did you tell him?" I demand, rounding on William. "Why *him*? Why the hell would you do that?"

"News flash," Kevin snaps, "he has actual friends."

"Guys, please," William says wearily.

Kevin focuses on him again, all intensity. "Seriously. Do you not get how textbook this sounds? Hearing voices telling you to hurt somebody?"

"I know. I know, I know. But it's not just me, Kev. That's why I called Skye. To prove it."

"Are you kidding? What have you been smoking?" He jumps to his feet, stabs a finger at me. "I don't know how the hell you managed to hypnotize him into this, but—"

William puts a hand on his arm, but he shakes it off.

"Why would you trust her?" Kevin demands. "Why would you believe a single thing she says? *Look* at her, she's like some sort of goddamn robot—"

"Oh, fuck you," I snap, goaded past endurance.

"Yeah, I see you," Kevin fires back. "I've *always* seen you! You're not as good an actress as you think you are!"

"Look," William pleads, "I know how it sounds, okay? But we both saw them. We were both right there. This thing was standing over her like—like it was going to eat her heart. Think about it for a second. Maybe this explains everything!"

"Does it explain why she tortured some guy? Or are you just going to ignore that?"

"That's beside the point," William says doggedly. "You have to believe me. You have to. If I don't do this—they already got Sophie. Don't you think they know you're here?"

"Sophie was in a car accident, William! Her mom was there!"

"And she said something stepped out on the road!"

"So, what, the deer are part of this conspiracy too, now? Listen to yourself!"

"I'm not asking you to help. Okay? I'm the only one who can do this. I know that. But I needed you to know what's going on. What I've gotten you into. If I'd told Sophie—"

"Sophie would tell you exactly what I'm telling you now. Which is *no. No fucking way.*"

Kevin pushes past me.

"Where are you going?" William calls after him.

"I'm telling your dad what you're up to, obviously!"

"You can't do that!" My voice goes shrill, beyond my control.

"Kev," William says, panic in every line of his face, "no, please—"

"I have to!" Kevin shouts. "Unlike *her*, I actually care what happens to you!"

I lunge after him as he's turning away from me, seize his arm in both hands, twist it back and around so he has to face me again. I can't marshal threats; I just stare him down, panting. But he meets my eyes steadily, not bothering to pull away.

"What are you going to do, huh?"

"Guys," William says, pale-faced.

"Are you going to drown me somewhere? Going to kick my ass? Great. That'll be super-convincing. You lay a hand on me, and how is that going to look for you?"

"*Guys.*" William drops his voice to a screaming whisper. "Kevin. Shut up."

Kevin opens his mouth to retort, but William puts a hand out to stop him, holds a trembling finger to his lips. A long, faint, whispering sound breaks the silence. Like a stick being dragged across the face of the house.

"Close the door," William hisses, "close the fucking door!"

Even when I let him go, Kevin doesn't budge. His eyes flick to the woods—a gray-green curtain beyond the screen door—and back to us.

"Not funny," he repeats. "Who the hell did you con into—"

But he stops short as something reaches into view through the sidelight, tapping its way across the glass. Something bony, purposeful, with too many fingers spread in a thin fan. A blunt fanged skull bobs into view, staring in at us from an eyeless socket, bones showing through the feathers on its winged crown. Kevin stumbles into me, away from it.

But all the creature does is lift the comb of ribs that forms its hand. Holds it edgewise to its muzzle in a stiff but unmistakable mockery of William's gesture a moment ago. A whisper drifts through the screen, a languid brush against my face.

Shhhh.

Then, with a bow, a flourish, it staggers out of sight, back the way it came.

Kevin slaps through the screen door to run after it, out onto the front walk, despite William's yelp of protest. He stands there gaping at the monster as it disappears into the woods. The snapping of branches is the only sign it was ever here, and even that quickly fades under the eaves of the trees.

Kevin looks at us. At me.

"Jesus fuck," he says.

"Get in here, you idiot!" William yanks him back inside, slams the door behind us, leans against it.

"Jesus fuck," Kevin repeats, his stare still fixed on the side window. He backs away from it until his heel collides with the stairs, and he sits heavily down.

"Do you get it now?" I demand. "Do you?"

"Shut up." He says it without feeling, sagging ghost-pale against the railing. "Oh my God. I'm going to puke."

"Just breathe," William says.

"How am I supposed to fucking breathe? You're telling me

that has been wandering around outside all this time, while we were—oh my God, they can't get into the *house*, can they?"

"I don't think so." I do my best to swallow my impatience. "Not…directly, anyway. Remember those roots I was telling you about? In the basement?"

"That is *so* not helpful." Kevin grinds the heels of his palms against his eyes. "This has to be a bad dream."

"I've been waiting to wake up for days now," William says. "You're lucky you didn't end up with some sort of job too."

"A *job*? That's what you're calling it?" Kevin looks up again, back and forth between us. "You're just *listening* to those things?"

Not this again. "Do you see an alternative?"

"What about all your ninja skills?" Kevin demands. "You're not going to fight them?"

"They have my sister." How many times do I have to say it? "I *can't*."

"I don't think we have a choice, Kev," William says hollowly.

"Of course you do! Come on, man. No. There's got to be some other way to get them off your back. We'll figure it out. We could take the zombie apocalypse, we can take these things!"

"I thought so too. I really did. And look what happened." William folds his arms, maybe bracing himself to hold his ground. It just makes him look smaller. Cold and lost. "Seriously. There's no choice. I can't delay any more. I can't risk anybody else getting hurt."

Kevin has rallied enough to glower at me. "Did she tell you that?"

"Kevin, for fuck's sake," I cry.

"She did, didn't she?" He laughs, incredulous. "Oh my God. Look, she's the one who dragged you into this! Why are you listening to her?"

"Maybe because I'm right! You think I wanted this to happen? You think I wanted any of this?"

"I think," Kevin snaps, "that you would shove anybody under a bus if it would save your ass. Including me. Including him."

"Come on, Kev, she's doing all of this to save her sister. If she was really like that, she'd have walked away."

"So what happens when they tell her it's you or her sister? What happens then?"

They both look at me. I glare back, stone-faced.

"Say it," Kevin insists. "What happens then? Who wins?"

"I don't know," I say raggedly. Truthfully. "What would *you* do, since it's so obvious? I could use the advice."

"He's not doing it," Kevin declares, and cuts William off when he starts to protest. "You're not! What the hell kind of friend would I be if I was okay with this? I'm not going to stand by and watch while you do this. I won't let you!"

"And how exactly do you think they're going to react if you stop him? You think they'll leave any of us alone?"

"Why are you even still here?" Kevin blazes. "You were here to convince me they're real. Fine, I'm convinced. Get the fuck out of my house!"

I start toward him, fists clenched, but a hand on my arm pulls me back.

"Skye. Don't." William looks beaten, his eyes shadowed, his shoulders hunched. "Look. You'd better go. I'll deal with this."

When I hesitate, William sighs and pulls the door open again, holds it there, waiting. Kevin shoves his hair out of his face, still glaring at me.

"I've made up my mind," William says. "This is on me now. You're just going to have to trust me."

Saturday is empty, endless. I could spend the day screaming. There's nothing I can do now, truly—literally. I'm in free fall, waiting to hit bottom, the air whistling past my ears. I'm the Queen of Swords for heartbeats at a time, frozen and regal, the knife-edge of calm. Mostly, I'm thin paper, smoldering, ready to go up in panicked flames. If I sit still, I'll burn to ash.

William said they would be leaving bright and early, his family and Kevin's rolling out in a convoy. Like an idiot, I unlock my phone a million times—what am I expecting, live tweeting? But whenever it's in my pocket, a conviction wraps itself a little more tightly around me, an awful, strangling thought: What if he didn't go? What if Kevin got him to change his mind? He can't change his mind now. I've bought and paid for this. What will I do if he changes his mind?

Once I've let the idea in, it's as if I'm possessed. It's not me flinging the door open, not my feet devouring the distance between my house and William's. I'm going for a walk, that's all. I'm going for a walk to clear my head. I repeat it to myself until I'm stepping over the fading bloody spot on the stones, until I'm knocking on his front door.

I have a breathless, dizzy moment standing on the step to wonder what the hell I'm doing before Angie opens the door. Her expression goes blank and closed when she sees it's me. She leaves the screen door closed between us. She doesn't say hello, doesn't say anything.

"Is William home?" It comes out shaky, but polite enough.

"No," she says shortly.

I want to be relieved. But if he *were* home, she wouldn't tell me.

"Do you know when he'll be back?"

"Not really." Getting this look from an adult is way worse than getting it from kids at school. It could scour me to the bone if I stand in it long enough.

"Okay." I give up, retreat, kicking myself. This was a bad idea. "Sorry to bother you."

But before I reach the end of the walk, she calls my name. When I turn back, she's leaning out the door, looking at me unhappily, biting her lip like she's not sure whether she should speak.

"You're going through a lot right now," she says. "I get that."

That statement is so absurd, I could laugh. I choke it down, expressionless, and shrug instead.

"It's just that William—he's got the kindest heart of any kid you'll ever meet. I don't want to see him get hurt."

But he's the kind of person who's doomed to get hurt. I knew it right from the start. I wish I'd never met him.

"I know." I cram my hands in my pockets, turn away. "Me neither."

TWENTY-FIVE

S UNDAY. THE END OF THE afternoon. I run full tilt across
the empty lot, rain misting down around me, clutching my
backpack full of monster-making supplies, just in case. All William's
message said was *meet me there*. It's done, it's over, it has to be.

He's slower than I am this time. When he ducks between
the leaning cedars, he looks terrible. Not just worn and tired, but
defeated somehow, a light gone out of him. His hair is wet, stray
curlicues plastered against his face.

"Here," he says, and pulls something from his pocket. A
heather-gray bundle of cloth. A T-shirt. Splashed with red-brown.
Stiff with it.

"It's mine." His voice is colorless. "My uncle used it to try to
stop the bleeding."

"William—"

"I don't want to talk about it." He drops down onto the log, puts his hands over his face. The bandage on his arm peeks out at the cuff of his jacket.

"That's fair," I manage. I don't really need to know. I don't really want to. But after a moment, he speaks again anyway.

"He'll live. In case you're wondering. It was—I hit—" He gives up on the words and slaps a hand against his knee instead. I clutch the bloodstained shirt in silence.

"I didn't think I could do it," he whispers. "There's no way I could have done it. But they got to Kevin."

The words flash through me, leave me numb. Just like Sophie. I don't want to hear this.

"We were on our way out to the blinds, all together, and... and Kevin and I had been arguing, so he was way ahead of me, and something...at first it looked like he fell. But then he started screaming. Something had his leg, he was halfway down this hole in the ground, and it wouldn't let go, it kept dragging him deeper. Bit by bit. I've never heard anybody scream like that before." His voice cracks; he folds his hands over his head. "So I did it. I fired. While they were all trying to get him out.

"They all think it was an accident. Even Dad. They got him on the stretcher, and he was all, *it's okay, William, shit happens.* Yeah. Sure. I told them—I said I'd drawn in case it was an animal or something, and something slipped. Something went wrong. And everyone *believes* me. Except for Kevin. Obviously. He didn't say anything, but...he just...he just *looked* at me. He was hurt worse than Dad. The guys who picked us up said his leg looked like he'd been attacked by a cougar or something." He closes his eyes. Tears escape down his cheeks. "I can still *see* it. It was like… raw meat, or…or that fucking raccoon, it was like—"

"You had to do this, William. You had no choice. I know, okay?" When he doesn't answer, I press on. "Look, you tried to warn Kevin. You did everything you could. You exhausted every other possibility." He passes his sleeve across his face, shakes his head. "You did! You slit your own wrist the other day! And when it didn't work, you did what you had to, even though it was horrible. You did it to save your friend. You look pretty heroic from here, all right?"

"But I did have a choice. I could have said no. I could have. Right up until the second I let the arrow go." He looks up at me, his eyes red-rimmed. "Did I do it to save Kev? I don't know. Maybe I did it to save myself. So they wouldn't come for me next. Maybe they just had to convince me that they really would."

The blood has turned the fabric into hard ridges that almost crunch when I tighten my grip. I don't want to look at it. I don't want to think about what's coming next, the half-glimpsed inevitability of it. But William's bleak honesty is a fishhook, dragging it into the light. I have to say something. He insisted on warning Kevin. I have to warn him.

"You should go. Before I try this. You did what they wanted. You should go home before they rope you into anything else."

"Probably," he responds, and doesn't move.

"William—"

"Look," he says, his voice tight, "they know where to find me anyway. Don't they? And I paid for this, all right? I just want to see what it was for. I just want to know that it worked."

I have to tell him. I have to tell him what he's walking into. But if he turns away—if I manage to convince him to run, to not look back—it means they lose their prize. It means I lose. It means I surrender. I think of the monsters, a bony antler-hand poised to strike. I think of the raccoon, guts spilling out.

I can't lose. Surrendering's not an option.

I can't think about this. I have to focus. Maybe we're supposed to summon them somehow to claim their payment, but the thought of their bony faces, their lurching movement, turns my stomach. Well, this is supposed to pay for the guide, isn't it?

Deirdre's creations were clothed, sort of.

I spread the bloodied shirt on the ground with shaking hands, dig Mom's scissors out of my backpack, slice through the stained fabric. Little rust-colored flakes fleck the blades.

The creature's waiting. Its glass eyes sparkle in the shifting light falling through the cedar boughs as I step closer. It already looks more alert. Hungry. I don't want to touch it. I drape the shirt around its stick and wire torso, fumble the cut edges into a clumsy knot below the skull so it hangs like a bloody cape.

Its body trembles, rattles, as if a gust of wind is blowing through it. Its head lolls, rocks back and forth, as if it's stretching, like an animal testing the wind. I stumble back as its stick arms swing out, flex back and forth. But all it does is cross them over its torso and bend toward me in a little bow. And then it lifts its stone feet and hobbles with surprising speed through the door of the clearing.

I run after it, but it's not going far. It reaches out to touch the shaggy back of the castle, and the dirt crumbles and slides away. A hole opens in the slope with a muffled thump and patter, wider and wider, until I'm staring into a tunnel that stretches into darkness, roots snaking down from the ceiling. My guide shuffles through that opening, disappears.

A sudden light at my shoulder startles me: the LED of William's phone. He holds it up high to illuminate the corridor. The monster's hitching movement is barely visible at its edge.

"Come on," he says, and hands me my backpack. "Before we lose it."

The tunnel is tall enough for me to pass, cringing away from the touch of trailing things that catch like hands at my hair and arms. William has to stoop down, stumbling along behind me. His breath is loud in my ears. The air is full of a secretive garden smell: wet, black earth, the sly cold scent of growing things.

Even when the walls and ceiling recede, the roots crowd closer around us, roping across our path, thick as my arm, twining around each other. We have to climb over, duck under, shimmy around them.

"Can you see it?" William pants.

"No." It's hard to force my voice past a whisper. It's hard to push myself forward, inching into something's lair against every screaming instinct. The dark presses down around us. "But there's only one way it could have gone."

Squeezing through one gap, I knock loose part of the wall; it comes showering down on me in pale, crumbling chunks like chalky gravel.

Like drywall.

I brush the debris off my sweater. I don't say *what the fuck*. Saying it out loud will make the fear real, a thing with teeth I can't escape. Instead, I hold out my hand for his phone—it's reading 33:33, with NO SIGNAL glaring at the top of the screen—and cast the light up over the passage before us.

"What?" William says behind me.

"Look. Do you see that?"

Between the roping black limbs of the roots, here and there, a flat surface is visible—buckled and discolored, but still paler than dirt. The shape of the corridor, however overgrown, is familiar underneath. Man-made.

"*What*, for God's sake," William says.

"It's a hallway," I whisper. "Like in a house."

We stand there peering uselessly into the dark. Somewhere water is dripping. Nothing moves. The ground between the roots has grown spongy, though it's still hard and steady underneath. Cautiously, I crouch down to touch it. It squishes wetly, fibrous, though too short and regular for grass.

Carpet. I lurch to my feet, away from it, scrubbing my hand against my jeans.

"Skye?"

"I'm okay," I say. My voice is thin, too high. "I'm okay. I'm fine. This is—this is really fucked up, is all."

"It's their castle," William says, and though he takes my hand, clutches it, he gives me a frail, uneven smile. "Of course it is."

How long is the tunnel we clamber through? It's an eternity, a maze. Eventually it opens up into a wide cavern, its floor humped and snaking, gleaming in places with water that throws back the blue-white light from the phone. The wall across from us is dimly visible, marbled with green and black. And like the hallway, its bones are vertical.

At least there's more space here, though I'm careful not to step in the puddles, reminded of the floor of the swamp, its sudden, unpredictable depth. I don't question how I know which way to go until I reach out automatically to grasp a wooden post, topped with a familiar polished knob, that stands straight and regular among the grasping roots. At the bottom of a set of stairs.

I pull my hand away, fold my arms.

"What's wrong?"

I want to say it makes no sense, but that's not really true, and that's the worst part. There's a dream logic to it, an inevitability.

"We're in my old house," I tell him, climbing carefully over the roots cascading down the stairs. "In the basement. Watch your step."

He just shakes his head as he climbs after me, holding the phone high. Nothing's surprising anymore.

The stairs creak and groan like they never used to, but they're sound enough. We come up past the landing, where the little window in the back door is choked with dirt, and the glass crunches all over the peeling linoleum, mixed with scattered clumps of spilled clay. In the kitchen, roots have pushed cupboard doors off their hinges, leaving dark gaping mouths. Black water fills the double sink, the tap dripping steadily to form a green trickle that snakes down the face of the cabinet, trailing rivulets of mildew.

A ghostly predawn glow seeps in from the dining room. It's empty, just like we left it. Four bare walls, old-fashioned built-in cabinets with the glass doors smudged and hanging ajar, a shaggy beige carpet. But a tree—a white-barked birch—has pushed its way up through the floor, leaving it as slanted and uneven as the earth in the woods. The trunk punches all the way through the roof, reaching for the sky, fracturing the ceiling with cracks like bolts of lightning. The light filters in between the crowded tendrils of some leafy vine that has crawled over the window.

Past the caved-in fireplace—red bricks and soot spilling out onto the carpet—the big picture window overlooking the garden is still intact, though dark and occluded with grime. Everything beyond it blurs into murky green shadow. Still, I know the neighbor's chokecherry tree by the tall sweep of its branches; it always framed our view.

"It still *smells* like our house." My whisper is too loud, out of place. "Underneath, I mean. Every now and again. How could they know how my house smelled?"

"The same way they know everything else, I guess," William whispers back, pressing his face up to the glass, trying to peer beyond.

The front door stands open into a strange purple twilight. Outside, the garden I remember has grown utterly wild, transformed into something monstrous and feral. The crowded trees of the swamp have shouldered up through the flower beds, taking over. The smell of peonies hangs in the air.

The path down to the street is no more than a suggestion, bits of broken concrete slab that protrude sometimes like bones. The street itself is still there, at least as a shadow, a broad shallow bowl of grass interrupting the trees. It's losing its clean, sharp edges, shaped more like a river now. Even here, out of the trees, William and I cast no shadows in the half light. It's directionless, a flare of sunset color lighting the edge of the horizon all around.

There's no sign of our guide. But I think I know which way we're supposed to go. The same way I've gone so often in my dreams. The one I can't forget. It's not even that far.

The path leading down to the valley, into violet shadow, stands untouched. The yellow line on the asphalt gleams in the twilight, a long plunge between the banks of trees on either side, the hills looming taller than they should. I clutch the straps of my backpack, unable to look away.

I don't want to go down there. Not again.

"Skye?" William prompts uncertainly. "Where are we? Is this somewhere you know?"

"Sort of." The sound bleeds out of my voice, leaves it a whisper. "This way."

And I step onto the path.

TWENTY-SIX

E XCEPT FOR THE LIGHT, I might never have left. Maybe
I'm still there, hurrying down to the river ahead of my enemy.
My heart thumping in my ears, every instant brimming with what
I'm about to do like I'm carrying a cup of water, trying not to let
it spill. It feels as if it should be getting darker, or lighter, but the
depth of the shadows never changes. Maybe I'll be here forever,
going down and down the ravine toward the river. With William
following me. Faithful. Clueless.

But the path has an end, just like it does in the real world:
through the last screen of trees before the river, over the footbridge.
Here's where I turned aside, the narrow, stony track of some
runoff channel. It winds down a scrubby slope to the riverbank,
slicing through thin whips of saplings just tall enough to swallow
us, thick enough to make the bike path behind us disappear.

Not far from here is the bank where Deirdre and I spent a thousand afternoons in another world. The last time was in the spring.

I lay next to her under the greening willows, my sword tossed in the grass beside me, poking the water with a long stick as she ripped her math notebook to shreds, page by page, grim and systematic. The water devoured the pieces. She'd gotten detention the day before for losing it. When it resurfaced in her backpack, crudely rendered dicks adorned every page.

Her mouth was marked by an ugly gash, a bloom of bruises. She wouldn't tell me how she'd gotten it. My heart gave another twist of rage every time I looked at her. They'd never dared to actually lay a hand on her before.

"It was Tyler, wasn't it?" I said. It was always Tyler. Never so you could prove it. But it was him, pulling the strings, inventing the names. For no reason, as far as I could tell. Because she was prey. For the lulz.

It had started with little things. Petty things. Making fun of the way she laughed. Pulling her hair when he sat behind her on the bus, and when she accused him, protesting that he would never; he didn't want to get fleas. And when all his little hench-men hopped on the bandwagon, sharpening their pitchforks, he thought it was hilarious.

If I was there to overhear, I could twist arms, dig into

pressure points, extract apologies. But I couldn't be everywhere. They laughed at me too, just more cautiously. And they stayed out of my reach. After I got suspended for giving David Emery a black eye—I'd launched myself into four of them as they stood over her, following her across the yard—they just turned invisible and kept at it. Leaving notes. Stealing things.

We'd tried telling a hundred times. Sometimes it had spurred a talking-to, a class lecture on bullying from the guidance counselor, non-apologies delivered with a smirk. After a while, we'd stopped bothering. Like the few kids whose attempts at kindness were quickly exhausted, the adults weren't really on our side. Deirdre was just too shrill, too brittle, too demanding. No social skills. She brought it on herself. What were they going to do?

"He's the warlord," Deirdre said darkly. "All the goblins dance for him." She threw the last handful of confetti, dabbed carefully at her face, wincing. "You're the Queen of Swords. You have to do something."

"So maybe we need to capture the warlord." I said it so calmly. Icy reason. The sun glinted on the water, the unfolding leaves. Everything was so sharp, so clear.

"And make him sorry." Deirdre glowered, then sighed. "Yeah, right."

"He's getting cocky. Usually they don't leave marks. We can't do anything that leaves marks." I trailed my stick in the water, ignoring Deirdre's look of surprise.

Water doesn't leave marks.

"I'll take care of this," I said.

I levered myself to my feet and waded out into the current, ignoring its knife-cold edge slicing through my shoes, and plunged the stick into the water.

"I will. By wood, stone, water, and bone."

I left the stick wedged upright among the stones, a seal on a compact. A promise.

I hardly notice the round rocks turning under my feet as I lead William down through the thicket to the black rush of the water. Onto the riverbank. The one I know so well. The water, flowing fast and deep here, glints choppy rose-gold, reflecting the false directionless sunset, bordered all around by shadowy brush.

On the narrow strip of shoreline is our guide, collapsed into inanimate pieces, a sad heap of wire and debris scattered among the river stones, eye sockets winking in the half-light. A signpost: This is it. End of the line.

"What the hell?" William pants.

Breathe, I tell myself. Keep breathing. Almost there. That was then. This is now.

"It's okay," I whisper. "Hang on."

I pull one of the monster's stick arms loose from the wire knotted around it, pick my way to the edge of the water, stab it into the silty earth among the rocks, twist it around as far as my wrist will go.

"Open up," I tell it. "By wood, stone, water, and bone."

The water swirls past, indifferent, as I stomp in a hurried circle around the twig.

"Wood, stone, water, bone," I pant. My kick at the pebbly riverbed sends a spray of water onto the bank. "Goddammit! Wood, stone, water, bone!"

"Is…something supposed to happen?" William ventures.

I turn to face him. And here we are. There's a price; there's still a price to pay. I sink to my knees. I can't catch my breath. I can't breathe. I can't do it. I can't do it again.

"Skye? Skye! Hey!" I try to push him away, but he grips my shoulders, gives me a little shake, kneeling down to look me full in the face. "Come on, don't fall apart now. You've got this. Okay? We're good. We're fine. We just need to figure out where to go, all right? We can go back to the path. It keeps going, doesn't it? Or should we follow the water?"

"I don't know," I sob. Because I do know. It's laid out before me, what I have to do. One way forward. What they wanted all along. Then and now collapsing into each other, no difference left between them. "I don't know, I don't know, I don't know—"

"Hey," he repeats helplessly, pulling me close, and I press my forehead into his shoulder and cry like I've never cried in my life, in sheer stormy desperation. Someone stop me. Someone wipe this out. Make it a bad dream. I'm hurtling down the tracks, falling from the sky.

Eventually I hiccup into hopeless silence. William shifts a little against me, but only to get comfortable, and leans his cheek against my hair. The water chatters endlessly past us.

"I'm sorry," I whisper into his shirt.

"It's okay," he murmurs back.

"It's not. I dragged you down here, and now—and now—"

"You didn't, though. You told me to go home. Remember?"

I can't answer, and when I stay silent, he presses on.

"Look, I made a choice. A stupid one, probably. But, well, here I am. So let's just get through this. Together. Okay?"

"You're a way better person than me, William." I push myself away from him, brace myself against one of the skinny trees instead. "You shouldn't be here."

"Nobody should be here," he returns, unfazed. "So let's go get your sister and get the hell out already. Right?"

When I shake my head, he puts his hands to my face, his fingers sliding warm into my hair, his eyes on mine bright and earnest in the twilight.

"Seriously," he says. "Who knows what use I'll be, but you're the girl who'd survive the zombie apocalypse. You can do this, okay? I know it."

I clutch his hand against my cheek, without a word to say. If everything is permitted, then I'm allowed to accept this. I'm allowed to pretend it will be all right for a few more minutes. He leans toward me, hesitant, every bit closer a question, until his lips meet mine.

When my mouth opens under his, he draws a shuddering breath, and I pull him closer, tangle my hands in his hair as his slide up my back. This is where I'll stay, where I'll lose myself, where I'll stop time.

But it doesn't work like that, of course. And eventually he pulls away.

"I've wanted to do that since basically forever," he confesses. His shaky smile might break my heart. It hurts to return it. When I reach out to tuck away the hair falling into his face, he leans into my palm, kisses it.

"I messed up your hair," I say, sniffling, and he laughs, yanks the elastic from it so it falls around his shoulders, starts to gather it up again.

"No, here," I whisper. "Let me."

I push myself up, leaning on his shoulder. Set the backpack carefully on the ground, still within reach. One, two, three steps, and I kneel behind him. Hesitantly at first, I run my fingers through his hair, combing it back.

"Is it safe here?" He peers nervously into the brush crowding the riverbank. "Maybe we should keep moving."

"They're not coming after us. Not yet."

He doesn't ask how I know, but he trusts me. He relaxes, by slow increments, into my touch, folding his legs, getting comfortable.

"If you braid it, it'll stay better." My voice still trembles. It's been a long time since I braided Deirdre's hair, and my fingers are clumsy parting William's. I have to try a couple of times before I manage to cinch that first plait tight enough to hold. "Why do you wear it so long, anyway?"

"Because my dad hates it," he says, and then, trying to look back at me, "Why, do you?"

"No. It suits you. Hold still."

One strand over the other. It goes so quickly.

"What did they say we're looking for?"

"A key. And a bell."

"So the stick was supposed to be the key, right? Where was it supposed to take us?"

"I...I don't know."

"Maybe we need the bell first. Did they hide it somewhere, or what?"

"I'm thinking," I whisper.

It takes me longer than it should to secure the elastic. I inhale carefully, flatten my icy hands against his back, slide them over his shoulders, press my cheek to his. He leans into me with a sigh.

When the crook of my elbow closes around his neck, my other arm pressing him down into the choke from behind, it takes him a second to sort out what's happening before his hands fly up to break my grip, to push me away, to hit me. To make me let go. And he can't. He doesn't know how.

It's not breath this hold cuts off; it's blood. So for ten seconds, forever, his frantic gasps fill my ears as he flails in my grip. Ragged single words. *No. Stop. Don't.* Worst of all: *Please.*

"I'm sorry," I whisper into his hair. Over and over again. "I'm sorry, I'm sorry—"

Ten seconds.

I told him.

His hands slacken and drop away, his heels stop their grinding scrabble against the pebbly ground, and he sinks back against me, dead weight. I allow myself one sob. And then I let go, heave him awkwardly to one side, let him slide to the ground.

My hands are numb and shaking, but a razor-edged momentum carries me through every ruthless step of what I have to do, a chasm I can cross if I don't look down, if I don't stop. The roll of wire is still in my bag. I loop it around his wrists, one after the other, over and over again until it pinches against his skin, against the white bandage on one arm that's almost luminous in the twilight. He twitches and shudders under my touch. Not much time left. I can't stop. It's him or Deirdre. It's him or I lose. I tried to warn him. They all did.

I'm twisting the wire around the nearest sapling, winding it through and around, weaving it tight, when his hands spasm open and closed, and he draws a sharp breath, like he's waking from a nightmare.

He tries to move. Tries to roll over. Tries to twist his hands free, to pull them loose. Yanks at them. It makes the leaves of the tree dance and quiver. He twists around, panting, coughing, and finally catches sight of me, standing frozen behind him with the willow branches snagging in my hair.

I close my eyes, but the look on his face sears into me. In a heartbeat, he's understood everything. Here it is—the very bottom. The ground rushing up to meet me. The end of the world.

"Oh no," he croaks. "No, no, no, no—"

He jerks at the wire with every repetition of the word, throws his weight against it, but it's merciless. Stronger than either of us. If I'm going to save Deirdre, this is the price. I have no choice. There's no going back.

"You don't have to do this." His voice is full of gravel. I must have hurt his throat. "Jesus, Skye, don't do this. Please. Please. Oh God. Please let me go."

I can't speak. I've swallowed glass. But a faint silver jingle twinkles through my silence, pauses, zigzags closer, bright and cheerful in the twilight. A bell.

Mog's bell.

William tries to sit up, to look for its source, but he can't get farther than leaning awkwardly on his elbows, pushing at the rocks with his feet. The sound bobs down the slope. I half expect the quirk of a tail to brush against my legs, but there's nothing there—just the sound, weaving around us once, twice. Urging me toward the water.

"Skye," William begs as I step around him and pick up the stick from where I left it among the rocks. "Don't leave me here."

I don't answer. I'm steel. I can do this.

But then there's another sound: a crunch, a rustle. All around us. Twigs snapping under uneven footsteps. Without thinking, I meet William's eyes, and I know exactly what he's remembering. The dead animals, torn open. Kevin's mangled leg.

He throws himself back into trying to escape, thrashing, scrambling to get his knees under him, to find some leverage. The branches stir all around us, parting before bony faces, cloth-bound arms, misshapen bodies, feathered and spiked and moss-covered. A dozen of them, more. Fanged jaws gape open, claws flex.

I shrink back a few steps. The icy river soaks through my shoes. William strains after me, against the bite of the wire, away from the monsters hobbling slowly, carefully toward him.

"You can't do this!" It's a sob. "Help me!"

The monsters peer cautiously at me, sink one by one into a creaky bow. There are so many. I could never fight them off. A rock rolls under my foot, and I lurch backward again. One splashing step. Two. The bell weaves closer and then away again, pinging impatiently, waiting for me.

"You can't just leave me here! You can't! Skye! *Skye!*"

They're closing around him now. He knocks one of them over with a flailing kick, yanks his knees up as a bony hand delicately pulls his shirt back to expose his pale stomach, jerks his head away from the caress of sharp, mismatched bone fingers. And I just watch. I'm cold and sick and very far away. This can't happen. The price is too high. Any second now he'll break through my makeshift bonds. Any second now he'll scramble up the slope away from me, back to the real world.

But there's no escaping them. I've made it so there's no escape. They bend over him, and there's just enough space between their bodies for me to see the point of an antler descending slowly, so slowly, toward his face. His breathless whimpers fracture into a scream.

It goes on and on, a scream like I've never heard, like Kevin must have screamed. It fills my head, rings into the sky. Do something, I tell myself. Come on. One way or another. You have to do something. Do it now.

And I plunge the branch I'm clutching, the key, into the water, and twist.

The world wheels around me, the sunset light slides from

the horizon, stars bloom overhead. Vertigo sends me to my knees in the water, and I clutch the branch with both hands. It's the only solid thing in the world. The rocks sink away beneath me into soft, sucking mud. William's voice is swallowed up by a tide of delighted, speculative whispers that fill my ears and then ebb away to the very edge of hearing. Silence finally falls, and I sag dizzily in place, shaking, retching.

Nightmare. That's what this has to be. I can't have done that, oh God, please don't let me have done that for real. But the truth burrows deep, past the depth of any roots. Inescapable as a hand pushing me underwater. It comes howling out of me as a wail, an ugly, animal sound that fills the whole world and changes nothing. I can't help it. I can't stop my awful, hacking sobs any more than I can stop breathing. It can't have happened. It makes no sense. There should have been someone to save him.

Instead, there was me.

And here I am. Without him. Still breathing, in spite of everything.

Because I have to. I have to keep going. I have to find Deirdre.

When I can finally lift my head again, the sky is full of a cold, green light, shifting and trembling like a field of wheat in the wind, stars glinting through it. The creek that I'm kneeling in is a shining path out into the wilderness, the smooth, glassy water reflecting the lurid sky. The house, the road, the empty lot have been erased—the forest is all there is, stretching out before me. Fireflies wink through the tangle like stars, but all around me it's utterly silent in a way these woods have never been. Except for the clumsy sloshing of my movement, the rasp of my breath. Except for the bell twinkling impatiently in the brush, farther down the creek, circling back to see if I'm following yet.

I won't think any more about what I've left behind. I can't think about it. There was a price, and I paid it.

Out there, that's where I have to go. It's a road. And at its end is Deirdre.

Under my hand, the prickly branch I held has grown smooth, heavy, warm—a polished hilt. When I pull it from the water, it catches the shimmering light as if it's part of the creek. A sword. Not the blunt wooden one I've always carried, but a true sword, liquid and sharp. It hurts to look at.

I stagger to my feet, making ripples shatter the perfect reflection of the shivering sky, and mop my face with my sleeve. Then I hold the sword out before me and splash forward, along the creek. Into the woods.

TWENTY-SEVEN

I T's NOVEMBER IN THE REAL world. In November, the creek
is barely more than a trickle. Here, in what feels like the first
green flush of summer, it quickly climbs past my knees, drags at
my thighs, threatening to unbalance me. I wade on slowly, pulling
my feet loose with every step, holding the sword up—but to one
side. I don't trust myself not to trip.

I've buried terrible things before. I'm practically an expert
at turning my back on things I don't want to think about. But
William…there's no way not to think about William. No matter
how sternly, how desperately I tell myself to leave it behind, memory
stalks after me, a kaleidoscope of pleas and screams and his hands
in my hair. It keeps catching up, forcing me to stagger to a nauseated
halt, leaving me doubled over, leaking awful, useless noises.

Every time, I force myself to keep walking. Remind myself why I had to do it. Why I'm here.

Deirdre. I have to be close. I have to.

Around me, the woods are waking, stirring, unseen watchers tracking my progress. When I stop to squint into the darkness, everything is quiet in a gleeful way that feels like a hand pressed over a mouth to hold in laughter. Every now and again I think I catch the flap of wings from the corner of my eye, something alighting in the branches, bigger than any crow. Sometimes I think I see antlers, the hollows of skulls. But in the trembling green darkness, nothing is certain, everything bleeds together into shadow. My splashing passage covers a chorus of tiny movements. Whispers. The only sound I'm certain of is the bell, drawing me on through the trees.

The water creeps higher, over my hips, over the banks, until there's no more floor to the forest. The trees are a band of tangled darkness uniting rippling light above and below. I push my way through an endless curtain of whispering cattails to emerge into an open, ghostly place—a swath of shimmering water punctuated by silver-gray trunks. All dead. They've been whittled down to tall spikes almost bare of branches, a battalion of pale spears reaching up into the belly of the sky.

The water is up to my breasts now, my armpits, lapping at Deirdre's golden necklace. I stumble to a halt and jerk away from the touch of long, clinging strings of roots underwater. If I go any farther, I'll have to swim.

I turn around and around, holding the sword out before me, sending waves rippling through the wide, black pool. The muddy bottom pulls at my feet, threatening to suck me down even farther. Was this just some sort of trap, in the end? Have they lured me here for nothing? Where is she?

"Deirdre." It comes out weepy, a plea. I raise my voice. "Deirdre!"

The word lands like a stone, sending ripples through the shivering light in the sky. The greenish radiance divides itself into a million silent, pulsing filaments. Lightning—no, floating hair, floating high as the clouds. I glimpse a thin crescent moon behind it in a two-horned crown, its points vanishingly sharp. The bare silver trunks of the trees become long pale limbs stepping out of the woods. The dark sky is a swath of robe hanging from mountains of shoulders. Some sort of giant stands towering over me, too huge to comprehend, stretching across half the sky.

I shrink back behind the sword and hold it up in an absurd attempt at self-defense, my face pressed into my sodden sleeve, a beetle not wanting to be crushed. Every breath a sob. If this is a monster I have to fight, then I've already lost. I can't do it.

"Sorry," says a familiar voice above me, and a hand closes on my arm, featherlight. A human hand, though it's luminous as the sky, lit from within.

"Sorry," Deirdre repeats. She's crouched over me, balanced on her bare toes on the water like its surface is as steady as any floor. "I forgot. Is this better? It's just me."

Her hair streams white over her shoulders, over her knees, glowing against the soft dark of some sort of fabric draped around her; it blurs into the water, into the night, its edges indistinguishable. The moon still lingers behind her head, as if it's been pinned there. It's hard to meet her eyes; they've turned silver, the color of the creek at nightfall. When I'm not looking right at her, the shape of her bones strobes to the surface, outlines flashing in and out of sight like fish underwater.

"Are you dead?" I whisper, and she bursts into peals of laughter. They ring out over the water, into the woods.

"Are *you?*" She giggles, snorting, and splashes me with one hand. "Come on. Ask a better question."

It must be a trick. It must be another test, another game, an image of her they've stolen and set loose to trap me. But it's so *her*. She rocks back and forth on the balls of her feet, biting her knuckles, her face alight with something she can't wait to tell me. I keep the sword up, but I'm blinking through helpless tears. It has to be her. My beautiful, impossible sister.

"Deirdre," I croak. "You have to come home."

She rolls her eyes, makes a *tsk* of impatience.

"No, no," she says. "You're supposed to ask me. Go on. You know you want to."

"Ask what?" She just grins at me. "Deirdre, please, you have no idea what I've been through to find you!"

"But I do," she says, and her smile widens. "You were amazing. You were better than in any of our games. I knew you'd come."

The conversation is shifting under me, giving way like the mud beneath my feet.

"Seriously," I plead, "please, let's just go. They'll let us go now, they have to. They'd better."

"Who?" Deirdre says, glancing over her shoulder. "You mean them?"

When I follow her gaze, the pale skulls of the monsters' faces gleam against the night behind her. They're shambling over the water without sinking. I stagger back a step, choking on rage and panic, before hurling myself at them, sword held high to beat them back from her—but Deirdre sighs and puts up a hand, and suddenly I'm blundering into a driftwood barrier, a long, gray trunk that wasn't there before, blocking my path, walling them off.

She giggles at my bewilderment, and the sound changes in the air, makes the reeds shiver and whisper. Her mouth moves, but it's *their* voices that speak, that flutter in the air to touch my face, making me start back in revulsion.

Relax, Queen of Swords, relax, don't you get it?

"This *is* a trick!" I cry, leveling the sword. "Where's my sister? You promised!"

"Oh, Skye," she sighs in her own voice again, "seriously. Think about it for a second." Her smile flickers back to life. "Sharpen up."

I stare at her.

"That was you," I whisper. She claps her hands, a delighted squeal escaping her. "That was *you*? That whole time?"

"Isn't it amazing?" She beams at me, splashes her hands in the water, like she can't contain herself. "Isn't it fantastic?"

I stagger back in the water, almost drop the sword. The world is unraveling around me, crashing in on me piece by piece, and William's horrified denials echo in my head. No. No, no, *no*.

"What did you do?"

"I made myself a kingdom," she says simply, ignoring the whimper in my voice. "A new one. Somewhere I could start over. And now you can too!"

"But Deirdre, they—you made me—"

"Made you?" Deirdre blinks. "I didn't make you do anything."

"You did!" It's a wail, desperate and childish, and I don't care. I could scream. It's not true. It's not real. "You *made* me! You made me—"

"I didn't think you'd actually do it," she says, like it should be obvious. "I thought they'd have to drag you in here kicking and screaming." She studies me, smiling. "This was way more fun."

"But I left him." The words fall like stones. Real and irreversible. "I left William back there—with those—those *things*—"

"You totally did," Deirdre says. The smile turns misty. "I knew you still loved me."

I can't stand still, the thought is cutting me open. I limp away from it, but it's closing in on every side, teeth sinking into me like knives, already done, already decided. I had no choice. I had no choice. This can't be true. This can't be happening.

"He was *nice* to you!" I cry. "He never did anything to you. He shot his own father with an arrow because his friends were in danger! We thought *you* were in danger!"

"No," she says crisply, "he told you himself. He thought *he* was in danger." Her expression darkens. "He thought he could take you from me. Well, you showed him. And now we're together again. Just us. You said you wanted to start over, didn't you? Here's your chance."

"I was starting over! I was doing fine!"

"With them? With *him*?" Deirdre scowls. "Who did you think you were kidding? I know you. You're the Queen of Swords. You're the top of the food chain. Compared to you, they're all rabbits. Haven't you figured that out yet? Look at what you did to Tyler."

"Don't talk to me about Tyler! I was trying to protect you!"

"Come on, Skye. I already know, all right? I know the real secret. You do too."

"I'm not talking about this! I already fucking confessed!"

"No, you didn't," Deirdre says. "Not the part that counts. Go ahead. I want to hear you say it. Why did you do it?"

I'm sinking. I'm sinking into time like it's mud. I'll never come up for air. I'll be there forever, walking away from the stick in the river, following Deirdre over the footbridge. Her step was lighter, mine deliberate. It wasn't rage that poured through me. It was something colder. I didn't know yet what I was going to do, but it would be terrible. I'd make them remember me when they looked at my sister. I'd make them fear my name.

"I did it because I could," I whisper. "Because I knew I could hurt him."

Deirdre smiles, almost gently. "And?"

It wasn't just that I wanted him to stop. I wanted to make him stop. I wanted the *power* to make him stop—that's the word for the sharp hungry edge that filled me that day. That carried me down through the valley to crouch among the trees, that kept my hand on the back of his head, pushing him down, pushing him under, straddling his back as he bucked and thrashed. Unable to escape.

"I did it because I wanted to." The words are ash in my

mouth. "I wanted to hurt him. I was stronger than him. And—and it felt good."

Deirdre's smile widens, grows pointed, sharp-edged as the moon hovering behind her.

"There." She sits back on her heels. "See? You don't belong there any more than I do. Don't you get it? That's what I'm doing here. I'm making a place for us. A place where there aren't any rules. Where *we* make the rules."

"But that's not what I wanted," I cry. "That's not what I paid for!"

"And what about me? What about what I paid for? Do you think this sort of thing comes for free?"

"Is that what happened to Mog?"

She withdraws at that, going dim, turns her face away. The shadows of her teeth flicker through her cheek.

"Everything has a price," she says. "And anyway, it doesn't matter." She puts a hand to her shoulder, and for a moment a cloud of shadow gathers there, a long tail, a head butting into her fingers, making the bell ping. "We're together now."

"I paid my price to bring you home!"

"I can't go home, Skye."

"Why not? What's out here?" I heft the sword, swing around in a circle, but there's nothing but the far black line of the trees. "Come on out, whatever the fuck you are! We had a deal!"

"Skye. Come on. It's just me."

"Something tricked you! Something talked you into this! You didn't do all this by yourself!"

"Nothing tricked me." She looks away, her brow furrowed, as if she's trying to remember something. Her bones shift and tremble under her skin. "We understood each other. Nobody else did. We both felt…betrayed. And angry. We had the same enemies. Together we could make…everything we wanted. For real. I gave them a way back." Her lip curls in a flash of inhuman disdain. "A way to hurt the invaders. And…and a way for me to find you."

"Who's *we?*"

Deirdre sweeps a hand across the landscape. "The trees. The water. All of this." She sighs at my uncomprehending stare. "It's hard to explain. But I paid the price they asked for. There's… no *we* anymore. No *they*. I'm the woods now. They're me."

"No. Bullshit. You're my sister. You have to come with me."

She shakes her head slowly, sadly. Like she's explaining something to a toddler throwing a tantrum. "It's not a two-way street. I've already left. I'm just holding the gate open because I wanted you with me. It's never the same without you." A slyness creeps into her silver gaze, a cat-like calculation. "Besides, you can't go back now. Can you?"

"You can't make me stay. Not if I don't want to." I say it out of reflex, out of stubbornness. But it's true. If I had a choice—if I always had a choice—I have one now. An open door. The last one.

"But you *do* want to." When I open my mouth to argue, she cuts me off. "You will. Just wait. I have something for you." Her smile is small, this time, a little sad. "I thought I would be enough to make you stay. But I guess it doesn't matter. I saved this for you in case. I saved the best for last."

She stands up with an imperious toss of her gleaming hair, and her silver gaze travels to a point above and behind me.

"Well, come on," she says. "Help her up."

I twist around to find a shadow standing over me, a stark silhouette against the sky. A person, bending down. Just above the hand held out to me, a white bandage glows in Deirdre's faint green light. The end of a braid dangles in my face.

For a frozen eternity, I can't move, can't speak, can't think.

"William?" It comes out a whimper.

"It's me." He sounds strange. Far away. Dreamy or feverish. "Come on, the water's cold."

His hand is cold, clasping mine, but his grip is strong, and as he pulls me up, my feet find steps—not solid exactly, but enough to bear my weight—to climb up to where they both stand. Deirdre full of ghostly light, and William dark, giving back none.

"I'm sorry," I choke out. "William, I'm so sorry. I didn't want to. I didn't—"

"It's okay." It's a contented sigh. As if he's talking in his sleep. "You had to. I understand."

"How can you say that?" I cry.

"It's okay," he repeats. "I'm here. We're together."

Should those words be comforting? They're sharp as knives. It's not possible. It's not right.

"But they were… What happened?" I can't see his face. I can't see anything. "Did they hurt you?"

"I don't really remember."

Dread blooms in my stomach. He doesn't sound right.

Why can't I see him? I almost reach out to touch his face, but I hesitate, pull my hand back. Remembering the antler poised above his eyes.

"It's the end of the world, isn't it?" he continues dreamily. "It's different than I thought it would be. I can see so much more clearly here. I can see everything. Even you. Right down to the very bottom. And it's—Skye, you're beautiful. You're a hero."

He takes a splashing, lurching step toward me. He moves like it hurts. He moves like one of *them*. And I scramble backward, away from him, and lift the sword between us.

"It's okay," he says again. "Really, Skye, it is."

"That's not William," I breathe.

"What do you mean, it's not William?" Deirdre demands. "Of course it is."

"You're making him say all of that! Stop it!"

"But don't you get it?" Deirdre says. "I'm giving him back. He's for you! He'll do whatever you want now. I don't *have* to make him. Neither do you. We'll be queens together. And you can have your own champion. Just say you want it. Use the words—our words—and it's done."

"But that's *not* what I want!" I cry. He stands there unmoving, not protesting. Silent. "That's not—that's not him!"

"Oh, come on! You only ever liked him because he does what you want. That's why you picked him from the start! That's what you've been *doing* all this time! He'll cooperate now, see? And you can keep him. You get him back, like I got Mog back. But only if you stay!"

I feel sick.

"What did you do to him?" I whisper.

Deirdre sticks her chin out, folds her arms.

"Everything has a price," she repeats.

"I don't want it. Undo it. Whatever it is. Let him go."

"Don't be like that," Deirdre pleads. "Stay. Stay with me! He's for *you*, Skye. Just like the monsters I made for you to fight. I made you a real sword, even. Isn't it beautiful? Mom and Dad won't even know we're gone. Not once the door is closed behind us. I promise." When I hesitate, she stomps her foot, sending a little ripple through the water. "How do you think it's going to work out if you go back? Do you think he'll cooperate if you go back? Do you think any of them will forgive you? You're better off here. Stay with me!"

I squint at William, trying to make out his face. I step one way, then the other, trying to catch a little bit of light. It doesn't work; the dark hangs like a curtain between us, Deirdre's glow casting only the faintest of halos around his hair, outlining his arms.

"Why can't I see him?" I demand. Deirdre doesn't look at me, doesn't answer. I clench my teeth, speak through them. "It's you. Isn't it? You don't want me to."

"I'm doing it for you," she says sullenly. "It's easier this way."

Oh God. "What do you mean?"

"Why are you still asking questions?" She comes closer, hugs my arm. Her touch is faint and cool. "All you have to do is say the words. You know the ones. And then you can look at him all you want. Okay?"

I pull away from her, focus on William's silhouette. I'm steel. Steel. I lift my hand slowly and reach for him. I have to know.

Under my fingers, his cheek is clammy. I feel blindly across his face. Lips and nose. I can't feel his breath. And under my touch, at the edge of his mouth, is a wet, ragged edge. Something tacky clings to my fingertips. Something gives where it shouldn't. When I jerk my hand back, it comes away stained with a dark smear of something that collects slowly at the base of my fingers, runs in a single drip across my palm.

Deirdre's light isn't bright enough to betray colors, red or otherwise. But I know what I'm looking at.

"It's okay," Deirdre coaxes. "It's not your fault. It's just the way you are. Stay here. I understand you. So does he, now. Come on, just say it. Wood, stone, water, bone."

"You can't make me stay," I whisper, looking up at her from my bloody fingers. "Can you?"

"I can't *make* you do anything," Deirdre huffs. "Nobody ever could."

"If I have a choice," I say, and my voice is stern and final, the voice of the Queen of Swords, "then I choose to go back. With or without you."

"But, Skye—"

"You don't get to tell me who I am!" I cry. "You don't get to decide who I'm going to be! If it has a price, then I'll pay it. I'm Skye, and I'm going back! By wood, stone, water, and bone!" I drop the sword at her feet. The water closes over the hilt with a gulp and a splash. Deirdre reels back a few steps, staring at me in disbelief, in anguish.

William staggers, stumbles against me, and I have to throw my arms around him to keep him upright. He sags in my arms, dragging us both down. The water rises around us, claiming my ankles, my knees, my thighs.

"You can't take him," Deirdre protests. "You're not allowed."

"You gave him to me, didn't you? I can do whatever I want!"

She balls her fists at her sides.

"You chose him. You chose *him*. Instead of me."

"Come with me," I beg. "I'm not the only one who has a choice."

"I've already made my choice." Her voice is hollow, made of the wind in the trees. "Maybe this is part of the price. My price. Giving you up."

"You don't have to!"

She's going dim, the moon shining through her hair as if it's caught in a net—no, caught in the branches. The tears sliding down her face are stars falling from the sky. I want to tell her I love her, in spite of it all, in spite of everything, but the moon is all that's left. The shifting green light fades from the sky. The water is closing over me, pulling at me. I hitch William up a little higher, trying to keep his face above the surface.

"Come on." His head lolls against my shoulder. "Come on, stand up, help me—"

"Skye?" he murmurs. "I can't—I can't see—"

After that, he's silent. No matter how many times I call his name.

So here we are, in the water, in the dark. I've made my choice. Deirdre is gone. And I'm so tired of fighting. William is the last thing left in the world. I cling to him, and I push my feet forward through the mud, one after another. I don't let go.

Somewhere, someone is crying. Maybe it's me.

The sound of my name is what pulls me back.

"Oh my God," someone says. Then they're yelling. "Over here! Quick!"

It hurts. I hurt. My head is too heavy to lift, cradled into the ground in a hollow that feels like it was made for it. When I open one eye by a crack, a strange white shape takes me a fuzzy second to decipher: my hand. Curled like a dead thing in the black mud, the sleeve of my sweater dusted with snow. Is it snow? If it was snow, I'd be cold, wouldn't I? Beyond it, cattails stand over me, tall sentinels.

"Skye," the voice says again. "Hey, kiddo, come on. Come on now."

Hands, searing hot, turn my head, so I have to face a silhouette bending over me, framed by a dim gray sky, crisscrossing branches. A man I don't know—kind of know—with a round face, a fuzzy military haircut. He's shaking me, patting my face, won't let me sleep. I manage a groan of protest.

"Come on, Skye, we've got you. Stay with us now. Let's get you warm, okay? I'm going to pick you up. Ready? One, two, three—"

Hands on my arms, pulling me up; arms under my knees, my shoulders. Gravity resents it, dragging at me. The sky, pale featureless clouds, swings over me, anemic with dawn. The branches part, recede.

"He's over there," the man calls, somewhere above me, a little breathless with exertion. "Under the trees. Hurry."

Other footsteps. Other voices. A confusion of them, shouting. Flashing lights stab through my eyelids until I peer out at them, and they resolve themselves into the ambulance, waiting by the road. That's not right. They left days ago.

I'm set down somewhere hard, unforgiving, hands all over me, a ceiling sliding over me with a jolt and a rattle, faces swimming in and out of view. One constant, tearful.

"Mom?"

I can't do more than shape the word with my lips, but she folds her hands over a wobbly smile.

"You're okay, honey," she quavers. "Everything's going to be fine."

And then it crashes over me. Where I've been.

What I've done.

"Whoa, whoa, slow down," says a male voice, stern and professional, when I try to fling myself upright. "Stay still. You could hurt yourself."

He eases me back down, ignoring my feeble flailing hands trying to push him away, holds me there. Someone else is slicing through my jeans with gleaming scissors, a sharp efficient snip, snip, snip, all the way up my leg, through my sweater, peeling the fabric away. I'm the only patient, but Officer Leduc's voice echoes in my ears. *He's over there.*

"William," I croak. "Where is he? I think he's—and I found—"

"He's safe, Skye." Mom clasps my hand, her face earnest. "Just relax."

They pile blanket after blanket on top of me, tuck them close around. There's a pinch inside my elbow, a slow, spreading bloom of warmth that loosens my joints, makes them start to jump and quake. My teeth clack together. I can't stop shaking.

"There," the man says soothingly, rubbing my shoulder. "That's good. Shivering's good. Keep it up."

"L-listen!" I can hardly talk. "Deirdre, Mom. I found Deirdre!"

Mom's eyes go wide. She clutches my hand.

"You what?"

"I found her. I found her. At the end of the creek." Hot tears spill over my cheeks. "She's gone, Mom. I couldn't bring her back. I tried. I tried so hard—"

"It's okay," Mom chokes, and kisses my hand. "It's okay. I'll go talk to the police."

She flies from the ambulance. I crane my neck, trying to follow her path, but she disappears into a sea of milling bodies, the hungry round lenses of cameras. Beyond them, the castle is a sullen, humped shadow, the trees a gray smudge behind it. The door of the ambulance swings closed, blocking them out.

TWENTY-EIGHT

WILLIAM'S ALIVE.

"He's in pretty rough shape," Officer Leduc says gently. "But he'll make it. Thanks to you."

Am I relieved? I can hardly tell. I wade through the questions like they're icy water. One foot after another. What were we doing? What kind of animal was it that attacked us? How did we get away? I repeat variations on *I don't know* until my voice gives out. It was dark. I can't remember. It happened so fast. All the clichés. They nod sympathetically. Squeeze my hand. Tell me I'm a real hero.

This time, when my parents called, the police had it easy. They found me almost right away, sprawled in the grass next to William, half in the creek at the edge of the woods. They can't believe I'm unhurt. I'm lucky I didn't freeze to death. I'm lucky I'm not losing fingers. The news is all over it: TEEN RESCUES FRIEND AFTER WILDLIFE ATTACK. Is there a bear on the loose? A cougar? That's their best guess, based on his injuries.

His injuries. I don't ask. Over and over again, I don't ask.

I watch the segment from the news on the computer. My dad gives a hurried, tearful statement. I hardly recognize myself on the stretcher. My face is slack, wax pale. Like a zombie's.

I feel like a zombie. Burnt out. A hollow shell.

Look at me. I've survived the end of the world.

A skirt and tights feels exactly as unnatural as the occasion. Deirdre's memorial.

It was a while before they told me. Hypothermia leaves you fragile at first, apparently. Prone to blood clots, heart trouble. But when we got home from the hospital, they sat me on the couch with snow sifting down outside, smudging the woods into gray shadow. Mom explained in a halting, broken voice that they'd checked the end of the creek, where it meets the long swamp, and found her dress. What was left of it. Nothing else, not yet. But that was enough, after what happened to Kevin, what happened to me and William, to draw conclusions.

She cries a lot. But at least she lets Dad hold her. At least she sleeps at night. That's something.

I don't sleep much.

The snow is still falling, softening all the edges, erasing the paths. I watch it through the tall church window as I drift through the songs and the hugs and the whitewashed stories about how "special" she was. It's tempting, it's so tempting, to let go. To let the snow bury me too, fill my mouth, erase my memories, all my crimes. Maybe they're right. Maybe it did happen the way they say it must have. Maybe trauma is messing with my head, mashing guilt and fear and childhood games together into impossible scenarios. If I'm not sure where my nightmares start and my memories end, maybe it's all nightmare. Maybe none of it really happened.

Maybe.

What shocks me awake—truly, painfully awake—is Angie Wright showing up among the murmuring, soberly dressed well-wishers that fill our house afterward. It's not my parents she seeks out first.

It's me.

"I'm sorry," she quavers, clutching my hand in both of hers, her eyes spilling over. "I'm so sorry. For everything. If it weren't for you—"

I think I might throw up. She won't let me go. "Listen, Mrs. Wright—you don't understand—"

"Angie," she sniffs, and manages a lopsided smile before pulling me into a tight hug, crushing my nose into the soft, scratchy wool of her fancy shrug. "Thank you for bringing him back to us."

This is hell, isn't it. I'm in hell. I'm paying for everything. I smile and smile and smile and extract my hand from her grip.

"Excuse me," I say, much too brightly, and flee the room.

Instinct draws me downstairs. To my room, to my refuge. But when I close the door behind me, I'm left facing a wall and ceiling stripped down to bare studs and joists, cracks snaking through the concrete foundation, filled with some sort of stabilizing compound. The crawl space yawns open, the doors off their hinges, empty again except for smears of sawdust. It all insists on reality. My reality, the one I remember. The one I wish I could forget.

My bed has been shoved over to the side, covered with a cloth. I sink onto it, drop my head into my hands.

She's never coming back.

That luminous, silver-eyed girl crowned with the crescent moon wasn't anything human anymore. Whatever's back there in the woods *did* devour her, in a way. I can still hear her laughing response to my question. *Are you dead?* She might as well be.

Could I have stopped her if I'd been paying attention, if I'd been there to wade after her, sword in hand? What's the point in even asking? I'm no one's hero. Not Deirdre's, and definitely not William's. I don't know if there's a word for what I am. Liar. Traitor.

Monster, maybe.

When the door swings open, I take a deep breath, determined not to snap at the intruder. My parents have been through enough lately. "Just give me a minute," I say through my teeth. "Okay? I'll be up in a minute."

No response. When I look up, it's Kevin looking back at me, hollow-eyed and tousle-haired in a jacket and tie. Leaning on crutches.

"Can we talk?" he says.

When I don't answer, he hobbles into the room and lowers himself slowly onto the bed next to me, grimacing.

"Ow. Fuck."

I lean away from him, my arms folded. "I don't have anything to say to you."

"Bullshit," he retorts. "You owe me."

I can hardly argue with that. We sit in silence for a while, footsteps creaking overhead.

"You weren't supposed to get involved," I tell him eventually. "None of you were."

He's silent, and I steal a glance at him. He's looking back at me. Wary. Puzzled.

"I'm trying to figure this out," he says. "They're saying you were attacked by some sort of animal."

He quirks his brows to say we both know what it really was. I look away.

"They're saying William could have died. And that you brought him out of the woods. They're saying you saved him." He waits for me to say something. "Is that true?"

I sniff, sweep my hair out of my face. "Ask him."

"I did. But he was…pretty confused when I talked to him. High as a kite. You know. His face…he got pretty messed up."

I'm not going to ask for details. I don't want to know. A memory flashes through my head: William sitting beside me. His hand on my arm. *I don't hate you.* But following close behind it is the memory of his sleepy, hypnotized, poisoned voice. *I understand.*

You had to. Words I made him say. Words Deirdre made him say. What's the difference?

"What happened?" Kevin asks. "For real."

Am I the only one who remembers, then? Is it up to me to decide what's true, what gets erased?

"It's—some of it's true. More or less."

"But it's not the whole story, is it?"

There's no more damage left to do. I've already burned everything down. Suddenly I can't bear the weight of another secret. It might crush me.

"You were right," I grate out. "About everything. I…I had a choice. Between him and Deirdre. And I chose wrong."

The silence is dense and heavy. A black hole. Explanations, excuses, lies couldn't fill it. Not in a million years.

"I brought him back, though," I whisper. "I did bring him back. I *chose* to bring him back. In the end."

The bed creaks as Kevin's weight shifts beside me.

"So was it worth it?" he asks.

It burns, hearing that question spoken aloud. The one that's been spinning through my head, half-formed, for days. "What the hell am I supposed to say to that?"

"I don't know. Tell me it meant something. Tell me you're sorry."

Not sorry enough to make Kevin think he has that kind of power over me. I study my hands in my lap.

"You are sorry, though." He says it slowly. As if he's working through a riddle, a tangled knot. "Aren't you?"

I wish he'd stop looking at me. "You think so?"

"Yeah. Yeah, I do."

"Well, so what if I am? What good does it do?" My stone face is cracking. I hide it behind my hands. Isn't he satisfied yet? Why is he still here? "Jesus, Kevin, what do you *want?*"

Another long silence. Beside me, he swallows.

"You want to hear a story?" He waits a few heartbeats for me to respond, but when I don't, he continues anyway. "So. Let's say there's this guy. He's pretty clueless. He's too—I don't know, he's too fucking nice. And his hair's not right, and his skin is bad, and…he just kind of needs someone to look out for him.

"Well. So, there's a princess. And, say, a knight. And they try to keep him from getting hurt. But there's this…I don't know, a dragon after him. A monster. Who keeps pulling…stupid shit. Calling him a fag. Knocking him down. You lose people's respect, you know, when you let that go on."

I blink. "Wait. The monster's after the knight?"

"No. The guy. The knight was protecting him."

"So some asshole was after you?"

"No, no, not *me*, it was"—Kevin rakes his hands through his hair—"oh, fuck it. The asshole was called Jared, okay? He had it in for William. And Bill—you know what Bill's like. He just kept telling William he needed to man up, grow a pair, fight back. Blah fucking blah. Except William wouldn't kick a dog if it bit him. So. Someone had to fight back. Right?

"So our asshole Jared was going out with…this girl. And he was in, like, sloppy, ridiculous, puppy-dog love with her. It was pretty nauseating, actually. So I told Sophie I saw this girl hooking up with someone else at a party. Someone I didn't know, conveniently, one of Dave Jablonski's friends. Sophie trusts me. It got around. And when Jared heard, of course he believed it. Because, you know, asshole. They had this big dramatic breakup. And then—*then* I told him. That it was all fake. Because by then, he couldn't even apologize to her, he'd already blown everything up." Kevin sits back, his arms folded. "He tried to beat the shit out of me for it. And that got him kicked out of school. Zero tolerance for the fucking win. And nobody ever knew."

"Right." A firelit memory flickers past: Kevin defending someone. Sort of. *Don't call her that.* "Except that now the girl—what was her name, Brittany?—she's the official Lanark Centennial slut. Isn't she?"

His mouth tightens.

"Collateral damage. I thought I was doing her a favor. Breaking them up. I didn't think…I didn't know people would take it like that. I didn't know they'd hang on to it for so long."

"But you didn't tell anyone you lied about her either."

"It wouldn't have done any good. It's not the sort of thing you can take back."

"Well. Nice story." Is he just trying to put me in my place? At this point, any secret he tells me is safe. If I tried to use it against him, nobody would believe me, anyway. "What am I supposed to do with this information?"

"I don't know. Maybe nothing. Maybe I'm just…trying to be nice. You know? A better person." He stretches his leg out in front of him, grimacing. "Maybe I'm trying to make up for being a dick.

I never trusted you. But maybe…maybe I'm not that different." He hesitates. "Maybe you were right about me too."

"Sophie said bullshit was your superpower."

Kevin snorts. "Yeah. That sounds like her."

I deal in bullshit too, though. "Why'd you do it, Kevin? For real."

My question is soft, but it nettles him into a glare. "I told you," he says, "I was protecting William. He was your collateral damage, wasn't he?"

I know how to take a punch. I don't flinch; I don't let up. "Who told you that was your job? Who signed you up for that?"

"Why the hell does that matter? Nobody else was doing it. I took care of it."

"But why? Why like that?"

"Because, okay?" He draws a breath, lowers his voice. "Just… because. Because reasons."

"Because you could," I whisper. "Because you wanted to."

We stare at each other. Recognition. It's ashy and awful.

I'm the one who looks away first. "So now what?"

"How should I know? I won't mess with you if you don't mess with me. And stay the hell away from my friends."

"That's not what I meant." I clench my fists in my lap. "I just…how do you go on? You know? When you know how far you'll go?"

His turn to look away.

"I have a choice, don't I?" I'm pleading. I can't help it. "I came back. I did. So how do I stop? How do I not be this person anymore?"

Kevin grabs his crutches, lurches to his feet.

"If there's a secret to it," he says, "let me know."

When I walk into school, my shoulders hunched, I part the crowds with a wedge of sharp-edged silence, leaving whispers and stares in my wake. Sophie hobbles past, leaning on a cane, without so much as looking at me. When someone sidles up to her, whispers something while glancing my way, she just shakes her head, her jaw set.

Between Sophie's icy silence and my supposed heroism, they don't know what to make of me. I can practically see the rumors swirling in the air. Funny how everyone got hurt except me. Funny how Sophie ended up in the hospital right after she crossed me. But I rescued William, didn't I? If I really rescued William, would Sophie be freezing me out?

Either way, the line between us has hardened, become impermeable. Me and them.

The whispers intensify as I slide into a seat in homeroom. *Fucking creepy* sifts through them, settles over my shoulders.

"Hey, shut up," Kevin says somewhere behind me. "Leave her alone."

And like magic, the whispers subside into a giggly, uncomfortable pause before the conversation turns to more normal things.

I twist around in my seat. Kevin's eyes flick up to meet mine, the barest acknowledgment, not even a nod.

Truce.

I'm at my locker, pulling it open, when a familiar laugh drifts down the hall. It's self-conscious, infectious. Inviting you to smile too.

The books slide from my hands to sprawl in a heap on the floor, and I run, shoving my way through the bodies milling across my path, ignoring the protests and scowls I leave behind. There, coming through the double doors from the parking lot, heading for the stairs.

"William!"

He turns in surprise just in time for me to throw my arms around him hard enough to make him stagger. His cheek against mine is cold from the walk outside. He smells faintly of vanilla. It's him. It's really him.

"You're all right," I gasp. "You're here; you're okay—"

I stop short of clasping his face between my hands. He looks back at me with one gray eye, the other hidden under a white bandage. A livid red seam winds out from underneath it, across his cheek, down his jaw to the corner of his mouth. Fading yellow bruises follow in its wake.

"William," I whisper. "Oh my God—"

He doesn't speak, but something passes between us as he steps out of my embrace. Something not quite seen, a shape underwater. Its shadow crosses his face. He backs away from me by a step, another.

"William," I plead.

"I'm…" His gaze flickers to the door, then back to me again, as if it's drawn unwilling. "I'm gonna go."

"William!"

He ducks away from me, slams back through the doors. Outside, he keeps walking, his shoulders hunched, the snow sifting into his hair, his steps as long as he can make them without running. Like that guy in the story—what was his name?—emerging from the underworld with a ghost trailing behind him.

He walks away like he'll lose everything if he looks back.

In the snow, twilight comes early. The woods, a band of shadow at the back of the yard, soften and blur behind a curtain of fat, drifting flakes that kiss my face as they tumble past. A fluffy few inches creaks under my shoes as I hurry across the yard.

The trees tower over me, mantled in white. Ice crusts the slate-gray water standing at their roots. I pace back and forth at the border, across the same shelf of rock where I first called the monsters.

But it's not the same at all. Something has turned its back on me. Some terrible attention has withdrawn into utter, blank indifference.

"Deirdre." The name dissipates into nothing, like the plume of vapor from my breath. The next time I scream it. "*Deirdre!*"

It echoes, fades away. Nothing answers me. No whispers. No movement. Not even the silver chime of a bell. She closed the gate. She said she would. It's firm and final as the rock under my feet.

I fold my arms against the pinch of my breath in my chest and the desperate spiral of half-formed explanations. I made a choice. I brought him back. Shouldn't that count for something? I have to tell him. I have to make him understand.

But the memory of Deirdre's shout stops the spiral cold. *Do you think he'll cooperate if you go back?*

I brought him back. But I can't make him come back to me. I'm not doing that, not anymore. It's a choice. I can choose.

That's not who I am.

If I walk away from him like I walked away from Deirdre, from her bone kingdom—if I let him go, if I choose to, if I choose again and again—does that change anything?

Mom's voice echoes down to me from the house, calling my name. Calling me inside. I'm not supposed to be out here, not with a wild something-or-other on the loose. Eventually I have to turn away from the woods, the gathering dark. No matter how many times I look over my shoulder, nothing stands between the tree trunks. The face of the forest is empty, blind and dreaming, filling up with snow.

ACKNOWLEDGMENTS

I've known since a certain wild winter night, when I was sixteen years old and watching a red crescent moon sink into the treetops, that I had to write something about the creepy, swampy woods that surrounded my family's home. What emerged at the time was a fantasy-world shadow of this story; I played with it off and on for a few years before finally giving up and burying it. It took me twenty years to figure out how to bring its bones to life.

So my thanks go out, first of all, to those who helped me wrestle with that first, early attempt: Janet Cover, whose encouragement I've always treasured; Nino Ricci and his 1996 summer workshop at the Humber School for Writers; Stephanie Bolster, who gave thoughtful feedback on a couple of different versions; and Rebecca Costello, my first internet friend and critique partner, who gave me the ending.

This time around, I'm indebted to Harold Pretty, who drew on his RCMP experience to outline for me how a missing-persons case like this might play out; to Kim Steele, once our neighbor, who let me spend an afternoon exploring her backyard; to Eric Workman, who's always up for answering weird medical questions; to Corey Yanofsky, martial arts consultant extraordinaire; to Liana, Zélie, and Louis Bérubé for sharing their memories of the woods and our old neighborhood; and to Marilyn Weixl, who sprang into action to recruit old friends into helping her daughter research a scary book.

Nova Ren Suma's 2016 Djerassi workshop was the greenhouse that got my first draft growing in earnest. My boundless gratitude goes out to Nova for that magical week, for her critique and encouragement, and for one observation in particular that bore wonderful, awful fruit. And thanks to all the amazing Sassy Djerassis—Bree Barton, Shellie Faught, Catey Miller, Jacqui Lipton, Aimee Phan, Melissa Mazzone, TJ Ohler, Wendy McKee, and Rachel Sarah—for their insights and their love.

I don't know what I did to deserve the creative fellowship of Allison Armstrong and Zélie Bérubé, but their wisdom and generosity made this book better and scarier, and I am inspired by and thankful for their incisive brilliance every time we meet. Wendy McKee, my sister in spookiness, has showered this story with fierce love, encouragement, and tireless rereading ever since those first twenty-five pages at Djerassi. My SCBWI critique group—Beth Elliott, Sarah Sambles, Chang Hong, Louise Bradford, and Madeleine McLaughlin—gave me the thumbs-up on my first tentative attempts at a few early scenes. And a host of other wonderful readers helped me fill in the gaps and figure out where to go next: Justine Hart, Rhen Wilson, Erica Mendoza Frey, Tracy Derynck, Averill Frankes, Rachel Sarah, Bree Barton, Shellie Faught, and Melissa Mazzone, thank you for being part of the village that shaped this book.

Thank you to all the wizardly professionals whose expertise and eagle eyes have brought it into the world: Lana Popović, sorcerer agent; and everyone on the Sourcebooks Fire team, especially Annie Berger, Sarah Kasman, and Cassie Gutman. They embraced my monster story, made it beautiful, filed its teeth into deliciously wicked fangs, and set it lurching into motion. It continues to be a joy and a privilege to work with you all.

Thank you to my own monsters, Rose Bérubé and Deji Yanofsky, for brainstorming with me and for always bubbling over with interest, excitement, and weirdness. I'm so glad you're with me on this wild, winding road.

And as a final note: The poem that graces the divider pages of this book is "Dark Pines Under Water" by Gwendolyn MacEwen, which has always reminded me of the woods that inspired this story. It is used here with the kind permission of David MacKinnon, the executor for her estate.

ABOUT THE AUTHOR

Amelinda Bérubé is a writer and editor with a small department in the Canadian public service. She holds a bachelor of humanities degree from Carleton University and a master of arts degree from McGill University. Visit her online metuiteme.com.

FIREreads

§ — #getbooklit —

Your hub for the hottest young adult books!

Visit us online and sign up for our
newsletter at FIREreads.com

 @sourcebooksfire

sourcebooksfire

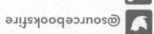 firereads.tumblr.com